All fiction is by nature revisionist and Motyl's surprising and ingenious novel, **Who Killed Andrei Warhol,** adds several dimensions to our understanding of this American icon, blazing new avenues of approach to a subject whose object was cultural depletion.

—Askold Melnyczuk
Author, *Ambassador of the Dead*

Who Killed Andrei Warhol will delight readers with its humor, its ability to capture the zeitgeist of America in the late 1960's, and its highly entertaining examination of the contradictions and absurdities of Eastern and Western outlooks on the world.

—Casey Dorman
Author, *I, Carlos*

With wit and great energy, Motyl invites us to reconsider the heroic forces that shaped Andy Warhol's life and work as witnessed through Communist comrade Sasha's eyes. After reading this book, I don't think I'll ever look at a Warhol painting quite the same way.

—Dzvinia Orlowsky
Author, *A Handful of Bees*

This novel is a riveting "Warholian" masterpiece. The diary takes the reader to the emotional inner conflict of Ivanov, who needs to decide where his loyalty lies. Written with such a sophisticated take on Ivanov, Alexander J. Motyl proves he is a writer to watch.

—Gloria Mindock
Cervena Barva Press

Who Killed
ANDREI
WARHOL

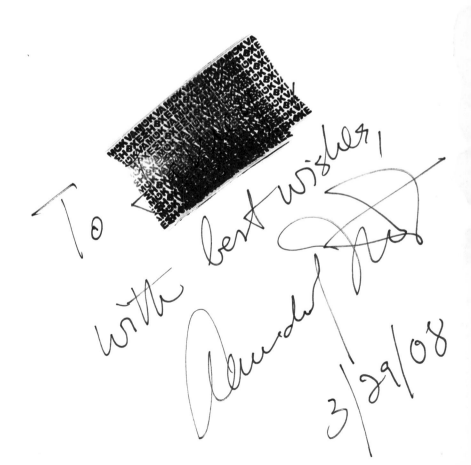

To
with best wishes,

[signature]

3/29/08

WHO KILLED ANDREI WARHOL

The American Diary of a Soviet Journalist

by

Oleksandr Ivanov

Translated, Edited, Annotated,
and with an Introduction
by

Vilen Abelin

Foreword by
Alexander J. Motyl

Alexander J. Motyl

SEVEN LOCKS PRESS

SANTA ANA, CALIFORNIA

Seven Locks Press
P.O. Box 25689
Santa Ana, CA 92799
(800) 354-5348

Individual sales: This book is available through most bookstores or can be ordered directly from Seven Locks Press at the address above.

Quantity Sales: Special discounts are available on quantity purchases by corporations, associations and others. For details, contact the "Special Sales Department" at the publisher's address above.

Cover Art by Kira Fulks © 2007
Cover and Interior Design by Kira Fulks • www.kirafulks.com

Printed in the United States of America

Library of Congress Cataloging-in-Publication Data is available from the publisher

ISBN: 0-9795852-0-1
       978-0-9795852-0-3

Foreword

What could be more Warholian than a friendship between Andy Warhol and a Soviet journalist? We read with fascination, and some horror, as Oleksandr Ivanov's encounter with Warhol evolves from a casual acquaintance into an increasingly intimate and unequal relationship in which Warhol dominates, affects, and distorts Ivanov's life—to the point of making it unlivable.

What could be more Warholian than Ivanov's interpretation of Warhol as a socialist realist painter? Ivanov's claim that Warhol opposed capitalism and promoted the interests of the working class in his art strikes us as nothing less than a classic postmodernist inversion. After all, by upending the modernist master narrative, postmodernism has created the theoretical space for a multiplicity of answers to the question of "What is art?" The irony is that Warhol made postmodernism possible and that postmodernism has made Ivanov's critique of Warhol plausible.

And what could be more Warholian than an insider's view of Warhol's private life that reveals it to have been almost disturbingly normal? Ivanov describes several visits to Warhol's home, where he eats potato dumplings, drinks copious amounts of vodka, and witnesses the touching closeness of a dutiful son and his doting mother. The juxtaposition of two worlds—the bizarre and the prosaic—forms the backdrop to the other, no less Warholian events depicted in this extraordinary diary that often reads like dramatic fiction.

Is the diary authentic? The simple answer is that it is as authentic as its translator, Vilen Abelin. In any case, the question is irrelevant. A text that is so Warholian in spirit can only be an accurate representation of Andy Warhol's life. Andy, for one, would surely have given the diary his seal of approval—and that is all that matters.

Alexander J. Motyl
New York City, 2007

Introduction

ભ

Oleksandr "Sasha" Ivanov came to the United States in early 1968 to write about what he believed was the impending American Revolution. A passionate Communist, he kept a fascinating, if intermittent, record of his impressions until his return to the Soviet Union in early June. His exposure to America, and especially his friendship with Andy Warhol, changed Sasha in subtle but important ways. Those changes eventually led him to dedicate his life to transforming the Soviet Union and, in time, his own country, independent Ukraine.

Sasha was born May 1, 1936 in the Soviet Ukrainian city of Kyiv. Both his parents were Ukrainian peasants-turned-workers. Five years after his birth, Germany attacked the Soviet Union, and Sasha's family was evacuated to Central Asia. They returned to a ruined city in 1946. After life returned to normal, Sasha became a leading member of the Communist Youth League, the Komsomol, and enrolled in the prestigious Moscow Institute of Journalism in 1959. The fifties were heady times in the USSR. The "thaw" initiated by Nikita Khrushchev was in full swing, and Soviet intellectuals were searching for the truth about their country and its past. Sasha joined in that search and, by the early 1960s, had become an influential journalist, writing articles for *Pravda*, *Izvestiya*, and other leading newspapers and magazines. In 1963, he began his career as a foreign correspondent in India, where he mastered the English language. In February 1968, Sasha was sent on assignment to New York City.

That turned out to be a fateful posting. Sasha's encounters with Columbia University student radicals and the Black Panthers gave him a deeper understanding of the contradictions of American reality. Sasha's closest Communist friend was an African-American named Jim (his last name remains unknown), who exposed him to the complexities of race relations in the United States. Sasha was also on a first-name basis with the head of the Communist Party, Gus Hall, a man he portrays as deeply sincere, slightly naïve, and somewhat cynical. What Sasha did not know, and could not have known, is that Morris Childs, Hall's right-hand man in the Party, was a long-time agent of the FBI. Childs, as we know from the diary, established a close relationship with Sasha, no doubt hoping to recruit him. (We may safely assume that Childs was responsible for placing a listening device in Sasha's living quarters.) Increasingly implicated in events beyond his control, Sasha eventually faced a series of profound moral dilemmas that, perhaps for the first time in his young life, led him to question the Communist Party's infallibility. His stay in New York culminated in two tragic incidents — one involving the accidental death of Jim, the other the shooting of three black activists near Columbia University. Both placed Sasha in the untenable position of being hounded by both the FBI and the KGB. At that same time, the FBI, ironically, was also investigating Warhol for possible violations of obscenity laws.

The primary value of the diary is its account of Sasha's friendship with one of America's leading artists, Andy Warhol. That friendship — and the people and ideas to which it exposed

Sasha — affected him in ways of which he was only vaguely aware in 1968. It is only in light of the future, when Sasha turned to Reform Communism, that we can appreciate just how deep these changes were. The first half of 1968 was also an important period in Warhol's life. We know in retrospect that moving the Factory from East 47ᵗʰ Street to 33 Union Square West marked the end of an era of outrageous license and pathbreaking cinematographic and artistic creativity. It was then that Andy began searching for new directions, and the diary provides some evidence of Sasha's influence. Andy's later important paintings of the Communist hammer and sickle, for instance, appear to have had their roots in an extended conversation with Sasha. We can only speculate how Andy's art would have evolved if Sasha had not returned to the USSR and their friendship had continued.

Sasha's diary does not contain much description of New York City. But it does capture and recreate many conversations with Sasha's Communist comrades, Warhol's colleagues, and various incidental characters who may be the filmmaker Paul Morrissey, the superstar Viva, the singer Nico, the rock and roll star Lou Reed, and the philosopher Arthur Danto. A certain Gerald — who may be Gerard Malanga, Andy's collaborator on many of his artworks — makes several extended appearances and proves to be an unusually sensitive, if somewhat vulgar, interlocutor for Sasha. (Curiously, Sasha refers to Malanga, Viva, and Danto as Gerald, Veeva, and Dante, perhaps to hide their identities from the prying eyes of Soviet censors; amusingly, Sasha also confuses Lou Reed with Dean Reed, an American pop singer who settled in East Berlin and dedicated his life to proselytizing Communism.)

Valerie Solanas, Andy's would-be assassin who believed that he had stolen her film script, also figures prominently in the text. Sasha's portrait of Solanas — with whom he had, despite her open lesbianism, a brief affair — is especially poignant. Believing her to be of Baltic background, he called her his "Lithuanian mouse." Sasha tried, and failed, to prevent Solanas from shooting Andy on June 3, 1968. It was this failure—of nerve and perhaps also of principle—that prompted him to board a plane for Moscow on June 4.

Sasha's portrait of Andy, and his interpretations of Warhol's art, are among the most memorable parts of the diary. Students of Warhol will find much here that is new, and unexpected. Among other things, we learn that Warhol (who was born Andrew Warhola in Pittsburgh, Pennsylvania) was acutely conscious of his ethnic identity as a Rusyn-Ukrainian—a facet of his life that his biographers have failed to recognize. We also learn of the important role that his mother, Julia Warhola, who touchingly called him by the diminutive "Andiku," played in Andy's life. Readers may not be entirely convinced by Sasha's suggestion that Warhol sympathized with socialism, especially in light of the prevailing wisdom that Andy's art was notable for its lack of social content. But conventional wisdom has been wrong in the past, and Sasha's argument is certainly worth serious consideration. I suggest that skeptics revisit some of Warhol's major artworks—his Campbell's soup cans, his Marilyn Monroe, and his flowers—as they read the diary.

A final comment on Sasha's role in perestroika: Not surprisingly, Sasha's career went into a tailspin after his return to the Soviet Union. The articles he had written about Warhol, as well as some of his misadventures, almost resulted in ejection from the Communist Party. Sasha survived the crisis, but his career as a foreign correspondent ended. Sasha then took to covering domestic affairs for the Soviet press, while also working on a variety of more analytical works critical of the direction Soviet society had taken after the invasion of Czechoslovakia in 1968. Sasha was never a dissident. He preferred to express his concerns from within Soviet institutions. It is for that reason perhaps that, by the mid-1980s, his ideas were sufficiently widespread among reformist circles of the Party to have influenced the newly elected general secretary. From what we know, Mikhail Gorbachev took his ideas about *glasnost* from Sasha, his close friend. At every step of the way, it was Sasha who advised Gorbachev on what to do. This is not to say that Sasha made perestroika. But it is to say that, without Sasha, perestroika would have been very different.

Sasha left the diary with me on June 4, just before he left for the Soviet Union. He requested that I not publish it until after the issues it raised were no longer politically sensitive. The collapse of the Soviet Union in 1991 spurred me to look at the notebook. Thanks to Sasha's oftentimes indecipherable handwriting, and my own preoccupations with becoming an American and acquiring U.S. citizenship, it has taken me over ten years to transcribe the diary. The printed text is completely faithful to the original. Unfortunately, Sasha's notebook perished in a mysterious fire that consumed my personal archive several years ago. I suspect the long hand of the Russian security service.

Readers will notice that, despite our close friendship, Sasha never mentions me by name in the diary. I assume he was trying to protect me from trouble with American or Soviet authorities. I am, in fact, the Comrade X he refers to several times. Although an officer of the KGB, I wish to emphasize that, unlike Russia's President Vladimir Putin, I joined the Soviet secret police to democratize Soviet totalitarianism from within. Indeed, I actually worked as a double agent for the FBI since the early 1960s. It was in the summer of 1991, just after the failed coup against Gorbachev, that I decided I could no longer live a double life and chose freedom in the United States. I have since then lived in Brooklyn, promoting human rights and civil society through investment in Russia's energy industry. It is in the spirit of my love of America that I changed my name to honor both the founder of the Soviet Union, V.I. Lenin, and the defender of the American Union, Abe Lincoln. I wish also to add that Sasha's account of the unfortunate death of three African-Americans is not quite accurate. Contrary to his version, it's a fact that I shot them in self-defense, and my subsequent exoneration by the FBI proves that point.

Unfortunately, Sasha cannot witness the happy occasion of his diary's publication. After his native land, Ukraine, achieved independence in 1991, Sasha moved to Kyiv. True to form, he continued his lifelong struggle for freedom by joining the Progressive Socialist Party. He passed away on August 24, 2000, after a long battle with cirrhosis of the liver.

Unlike most diaries, which have entries for specific dates, this one does not. It was actually a notebook, and the entries were never dated. We know that Sasha arrived in the United States in mid-February 1968 and that he left on June 4, and we can often guess when certain entries were written. It is also clear that Sasha kept the diary sporadically. In that sense, the diary is misleading. It suggests that Sasha led a life of non-stop adventure. In reality, most of his days must have been filled with mundane research, writing, and interviewing.

Sasha loved language, words, and wordplay, and it is no wonder that he kept his diary in Russian, Ukrainian, and English. Russian was, of course, the language in which he exercised his profession in the Soviet Union. At about the middle of the diary, however, Sasha increasingly turned to Ukrainian, the language of his childhood and youth. Often, he wrote in English, especially when attempting to convey the linguistic idiosyncrasies of his conversations with his African-American comrade, Jim. Needless to say, Sasha's

English was full of mistakes, misspellings, and the like, which I've generally removed or corrected, unless they were critical to some immediate impression.

I have, as a rule, retained Sasha's phonetic renditions of the dialogues. Where they struck me as being obviously incorrect versions of slang, I took the liberty of making minor changes. I have also retained some of Sasha's awkward English-language phrases or terms, even translating his phraseology literally, so as to convey the spirit of the original. For example, Sasha often says "it struck me in the eyes" in the text. That sounds awkward in English, but Russian speakers will easily recognize the sentence. I also rewrote some of the dialogue, especially Sasha's garbled versions of certain American colloquialisms. Sasha generally avoided writing out obscenities, preferring to write F for some variant of fuck, S for shit, and so on. Otherwise, the diary contains only Sasha's words.

Who Killed Andrei Warhol is my title, not Sasha's. His, which sounds awkward even in the original Ukrainian, translates as *Who Was Ultimately Responsible for the Killing of Andrei Warhol*. Note the absence of a question mark. My sense was that a pithy title that captured the spirit of Sasha's would be more appealing to a Western audience. The subtitle is also mine.

Consumed by guilt, Sasha obviously felt responsible for what he mistakenly believed was Valerie Solanas's assassination of Andy. Sasha's diary is, thus, a confession. I suspect that's the real reason he left it with me before returning home.

Vilen Abelin
Brighton Beach

Who Killed ANDREI WARHOL

or

Who Was Ultimately Responsible for the Killing of Andrei Warhol

IT is settled: I am going to imperialist America! The decision was made today. We discussed the question for hours, and all the comrades agreed that it was imperative for a trusted cadre to be in the citadel of imperialism when the revolution breaks out and socialism triumphs. And who better to fulfill this strategic role than an experienced journalist? The only disagreement centered on when the revolution was likely to occur. Some comrades believed that dual sovereignty had not yet manifested itself. In that case, revolution was still some way off. Others claimed—more persuasively—that the ongoing mobilization of the American workers and peasants was a clear sign of dual sovereignty and that revolution was likely this year. The symbolism of my arriving in the United States in February—exactly fifty-one years after the outbreak of the February Revolution that brought down the tsar—did not escape anyone. Our working assumption was that, if the Communist Party of the United States executed its world historical mission as leader of the revolution, the collapse of the capitalist order would take place later in the year—

perhaps even in November. And would that not be a fitting way to celebrate the fifty-first anniversary of the Great October Socialist Revolution? We agreed that I would live separately from the workers of the Soviet, Ukrainian, and Belorussian Missions to the United Nations, and that I would work in close cooperation with the American Party vanguard.

I say good-bye to Katyusha. She says she will write every day. I promise the same. Both of us know we will not. What saddens me more? To be leaving my Soviet Motherland or to be exchanging mechanical good-byes with my wife? My Uzbek driver takes my bags downstairs and heaves them into the trunk of the Volga. As we drive away, I notice that she is waving at me from the window. It is snowing lightly.

An extraordinary occurrence the day before my departure. Is it an omen? Kelebek, Kolibri, Katyusha, and I are sitting in a terrace café overlooking the gray waters of the port. Below us, railroad tracks snake their way among dusty warehouses and neat piles of coal. To the right lies a red freighter, tilted on its side, a rusty chain extending diagonally from its prow to the water. I do not recall when it appeared there, stranded like a whale, but it has become an integral part of the landscape we love so much. Katyusha is smoking, and she is irritable. Kelebek is characteristically cautious, while Kolibri and I are reading *Pravda*.

"I saw something beautiful on the ferry yesterday," says Kolibri. "Flocks of seagulls flew alongside the boat. People threw pieces of bread at them, and the gulls caught them in mid-air."

"Probably Finnish tourists," says Katyusha.

"I don't think so," says Kolibri.

Katyusha takes a deep drag, ready for a fight.

"How could you tell?" she asks.

"They weren't dressed like tourists," Kolibri says. "They looked like us. They looked Soviet."

"And just how do we Soviets look?"

I roll my eyes at Kolibri. He takes the hint and says, "You're probably right," and returns to his newspaper. Katyusha appears satisfied by her minor victory. She twists the butt into the ashtray and lights another cigarette.

Kolibri has a glint in his eye, and I know that he is getting ready for another round with Katyusha. I produce a slight frown, as a warning, but he turns away. Kolibri folds his paper and looks out at the water.

"Katyusha," he says slowly, "there is something in the newspaper I want to show you. It says here—"

At that moment, we hear a crash, followed by hysterical screaming. The waiters disappear, and all heads turn in the direction of women crying. Kolibri rises from his chair, as does Kelebek. Katyusha looks about uncertainly.

"Was that a robbery?" I ask.

Kelebek, Kolibri, and I run off to the winding staircase in the middle of the hotel. The lift, an ornate wooden contraption built in the nineteenth century, is standing, doors flung open, on the ground floor. People, red faced and perspiring, are milling about. A man in a tuxedo is carrying a weeping woman. Waiters are holding towels, though to no discernible end. Behind the lift we see a body. A man, wearing brown pants, a white shirt, and a black vest. His shirt is unbuttoned and his tie has been loosened.

He is bald, or balding, and the marble floor near his head is covered with a dark fluid.

"Is that blood?" asks Kolibri.

"Of course," says Kelebek. "He is dead."

We return to the table and Kelebek tells Katyusha that the man is lying in a pool of blood.

"Was it rectangular, the pool?"

"No," says Kelebek. "How could it be? He cracked open his skull. The blood flowed out. How could the pool be rectangular?"

"Then it wasn't a pool," says Katyusha, "was it? Pools are rectangular. Then it was a lake or a pond. You should have said he's lying in a lake of blood."

"No one would say that, Katyusha," objects Kolibri. "It's a figure of speech. A pool of blood is a figure of speech. It doesn't have to resemble a swimming pool to be a pool of blood."

"Then it's an absurd figure of speech," she says, livid. "Say what you mean."

"I wonder who the man was," Kelebek says timidly.

"He probably jumped," says Kolibri. "He probably committed suicide."

"Who commits suicide by jumping inside an old hotel?" asks Kelebek.

"Why not?" Kolibri shrugs. "Why does it have to be a bridge? Or a tall building? Why not a hotel?"

"Because jumping over a hand-carved balustrade on an upper floor is a spontaneous act," says Kelebek. "No one plans on jumping from the third or fourth floor of some hotel. That might happen by accident, or even on the spur of the moment, but it's not what a suicide would do."

"He couldn't have slipped," I say. "The balustrade is too high. Was he pushed? He could've been pushed. That would've been easy enough."

"But then we would've heard a scream," says Kolibri, "but we heard no scream. Remember? We were sitting, chatting. And then, without any warning, that thud. There was no scream, no shout—until *after* the thud."

"A murder?" says Katyusha gleefully. "How exciting."

"But that's my point," says Kolibri, his forefinger extended. "It couldn't have been a murder. We would've heard a scream. And it couldn't have been an accident. We would've also heard a scream. So it *must* have been suicide."

"But why commit suicide by jumping into the stairwell of a hotel?" says Kelebek. "Don't suicides always leap from bridges or buildings? Why a stairwell? And here? Why *here?*"

"Why *not?*" says Katyusha, aroused and ready to do battle. "It makes perfect sense—to a woman. Maybe he had just opened the door to his room and found her in the arms of another man? Or maybe she decided, after much hesitation, to tell him that she no longer loves him? That she wants to leave him? She tells him it's over, his world collapses, he pleads for her to come back, she says no, he cries, she remains hard, he stumbles out the room, desperate, hopeless, despairing. He sees the balustrade. All it takes is one quick leap and his troubles are over. He leaps. He falls. We hear the thud. His troubles *are* over."

"A man wouldn't do that." Kelebek speaks slowly and deliberately. "A man wouldn't do that. A man wouldn't kill himself if some woman said she was leaving him. A woman might act that way. But not a man. A man would get drunk. A man might break furniture. A man might beat her. But kill himself? Kill himself because she left him? Kill himself because she has a lover? *Never*," says Kelebek with finality.

The conversation, clearly, is no longer theoretical. Kelebek and Katyusha appear to be talking to each other.

We fall silent.

At the airport. I am greeted by Kelebek and Kolibri, my closest Party comrades and my best friends. Kolibri has the vodka. We pass it around and drink straight from the bottle. As I kiss and hug my friends, we break into tears. How long have we known one another? Ten years? Fifteen? We are all different, but we are all united in our love of the Communist Party, the Soviet Union, and one another. This is our special tradition. We always accompany whoever happens to be leaving on a trip, especially if it is a long trip abroad. The ritual is always the same. Two of us wait for the third with a bottle of vodka. We drink, we embrace, we hug. Our relationship is simple and straightforward, like a tall birch tree.

The plane departs after a delay of two hours. We Soviet people are used to this, but the Americans on board get flustered, incessantly calling the stewardesses and demanding to know when, *exactly*, we will leave. How unfortunate these poor people are—always in a hurry, always concerned with not wasting time, making money, and rushing to the next opportunity to make money. I sit back and open my own bottle of vodka, which I share with my neighbors. We are Soviet men. We certainly know how to enjoy life.

The first thing Kelebek told me when I met him was that his name means butterfly in Turkish. I responded by saying that I had a good friend, Kolibri, whose name meant hummingbird in German. This exchange of intimacies quickly led to a solid and lasting friendship. We would see each other at least once a week in those days, usually after Party meetings. How proud we were of our friendship— Kelebek the Crimean Tatar and Ivanov the Ukrainian—a symbol of the international solidarity of the working people. Workers of all countries, unite, said Marx. Well, Kelebek and I, and Kolibri the Volga German, were a shining example of just what the great founder of Communism had in mind.

True friendship is an extraordinary thing. It is attainable only by toilers who share in the proletarian internationalism of workers and peasants who love other nationalities as much as their own. When true friendship exists, even betrayal cannot negate it. I could betray Kelebek or Kolibri, or Kelebek or Kolibri could betray me, but our friendship would remain unaffected because it is larger than Kelebek or Kolibri or me.

Am I an idealist? Kelebek says that I am, but Kolibri disagrees. Kolibri and I think that Kelebek can be excessively cynical. Oddly enough, despite—or perhaps because?—of his cynicism, Kelebek is unwavering in his loyalty and love. If you are his friend, there is nothing you can do to lose his friendship. Kelebek's male friends like that side of his character. His female friends are less inclined to embrace that trait. I think they like it at first. What woman would not admire loyalty in a man? But then, after a brief while, they feel resentful and aggressive. During their break-ups, they characteristically accuse him of wanting to control their lives. As far as he is concerned, Kelebek wants anything but to control them. Unfortunately, he does not appreciate that his unconditional loyalty places an enormous burden on others. His male friends can elude that burden by laughing or joking or teasing him. His women cannot, or in any case they do not. So they suffer quietly, until they resolve no longer to suffer, a moment that usually heralds a tumultuous end to the liaison.

Just as Kelebek takes pride in his name meaning butterfly in Turkish, so too Kolibri takes equal pride in his name meaning hummingbird in German. Not only that, he once whispered to me as we were standing before a store that sold old typewriters, Kolibri is a brand of German-made typewriter.

"Does it hum?" I asked him.

Well, Kolibri the hummingbird and Kolibri the humming typewriter are one and the same person, and that person is, fittingly, as simple as a hummingbird and as reliable as a German product. Kolibri's main quality is that he does not care what people do or say or think. That attitude is useful for dealing with ideologically lax Party members, but it invariably complicates his liaisons with women. Regardless of what they do or say, Kolibri remains indifferent, and the more they try to provoke a response, the more indifferent he becomes. His insouciance drives them crazy, but, before they become hysterical, it usually drives them to fits of exasperation, by which, unsurprisingly, Kolibri refuses to be exasperated. Needless to say, Kolibri, like Kelebek, has been unlucky in love. Kolibri would probably agree with this assessment, but I doubt that he would agree that luck matters much to his happiness. Kolibri has always insisted, whether sober or drunk, that he is a happy man, which is his backhanded way of saying that love is irrelevant to happiness and that the Party is all that matters.

An excellent Soviet meal accompanied by Russian vodka and Crimean wine. It is almost exactly fifty years since Vladimir Illich Lenin and the Bolsheviks stormed the Winter Palace and began the Great October Socialist Revolution. Like John Reed,[1] I am traveling to observe another revolution. I wonder: Which ten days within my ten months in imperialist America will shake the world? A stupid and arrogant question. When the workers of the world's leading capitalist state finally rise up, every day will shake the world.

I look at my diary and it strikes me in the eyes that I—who am about to embark on a wonderful adventure in a country on the verge of revolution—have just spent several pages writing about my dearest friends. But why should I be surprised? We are proletarians, Stakhanovite workers, builders of Communism, architects of a new society. What binds us is far stronger than good times and pleasant experiences (although there have been many of those, too!).

I sleep for an hour or two. When I awake, the captain informs us that we shall be landing at Kennedy Airport

---

1   The world-famous American Communist who witnessed the Russia Revolution; author of the brilliant *Ten Days that Shook the World*.

in an hour. What do I expect to find in the stronghold
of capitalism and imperialism? An impoverished and
immiserated population. A desperate working class. And
good Communist comrades. There will be more, of course.
There always is. Just as I expected to find only socialism in
India, but instead came upon feudalism and capitalism and
poverty as well, so too I am certain that there will be many
surprises here, in the bastion of the global bourgeoisie.
Less poverty? More poverty? Less class struggle? More?
Who knows? I do know that the essence of capitalism is
man's exploitation of man, just as the essence of socialism
is man's cooperation with man. Superficial observers forget
this obvious fact. They see children on a playground in some
capitalist country and conclude that capitalism makes
them smile. But children are children everywhere. I used
to play in the ruins of Kyiv. Some comrades also think that
the American people must be like their system. They are
not, of course. They are the sad and unconscious victims of
that system.

A comrade meets me at the airport. He is a tall, majestic
Negro dressed in a thick red sweater and brown corduroy
pants. His broad nose is flat in the typical African style.
I cannot help thinking of a Kazakh nomad I knew while
harvesting corn for the Komsomol in the virgin lands.
Nursultan was a master horseman, but a disaster on
the combine. We teased him incessantly, but he always
remained good-natured, responding to our jibes with a
toothless smile and incomprehensible native sayings.

The big Negro says, "Hi, Comrade Ivanov, the name's
Sam," and extends an enormous workingman's hand.

I like that "Hi" and the use of the first name: It is the informality and collegiality of the working class. He takes my suitcases and says to follow him. We weave through the crowds—I sense for a moment that I am in Moscow—and walk through a wide glass door. We cross several roads—there are yellow cars and large buses everywhere—and enter a parking lot. We walk past rows of glistening chrome fenders. I have seen photographs of American cars, but, except for jeeps, this is the first time that I have seen so many, and all in one place. Comrade Sam stops and says, "Here we are." He opens the trunk of a battered, olive green Volkswagen. I smile. How appropriate, I think, that we should be driving in the people's car. I climb into the front seat.

"Like a smoke?" Comrade Sam offers me a pack of American cigarettes. I take one, but it is bland. I offer him a Belomorkanal. He pulls on it and starts coughing. I laugh as he says, "How can you smoke that shit?" But he keeps smoking it, and I keep smoking the American cigarette. *That* is proletarian internationalism in action.

Endless highways and nothing but cars. Fences divide us from the little white wooden houses beyond. Nothing and no one must interfere with the primacy of the automobile in the land of capitalism. Comrade Sam is quiet, his steely gaze focused on the cars weaving in and out of the three lanes before us. And then, suddenly, there is Manhattan. As we approach a tunnel, a panorama of enormous towers strikes me in the eyes.

"First time here?" he inquires.

"Yes, comrade."

"Pretty fucking impressive, ain't it?"

I am dismayed by the obscenity. "Yes, I have never seen anything like this. Karl Marx wrote of capitalism's powers to transform the world."

"Uh-huh."

Comrade Sam is an excellent driver. He swerves to the left, to the right, misses cars by centimeters, but always he manages to get ahead. A true Leninist. Vladimir Illich[2] would have been proud. We wind our way through a porcelain-tiled tunnel and emerge in Manhattan itself. The first thing I notice is that the sidewalks are buried under mountains of refuse. I can smell the sickening stench even in the car.

"What is that?" I ask, as I roll up the window.

"Garbage strike."

"Excellent." I say, "The rot of capitalism is fully visible for all the world to see."

We rattle along canyon-like streets—they are as dreadful as the comrades have told me—and enter a wide street. The desks and cabinets in the store windows are barely visible behind the garbage.

"Where are we?" I ask. "The Wild West?"

"Twenty-Third," he says, "almost there." He pulls up alongside a large red building with delicately woven balconies running up the steep facade.

"This is it." He turns off the motor and, with another Soviet cigarette dangling from his mouth, the smoke curling up his face, his eyes squinting, climbs out and opens the trunk.

I too get out. We walk into the lobby and approach the desk to register. I take out my passport, but the hotel

---

2   Vladimir Illich Lenin, of course, the world-famous Bolshevik
       and founder of the Union of Soviet Socialist Republics.

manager, a dark-haired man who could be a Georgian fruit seller, waves it away with his hairy hand. He drops a large key onto the polished wooden surface and grunts, "Welcome to the Chelsea."

Comrade Sam says he will be waiting for me in the lobby tomorrow at eight in the morning. I embrace the brave Negro and take the lift to the fifteenth floor. I pour myself a glass of vodka and fall asleep immediately.

I awake before the sun rises. I have a hundred grams. My room is small, perhaps twelve square meters. Next to the bed are a wobbly nightstand and a brown lamp. A small television stands on a dented dresser. The paint is peeling from the ceiling. The faucets in the bathroom are rusty. I feel at home. I drink another glass, wash and shave, put on my gray suit, blue shirt, and beige tie—and, after seeing that I have another forty-five minutes before Comrade Sam arrives, decide to take a walk. The lobby is empty, save for a thin pale woman slumped in one of the chairs. It is dawn as I walk out into the cold air. I turn to look at the hotel. It is an old structure, built of dark red bricks, not at all American in appearance. The comrades chose well, I think. Save for the foul-smelling garbage, the sidewalk is empty. I turn right past a musical instruments store and walk to the corner. At Seventh Avenue I turn right again. In the middle of the block I see an American *gastronom*.[3] Inside sits a worker, smoking and reading a newspaper. He looks up at me as I walk in. He has the pale face of a Latvian writer I once met in Riga.

"Good morning, comrade," I say. He says nothing. As I recall, my Latvian colleague was equally reticent.

---

3   Russian: grocery store.

"May I look at your commodities?" I ask. Again he says nothing. Soup cans, vegetable cans, fruit cans, dog food cans line the dusty shelves. Why do American dogs have their own food when millions are starving? Precisely because millions are starving. No: precisely so that millions will starve while the dogs of the rich grow fat. I return to the counter and look at the poor worker. I reach into my coat pocket and ask, "Would you like some vodka?"

"Hey, man," he says, "a little early for that, ain't it?"

"I am from Russia. Come drink with me, *man*." That "man" is a nice proletarian touch. I shall have to use it more often.

"You from Russia?"

"I am a Communist," I say proudly, "a citizen of the Union of Soviet Socialist Republics, and a proletarian journalist."

"No shit?"

"It is anything but that," I respond, hoping to adopt a more civilized tone. "Let us drink to peace."

"Awright," he says. His name is Moe, and he is smiling as I leave his store. Communism, I think, is best built by revolution, but that is no reason to ignore small steps.

I turn right on Twenty-Second Street. I am struck in the eyes by the practicality and fairness of the American mind. Streets *should* have numbers and they *should* be arranged in a horizontal and vertical grid. The system is simple, direct, and just: It smacks of proletarian inspiration. And it has the virtue of rationality. It is like a Five-Year Plan, in which everything has its place and function and task. It occurs to me that the victory of Communism may be easier here than I had thought. The American people see things straight. How can they fail to see that Communism is best for them?

Twenty-Second Street is what I imagined New York to be like. Small four-, five-, and six-story buildings, streaked and dirty windows, uneven sidewalks, litter, dog droppings, a few trees. I look into people's homes and am struck by the absence of curtains. How unlike our Soviet Motherland. I reach Eighth Avenue and turn right. A man is slumped in some doorway; his crotch is stained, and I can smell him even as I rush by. Two longhaired boys are standing on the corner smoking sweet-smelling cigarettes. On Twenty-Third Street I turn right again. A synagogue, stores selling desks and chairs, yellow taxis. And then my hotel, and next to it a restaurant, El Quijote. I cannot resist laughing. And I am the Sancho Panza of Communism!

As promised, the punctual Comrade Sam is waiting for me in the lobby.

"Had breakfast, man?" he asks. I shake my head. "Here's some." He hands me a brown paper bag.

"Let us go, man," I say. "I am eager to begin work. I can eat on the way."

"Your call, man."

I open the bag after we exit the hotel. Wrapped in unusually thin wax paper is a soft buttered roll with poppy seeds. It is wet from the coffee. I hold it gingerly in my right hand and spill some coffee on my coat. Comrade Sam laughs.

"Welcome to America," he says. I also laugh.

We walk down Twenty-Third Street, past dusty stores

with office supplies and still more desks, bookshelves, and chairs. We cross several avenues and finally reach the infamous Broadway. But it is a regular street, no different from the others and not especially broad. I must be visibly disappointed because Comrade Sam says, "The theatres are uptown, man, not here." We turn right at a thin triangular building and walk for another ten minutes.

"This is it," Comrade Sam says, "Union Square. This is us."

Before me is a small park that does not do justice to the beauty of its name.

"The Party is based here?"

"Yep." Comrade Sam points to a tall, white, narrow building on the right. "That's us. Number thirty-three."

"Thank you, Comrade Sam," I say with profound excitement in my breast. "I feel just like John Reed."

"Huh?"

We take the small lift (so reminiscent of Soviet ones!) next to the twisting staircase and reach the eighth floor. On the door is a sign that proudly proclaims "Communist Party USA."

"I feel home," I say to Comrade Sam. "*Spasibo,*[4] my friend."

"Yeah, cool," he says, "A-Okay."

Comrade Sam opens the door and I step into a large room filled with ancient wooden desks, olive green file cabinets, and metal bookshelves. Posters adorn the walls. A large plant stands near the unwashed windows. The air is thick with cigarette smoke. Four comrades—three men and a woman—are sitting at a table, drinking from typically American paper cups.

---

4   Russian: thank you.

"Comrade Ivanov," says Comrade Sam. The others look up at me. They rise from the table with outstretched hands and broad smiles on their kind faces. The three men embrace me; the woman shakes my hand.

"How was your trip?" asks a round-faced man with a goatee and glasses, who could be a pre-revolutionary intellectual from Odessa.

"A-Okay, man," I respond.

"Hey," another man says, "he's already talking like us!"

"Welcome to the citadel of imperialism," says the woman dryly. Her auburn hair is cut short, like a man's, and she has the demeanor of a Soviet television announcer.

"And of racism," says the third man, round, bald, and with a prominent Armenian nose.

"Long live the revolution!" I reply, impressed by the multinational contingent of comrades before me.

"Right on," respond Comrade Sam and another large Negro named Jim. They raise their right fists.

So do I.

"Lemme show you yo' office," Comrade Jim says. As the others return to the table, he takes me down a narrow corridor and opens a door into a small room filled with boxes and chairs. A desk sits in one corner.

"Hope you don't mind, comrade," he says. "This here's our storage room. We'll clean it up, OK?"

"A-Okay, man," I say. I like Comrade Jim. Like the other Negro comrade, he is direct and to the point, and he does not waste time on formalities. Although I am a guest, he treats me like a friend. Is that a Negro cultural trait?

I also like the other comrades. They greet me, they ask about my trip, and then they get back to work. They can laugh, but they are serious. I shall like it here. I feel at home. The only problem is Comrade Jim's pronunciation of the English language. He drops consonants and slurs word endings, creating the impression that his sentences are long words. What a contrast to the singsong English of my Indian comrades.

"We can get you a typewriter," Comrade Jim says. "We're outta ribbon, but we'll get some tomorrow."

"It is A-Okay, Comrade Jim," I say. "I have my own typewriter. Russian."

"Just in case," he says. "If you change yo' mind."

At that moment, a small fat man lumbers in with a stack of newspapers under his arm.

"*The Daily Worker*," he says, as he drops them on the desk, producing a cloud of dust. "Thought you'd like to have it." He rubs his hands as if in anticipation of a plate of cheese *varenyky*.[5]

"An excellent newspaper," I say with genuine enthusiasm. "I will read it with great pleasure."

"The name's Arnold." He opens one of the newspapers and points to the masthead. "I'm on the editorial board. Got a sec?"

"Well," says Comrade Jim as he moves to the door, "make yo'self at home. If you need anythin', just holler."

"Thank you, comrade," I say, "I shall indeed holler." Comrade Arnold and I shake hands. "Your party organ," I say, "reminds me of Lenin's *Iskra*."[6]

5   Ukrainian: dumplings
6   *The Spark*, a brilliant newspaper published by the great Lenin.

"We do our best," Comrade Arnold replies. He scratches his ear. "I was hoping you'd write for us."

"What would the proletariat be interested in knowing about the Soviet Union?"

Comrade Arnold pulls up his pants. "Anything that'll give them hope." He hesitates for a moment. "Is life in the Soviet Union really as good as they say?"

"It is even better, Comrade Arnold. It is the *only* way to live."

"Then teach us how to dream, comrade," he says solemnly. "Capitalist America is a nightmare."

After Comrade Arnold leaves, I sit down and think: My first day, and so much has already happened. I am excited. I am genuinely excited. I had expected to be excited— especially by the thought of witnessing a revolution fifty years after ours—but I did not expect to be quite as excited as I am. My hands are almost trembling. My heart is beating. I sense that great events are in store for me.

In the evening, as I ride the lift, two men enter on the sixth floor. They are complete opposites in appearance. One is about forty, but his hair is completely white. He is also wearing sunglasses—*inside* the building. His friend, a strikingly handsome young man with magnetic eyes, has long dark curly hair. He could easily be an actor in a Mosfilm production or a dancer in a Bolshoi ballet. I move to a corner as they enter. They say nothing to each other. Once outside, the white-haired man raises his bony hand, a taxi stops, and he climbs in. His movements are awkward and he is remarkably thin for an American. But something else about his physiognomy strikes me in the eyes: I have seen his bulbous nose on the faces of our collective farm workers near Kyiv.

I turn left twice and walk to Fifth Avenue. Comrade Jim told me that the Soviet bookstore is a few blocks north. I pass a Chinese store with posters of a benevolently smiling Mao and copies of his absurd little book in the window. Our store is called Four Continents, and I recognize the familiar aroma of Soviet paper as I step inside. What a contrast to the putrid capitalist smells outside! The newspapers are all several days old, but I look through the books and decide to buy Leonid Illich Brezhnev's *Collected Speeches* and a book by the American revolutionary, Angela Davis. I intend to write several articles on the Negro struggle for Communism.

On the way home, I stop at Eisenberg's sandwich shop and do as Comrade Sam suggested.

"Mister Eisenberg," I say to the man in the apron, "I would like to order a cup of coffee and a BMT."

"You wanna subway, fella?"

"No, Mister Eisenberg," I say, "I would like a sandwich with bacon and—"

"A BLT?"

"*Da*," I say, "yes, yes, a BLT." I feel embarrassed and turn red. Mister Eisenberg, the good Jewish worker, just grins benignly.

"Coming right up," he says.

As I emerge from the sandwich shop, my stomach full and my spirits high, I see a metro entrance and laugh at my own stupidity.

In the hotel. I am exhausted, but I cannot sleep. I finish

the bottle, lie down, and smoke the last of my Belomorkanals. I wonder what Kelebek and Kolibri are doing. Probably drinking vodka at Kelebek's. The Party meeting would have been today. Kelebek probably delivered a speech on the worrisome situation in the Czechoslovak Socialist Republic. He is an excellent propagandist, and I am sure that his talk left a mark on his listeners. Kolibri would have presided. And where am I? Not with my comrades and friends, but here—thousands of kilometers away. I read Leonid Illich's speeches. The one on agriculture, which he delivered to the Central Committee plenum two years ago, grabs my attention. Shortly after midnight, aware that I must get some sleep, I reluctantly place the book aside.

I awake with a start in the middle of the night. I dreamed of the incident in the hotel just before my departure for America. I distinctly recall the dream, but its details are different from the reality. My dream also begins with the four of us sitting in a café. We hear a crash, followed by hysterical screaming. The waiters disappear, and all heads turn in the direction of the crying women. Kelebek, Kolibri, and I run off to the winding staircase. The ornate lift is standing, door flung open, on the ground floor. Behind the lift we see the body of a man in brown pants, a white shirt, and a black vest. His shirt is unbuttoned and his tie has been loosened. He is bald, or balding, and the marble floor near his head is covered with a dark fluid.

"Is that blood?" asks Kolibri.

"Of course not," says Kelebek. "He is dead."

Why does Kelebek say "Of course not"? What an odd twist.

Morning, and I feel better. I wash and shave. I decide to

shower tomorrow. I also unpack my things. I always travel light. One suit, two pairs of shoes, four shirts, two ties, one sweater, one additional pair of pants. Katyusha insisted on that second pair of pants and the four shirts. She said that, as a leading representative of the Soviet working class, I must look prosperous in America. I see her point about looking prosperous in America, but feel uncomfortable about looking more prosperous than workers. We are all proletarians, I said to her. Yes, of course, she said, but even Leonid Illich dresses in a suit when he travels. I could have said that Leonid Illich Brezhnev is the general secretary of the Party and that I am a journalist, but decided to drop the point. You cannot argue with women, as I have come to learn. And even if you could, you could not argue with Katyusha.

I take my typewriter and leave. In the lobby are three women with short skirts, enormous hair, and pale skin. Prostitutes? Drug addicts? I walk to the gastronom on Seventh Avenue and order a tea. The same worker, Moe, who was there yesterday, is there today. His name reminds me of how Comrade Jim pronounces the word "more."

"Milk?" he asks.

"No," I say, "tea, please."

"Sugar?"

"No," I say, "just tea." We smile at each other.

I walk down the avenue sipping my tea. On the way, I buy two small bottles of American vodka.

The refuse towering above the streets is both utterly incomprehensible and utterly comprehensible to me. How can a government mistreat its workers to such a degree that they are forced to go on strike? And how can it disregard the health of its citizens by permitting so much garbage to pile up? I understand: This is the way capitalism functions, exploiting the working class and ignoring the needs of the people. Even so, the landscape leaves me feeling flabbergasted. The symbolism of the garbage—which had struck me in the eyes as Comrade Sam drove into the city— is worth some reflection. And it is a perfect opening for my article about the United States. Like me, Soviet readers will shake their heads in wonder at this inhumanity. And it will take little commentary for them to appreciate that these mounds of putrid and decaying offal are nothing less than capitalism itself. We speak of the "garbage heap of history" and of how capitalism is doomed to finish its days on that heap. A few photographs and an extended essay on those mounds will transform that image into an unforgettable reality.

I make an interesting observation.

All young Americans appear to wear long hair—the men as well as the women. Sometimes it is impossible to tell who is who. As I approach Union Square, I see what I take to be a shapely woman. It is a man. A minute later, I see a man. It is a woman. Or is it a man dressed as a woman? I would not be surprised: Capitalist alienation can easily confuse workers. If they can fall victim to bourgeois propaganda, why should men and women not lose sight of whom they really are?

These longhaired people are the infamous "hippies." This curious word surely derives from the pronounced tendency of hippie women, and sometimes of hippie men, to swing their hips when they walk. I am heartened that hippies reject capitalism. I have read that they have even established communes, but I suspect that they are at best only modern-day variants of nineteenth-century utopian socialists. At worst, they may objectively promote counterrevolution. Their drug-taking and sexual adventurism suggest to the healthy sectors of society that only asocial elements reject capitalism. Worse, these behaviors imply that the proletarian values of the working class—honesty, solidarity, and love of work—are relics of the past, whereas they are, in reality, harbingers of the future. The hippies and their "flower power" will, I fear, be of little use to the revolution. I for one like flowers as much as any toiler, but their pleasant smell and attractive appearance are powerless to affect the international correlation of forces between capitalism and socialism.

As I step into the office, Comrade Jim winks at me.
"Know who's gonna be here today?" he asks slyly.
"Who?"
"Gus."
I say nothing. He looks puzzled.
"Gus Hall," he says.
"*Comrade* Hall?"
"Yep," he grins, "the one and only."
"I am honored. When?"
"In one hour. Wants to meet you."
"Me?" I am astounded.
"*Da,*" Comrade Jim says. "L'il ol' you."
I truly am honored, but I am also worried. I know that Comrade Hall, as befits the leading representative of the American working class, desires only to greet me, a simple

journalist from the Union of Soviet Socialist Republics. I know that I would be surprised if he did not want to greet me in person. And yet, I am worried, however slightly. Meeting the *nachalnik*[7] is never easy. Too much has to go right, and too much can go wrong. I decide to go for a walk in the park. I take the stairs. On the ground floor, the thin, white-haired man in sunglasses is standing, chewing gum, and evidently waiting for the lift, together with an even thinner woman. She may be the one who sat slumped in the chair in the hotel lobby.

Outside, I breathe deeply. I enter the park and am shocked by what I see. The benches are filled with sleeping, filthy men and women, their legs sprawled, their heads thrown back. We do not have such squalor anywhere in the Soviet Union. Even other capitalist countries do not have such open misery in the midst of wealth. I am reminded of India. To think that here, in this very square, is where Communist demonstrations with thousands of workers have taken place in the past. I walk along the cracked asphalt paths. Two young Negroes approach me.

"Spare some change?" one of them says.

"You are quite right," I say. "This country desperately needs change."

"Watcha talkin' 'bout, bro? Got some money?"

"Of course, friend," I say, "of course." I reach for my wallet. At that moment, one of them pushes me in the chest and the other grabs my wallet. I fall against a hedge.

"Fuck you," they laugh, and run away.

I extricate myself from the branches and look around.

---

7   Russian: boss.

No one has noticed, or no one cares. I feel ridiculous. The boys will have little profit from their hooliganism. Photographs of Katyusha, a few rubles, a few dollars. And my Party card. All easily replaceable. Perhaps the symbol of Communism will bring them to their senses.

I return to the office. The comrades are conversing at the large table. Comrade Sam asks me if I want some coffee, and I say yes. He also offers me his comb and suggests I fix my hair. I tell him what happened, and he says, smiling, "That's capitalism, man. Don't worry, the Party'll take care of you."

Comrade Gus Hall greets me with glowing eyes. I like this man as soon as I see him. He looks exactly like his photographs: a workingman's build and the smile of an angel. A quintessential worker, he could adorn our electoral posters.

"Comrade," he says, while giving me a hearty bear hug, "the American working class greets you." As I return the embrace, it strikes me in the eyes. A Russian bear! The great Gus Hall is a gentle Russian bear!

We kiss three times on the cheek, and he is un-embarrassed to do so. I can see that this is a man who knows the ways of the Soviet working class. French, German, and Austrian comrades, despite their far longer Communist roots, kiss with stiffness, almost reluctance. We Soviet people sense it in their bodies. This American, as distant from Europe and the Soviet Union as any man can be, is different. He is one of us. He is a worker by nature—in his heart.

"Comrade Hall—"

"Gus," he says.

"Yes," I say. "Comrade Hall—"

"Gus," he says, "just call me Gus."

I smile. I am touched by this great man's simplicity.

"Sasha," I reply, "just call me Sasha."

We go to the conference table and Gus sits at the head.

"I hear you had your first taste of American capitalism today."

"It is nothing, just some hooligans."

"Negro workers are terribly exploited. They're desperate and they sometimes do desperate things."

"But they are fighting back," I say. "That is all that matters."

"Yes," says Gus, slamming his hand against the table. "Their asocial behavior is the product of objective conditions. As those conditions change, so will their subjective consciousness."

"Quite right," I nod. "The base always determines the superstructure."

"Exactly! Sasha"—he looks slightly embarrassed—"may I give you something?" He rummages in a large bag near his feet. "A gift from the working class."

Comrade Gus hands me a stack of books—all his. Some of the titles are familiar: *For a Meaningful Alternative, For a Radical Change, Paths to Revolution, Toward a Peace Ticket in 1968.* I am especially excited by his latest contribution to Marxist-Leninist theory and practice, *Imperialist Rivalries and the World Struggle for Peace.* I am moved to tears by his generosity.

"Gus," I say without any false emotion, "this is more than a gift. This is a privilege."

"I try," he says with typical proletarian modesty. "We all do our share for the revolution."

"This is more than a share, Gus. You are the Mikhail Suslov[8] of America!"

"I'd *like* to be, Sasha," he smiles. "In the meantime, I just do what I gotta do."

"Your work has already borne fruit, Gus. The revolution has begun."

"I think so, too. So does Morris."

"Morris?"

"Childs, my right-hand man. An excellent comrade. He's in Prague now. You'll meet him in a few weeks."

"Prague?" I shake my head. "Developments in the Czechoslovak Socialist Republic worry me, Gus."

"Morris is fixing things, Sasha. If anyone can, he can."

"I hope so. America is on the brink of another October," I say, "and the working class does not need a counterrevolutionary diversion."

"The Party is ready, Sasha. Don't worry."

"The *world* is ready, Gus."

"*I* am ready, Sasha."

"So am I, Gus."

As I emerge from Comrade Gus's office, Comrade Jim motions me into his, a tiny space crammed with piles of newspapers, journals, and books. A large ashtray overflowing with cigarette butts sits among the papers strewn about his desk. The floor is covered with paper clips.

"It's a mess," he grins. "I've tried puttin' it in o'der." He pauses. "Sasha?"

8   World-famous Soviet ideologist and comrade of L.I. Brezhnev.

"Yes, Comrade Jim?"

"OK if I call you Sasha? I ain't used to fo'malities."

"Of course, Com—," I catch myself, "Jim." We laugh.

"Sasha," he says, "the Party's here to serve you. You know that, don't you?"

"Of course, Jim. Thank you."

"Don't thank us," he says, "thank the workin' class."

"I do, Jim."

He offers me a Camel cigarette and takes one himself.

"The class struggle is pretty intense here." He takes a long drag and exhales toward the ceiling. "It don't look it, but it sure is. Believe you me."

"I do, Jim. I do believe you."

Again he pauses and looks me in the eyes. "Particularly in the Party."

I nod—slowly.

"Be vigilant," he says. "I don't need to say that to a Soviet Communist, do I?"

I shake my head.

"Be on guard, man," he says, "and everything'll be OK." Jim rubs the cigarette into the ashtray. "I gotta stop. This stuff'll kill you."

I go to my office and close the door. I open my typewriter case and remove the machine. I place it on the desk next to the stack of blank paper that some solicitous comrade has given me. I sit back in the chair and close my eyes. So the Party is penetrated. I am not surprised. The enemies of the working class are everywhere, and they are strongest in the citadel of capitalism. But I am also saddened. Vigilance is something I am used to. But it dampens enthusiasm and spontaneity. Perhaps that is just as well, however. The revolution requires careful planning and strategizing. Spontaneity and voluntarism are for the Maoists and other revisionist hotheads.

I make a decision. My first article will be about the Negro working class. I spend most of the day reading the back issues of *The Daily Worker* given me by Comrade Arnold. I am appalled. Conditions are worse than I had imagined, worse even than the reports in our press. Negro poverty is immense, discrimination is ubiquitous. Beatings, shootings, lynchings are the order of the day. The Ku Klux Klan runs the South. The Rockefellers run the North. And where are the Negroes? Forced to steal from Soviet journalists. I resolve to visit Harlem, Bedford, and Stuyvesant and see race relations in imperialist America firsthand.

I understand now why the capitalists are trembling. Reports of an imminent revolution in the stronghold of imperialism are not exaggerated—even if they have been mostly produced by our journalists and other Marxists. I confess to having harbored a slight suspicion that they were not quite true, that the comrades might have let themselves confuse wishes for reality. Not at all. I can state with complete certainty that the revolution is in its first stages here in America. Maybe even past its first stages. Revolutionary cells exist. They have leaders, they consist of cores of committed fighters for socialism, they have well-developed propaganda apparatuses and organizational structures, and they have money—not much, but enough to agitate among the Negro masses and mobilize them for the revolutionary struggle. And not without success. Communist propaganda is beginning to overcome the traditional trade union mentality of the American working class. Significant inroads have been made into the Negro nationality. Students—admittedly not a class, and a fickle social group to boot—support the ideals of Communism. Popular fronts of Negroes, students, and workers are in the process of being constructed. The news is good.

I leave the office when it is already dark.

"Careful, Sasha," says Comrade Jim, as I say good-bye. "You don't wanna get mugged again."

"Thank you for your concern, Jim. Material existence has taught me a lesson I will not soon forget. Do not worry: I will avoid poorly lit and empty streets."

"Best," he says, "you head up Broadway and cut across. Or down Fo'teenth and up Seventh or Eighth."

"So many numbers!" I laugh, touched by his kind-hearted sincerity.

Fourteenth Street is lined with brightly lit stores displaying clothes, televisions, radios, shoes, socks, underwear, and other useful things. The abundance of commodities is impressive, but at what cost to the laborer who must sell himself to capital? The poverty of the people strikes me in the eyes. Little men and women carry enormous bundles. Suspicious types lurk in doorways. Women in astonishingly short skirts parade up and down the sidewalks—prostitutes, no doubt. A capitalist heaven. And everywhere the long hair. I resolve to taste another variety of proletarian food, pizza, but realize that I have no money. I am amused by my plight, which is that of all toilers. I turn right on Seventh Avenue and stop before a large clothing store with boy mannequins wearing nicely pressed suits behind the large windows. They stand straight, their hands at their sides, palms turned inward, hair combed back, identical smiles on their cherubic faces. Mister Barney's boys' town could just as easily be a Young Pioneer choir in some Ukrainian village.

A remarkable coincidence in the hotel lobby. I see the white-haired man in sunglasses, his dark-haired companion, and the emaciated woman with languorous eyes and magnificent hair. They are sitting in a corner, smoking. The white-haired man says nothing; the other two gesticulate wildly and speak rapidly. They appear to be arguing. A film camera lies at the white-haired man's feet. In my room, I find my dollars, take a few, and rush out. The troika is gone.

The pizza restaurant to the left of the hotel looks like a *stolovaya*[9]—small and cramped. People eat standing up. They fold the pizza in half and appear to drink it. The large ovens remind me of our village houses, except that there is no *baba*[10] curled up on them. Three dark-haired boys in yellowing undershirts prepare and sell the pizzas. One kneads the dough, the second flattens it and spreads the sauce and cheese, the third cuts the pizza into pieces, places them on white paper plates, and hands them to the customers, in exchange for almighty dollars. The process is simple and efficient. The division of labor is clear. They work with Stakhanovite speed.

"One pizza, please," I say.

"You wanna whole pie?"

"I do not want a pie," I say. "I would like a pizza." I make sure to enunciate as clearly as possible.

9   Russian: Soviet-style bar.
10   Russian and Ukrainian: old woman.

"Look, buddy, you wanna whole pizza or a slice?"

"I would like a slice, please."

"Regular or Sicilian?"

"Italian."

"OK, regular. To stay?"

"I would like to eat it like proletarians—walking on the street."

Minutes later, the boy hands me a white paper bag. I pay twenty-five cents and leave the restaurant. Inside the bag is the slice, folded in a white paper plate, and some paper napkins. I remove the pizza and plate with my right hand, but how do I grab the napkins? I take hold of the pizza and plate with my three middle fingers and the bag with my right thumb and little finger. I quickly remove the napkins with my left hand, and then seize the bag with my left thumb and little finger. As I drop the bag into an enormous pleated trash basket, I notice that the tip of the pizza is bent and that cheese and oil are slithering down my hand. I raise the pizza, open my mouth, extend my tongue, and take a bite. The oil scalds the roof of my mouth and I cool the dough and cheese mixture by moving it from side to side with my tongue. Finally, I swallow. By now, my right hand is covered with oil and I fear that my shirtsleeve is also stained. But I am determined to defeat the class enemy, whatever the cost! I embark on a tactical retreat and use my left hand to unfold the pizza and position it for attack and defeat. It sits before me, helpless, on the greasy white plate. Victory is mine. Leninist tactics triumph once again!

I deposit the plate into a receptacle, wipe my hands

with the napkins, and continue my walk. One hundred grams would be good now.

The pub, Wilson's, is filled with thick American cigarette smoke. A long wooden bar lines the left side of the elongated room. Mirrors cover the wall, and before them stand, like Mister Barney's boys, neatly arrayed bottles—of everything. I see vodka, gin, whiskey, cognac, and many alcohols I do not recognize. A fat man with large eyebrows—he could be a relative of Leonid Illich—wearing an unpressed white apron, stands behind the bar, a cigarette precariously balanced on his fat lower lip. Several men, all wearing hats, sit quietly on stools, cradling small glasses in their hands. I take a stool in the corner, from where I can watch them. No one speaks, and this audible silence—so different from the raucous nature of a Soviet stolovaya—strikes me in the eyes. Their hands tremble as they raise their glasses and take short sips.

"What'll you have?" asks the fat man.

"Good night, Mister Wilson," I say. "I would like some vodka. One hundred grams, please."

"You wanna double?"

"One hundred grams," I say, "not two."

"Rocks?"

"No rocks," I say. "Vodka."

He pours the vodka into a glass. It is warm.

"You do not have cold vodka?"

"I got rocks," he says. "You want rocks?"

"Then, please, rocks. I will have the rocks."

He takes a handful of ice from a bucket and drops it into my glass. The vodka tastes watery, and the "rocks" make it impossible to drink in one motion, but I am happy nonetheless.

The mountains of garbage are proof of how differently capitalism and socialism approach nature. Here, everything is disposable and everything—including man—is potentially refuse. At home, everything has value and man is valued above everything. Ironically, the garbage has blended into the landscape of the city—almost becoming part of capitalist nature. Amid the tall buildings and wide streets are humanly constructed hills of trash. In the gutters flow streams. Cockroaches, rats, mice, and other vermin abound, jumping playfully from hill to hill. A veritable capitalist utopia! Small wonder that our propagandists speak of capitalism as being on the "garbage heap of history." I used to think of that as a metaphor, but now I see that they were only being literal.

As I approach our building, I encounter several men carrying large canvases. I stand aside at the entrance as they maneuver past me, two to a painting, each holding one end. It is an awkward undertaking, and the thin, white-haired man is standing on the sidewalk, smiling, gesturing, occasionally raising a hand to his mouth as if he were surprised.

"How many more, Andy?" one of the men says.

So his name is Andy, I think, and he must be the artist.

"Uh," he pauses. "Uh, I think that's it."

This Andy is soft-spoken, almost shy. As I observe him, another man stumbles down the stairs and almost falls onto the canvas he is holding.

"Shit!" he cries.

"Oh, dear," says the man called Andy.

I rush to the man who has stumbled. I recognize him as my companion in the lift several days ago.

"Come, comrade," I say, "permit me to help you." I place my right hand on the canvas in order to steady it.

"Hey, man," he replies, "thanks."

We carry the canvas together to the van and push it among the others in the back. After the door is closed and the van drives off, the man I helped extends his hand and introduces himself as Gerald.[11] He gives no family name, but I am no longer surprised by the American preference for casual forms of introduction.

"Sasha," I say in return.

"Sasha?" he says. "You Russian? Andy's Russian."

"I am from the Soviet Union," I say. "I am a Soviet journalist. I work in the office of the Communist Party in this building."

"No shit?" he says. "Hey, Andy, get this. This guy's from the Soviet Union. And he works here."

"We are above you," I say, "on the eighth floor."

"We just moved in," says Gerald. "Fuck, Andy, this is far out. This Sasha guy's a Russian Communist!"

The thin man called Andy is smiling broadly. As he slides past us into the building, he motions me to follow him. I notice that he has paint under his fingernails and on his ears.

We are in an artist's studio, and it is called the Factory. *Zavod!* The name is music to my proletarian ears, and I think that perhaps this thin man Andy has more to him than meets the eye. He walks toward a beaten couch in a corner of the large room and sits down, crossing his spindly

11   Gerald would appear to be Gerard Malanga, and yet there is evidence to suggest that Malanga may have been in Rome at this time. This discrepancy in the text remains an unsolved mystery.

legs. I sit down next to him. He waves his hand at Gerald who is carrying a tripod and a film camera toward us. Gerald places the tripod a few meters away, focuses the camera on us, and starts filming. As he walks away from the camera, I turn to the man called Andy with a quizzical look on my face.

"We're, uh, filming you," he says.

"*Me?*" I say, astonished. "But why?"

"Shhh." He places a thin finger on his lips. "Hear the film?"

"Of course."

"It makes a nice, uh, sound."

"Yes, but what should I do?"

"Uh, nothing." Andy uncrosses his legs. "Just listen."

"Nothing? I am a builder of Communism! How can I do nothing?"

"Stay cool," he says and places his hand on mine. "Stay cool. Do what you, uh, want."

"It's OK, man," interjects Gerald. "We do this all the time. It's OK. It's just film, man. That's all it is, man, just film."

"But what do you want me to *do?*" I cry. "Should I *say* something?"

"That's the thing, man," says Gerald. "Nothing. Anything. Just look at the camera. Want some gum?"

"I have *never* seen such filmmaking!" I rise, as if to leave, but sit down again. I am exasperated, as much by the filming as by the vacant expression on Andy's face.

"Hey, man," says Gerald. "This is the Factory and that's Andy Warhol."

Varkhol? Vargol? The name is not Russian, but it does

sound Slavic. Is it a shortened version of Varkholsky? Vargoliak? Vargolenko? Is he Ukrainian, this thin man called Andy? Or Slovak? Is he Polish? Belorussian?

"You are Russian?" I turn to face this Andy Warhol.

He smiles. "Czechoslovakian."

"Czechoslovakian? There is," I say very emphatically, "no Czechoslovakian nationality, man. There is a Czech nationality and there is a Slovak nationality."

"My parents," he says softly, "they're from, uh, Czechoslovakia."

"Prague? Bratislava? Brno?" I doubt that someone with his nose would be from a large city, but I do not want to offend him by asking if he is from the country.

"Some, uh, village. In the east."

"In the Carpathian Mountains?"

"Uh-huh," he mumbles.

"Then you must be Ukrainian!" I say. "That region is populated by the Ukrainian nationality."

"Uhhh," he says. He appears to be thinking. "We, uh, used to say we were *nashi*."[12]

"Are you Rusyn-Ukrainian then?"

"Uh, yeah," he says, "something like that."

"Then we are brothers!" I cry. "My nationality is also Ukrainian. Look at my passport. See?" I point to Article 5.

"Hey, man," says Gerald, "I thought you were Russian."

"I am Soviet," I explain, very slowly and very deliberately. "I am a Soviet citizen. But my nationality is Ukrainian. I am Ukrainian—like Andy. No"—I correct myself—"like *Andrei*."

Andrei smiles, while Gerald claps his hands.

---

12   Ukrainian: our own.

"Fucking Andrei fucking Warhol!" he cries. "Fucking Andrei fucking Warhol! Oh, this is too much." He laughs and drops to his knees.

I suddenly realize that, throughout this scene, the camera has been rolling and that we have been captured on film. Somehow, in an oddly dialectical fashion, I managed to do something by doing nothing. How was that possible?

It is time to go and, while Gerald is still writhing on the floor, I shake Andrei's moist hand and ask him if he would like to join me for supper tonight.

"Drop by at, uh, six," he says, squeezing my hand. I leave for Party headquarters, feeling both elated and slightly shaken by this unexpected encounter with a fellow countryman.

Only Jim is there, and he smiles his broad Negro smile as I walk in. He is seated at a large table covered with piles of letters and envelopes.

"Mass mailin' to our suppo'ters," he says. "This here's the only thing 'bout bein' a revolutionary I hate."

"I understand," I say and smile sympathetically. "Outside militant Negroes and young people are on the barricades, and inside we are doing the dull work of the *apparat*.[13] But that, too, is important, Comrade Jim. Without the machine, there can be no Party, and without the Party, there—"

"—ain't no ree-vo-lu-shun."

"Exactly," I say. "We are Leninists, and we know that revolutions are never spontaneous."

"Right on, man," he says and resumes his work with renewed vigor.

---

13   Russian: apparatus.

I am glad to have helped revive his flagging enthusiasm for the organizational work that is indispensable to the class struggle. This is something too many young comrades do not understand: that class struggle is nine parts organization and one part marching. They think it is, or should be, the other way around. But that is an infantile view. I suspect that the youthful student revolutionaries in American universities share that belief. If so, their revolution will go nowhere. That will be unfortunate, but their failure will still destabilize the capitalist system and prove our superiority. And, ultimately, that is all that matters—all that *really* matters.

I spend the day reading about the Negro movement and arranging for meetings with Negro revolutionaries in Harlem. I leave the office at a few minutes before six and walk down to the Factory. I feel certain that Andrei comes from a working class background. I must see his art. Perhaps he is a proletarian artist?

The handsome Gerald opens the door. "Andy's in the back." He burps loudly, without any embarrassment. "He's waiting for you." He motions lazily with his hand. "That way." I like this Gerald, even though he has the easy mannerisms of an Italian aristocrat and the cultural level of a Chukchi seal hunter.

As I walk through the room, I notice the large windows looking down onto the park on Union Square. I also notice what I had failed to see in the morning—the paintings, presumably by Andrei, hanging on the walls. I pause to examine them more closely. They are meticulously executed portraits of everyday things. My excursion along Fourteenth

Street comes to mind. I see bottles, cans—many, many cans, all by a capitalist food-producing company called Campbell's that I have seen in the stores—and other simple things that workers use in order to survive in the capitalist world. There are even paintings of money—plain green bills that dominate the whole canvas just as they dominate capitalist life. I am astounded. I have never seen anything like this. The objects—all everyday material objects, the objects that capitalists fetishize and that workers use, just use, in order to live and reproduce their labor power—are all painted in a completely realistic style. The paintings are so direct and straightforward that they remind me of photographs. Photographs of working class life. Photographs of the things that comprise working class life. Photographs of material existence. I do not know if Andrei is a Marxist, but I begin to suspect that he is a socialist realist painter.

"Good shit," says Gerald, as he walks by and holds open the curtain for me to enter.

Andrei is crouching before a painting of enormous flowers lying flat on the floor. Gerald joins him.

"Good shit, Andy."

"Uh-huh," says Andrei.

Their laconic exchange stands in sharp contrast to the excitement in my soul.

"Andrei!" I cry out. "Your paintings, they address the material and spiritual needs of the working class!"

"Huh?" He turns his white head toward me.

"Your paintings are magnificent," I say. "You should exhibit them in Moscow, in Leningrad, in Kyiv—in the entire Land of the Soviets! I could organize a speaking tour for you. We could even visit your relatives in Soviet Ukraine."

"Yeah, fab," he says. "Hey, uh, let's have dinner."

"You like Chinese?" Andrei pointedly asks me once we are outside.

"The people, yes," I reply, "but the reactionary leadership under the Mao Zedong clique that is doing great damage to the cause of socialism, no." I can see from Andrei's quizzical expression that he wants to know more about Chinese revisionism.

"The Great Proletarian Cultural Revolution was a catastrophe, Andrei. Millions of Chinese workers and peasants died, and the Mao Zedong clique is now fanning the flames of bourgeois nationalism and anti-Sovietism. They are a terrible deviation, Andrei, proof of what inevitably happens when Leninist revolutionary principles are abandoned for voluntarism."

He remains thoughtful and says nothing. We walk through the park—an unemployed man is urinating in public, other unemployed Americans are sitting slouched on the benches—and cross the street near a "department store," Klein's, that looks like an incomparably smaller and poorer version of our magnificent GUM.

"Let's do Luchow's," Andrei says.

On Fourteenth Street we turn left, go a few meters, and come upon a small building with a striped awning.

"I just *adore* Schnitzel," Andrei says, as we walk into a cavernous dining area with portly waiters in white aprons and a German brass band lumbering from table to table. The headwaiter recognizes Andrei and guides us to a small table in the far corner, away from the band and away from the kitchen. The table is covered with forks and knives and glasses and a basket full of pretzels. Andrei immediately takes one and proceeds to munch on it. A waiter pours water into our glasses, and another asks us what we would like to drink. Andrei looks at me, and I say "vodka on rocks," and then he orders champagne.

"Andrei." I decide to be direct and take the bull by the horns.

He giggles. "No one's called me that in, uh, years."

"Andrei," I continue, my heart pounding, "your art is proletarian. It is the art of the workingman. It is revolutionary!"

"Uh, yeah? No kidding? Fab."

"Yes, Andrei, you speak with the clear and pure voice of the simple toiler—the man who struggles for his material existence on a daily basis and who knows that the objects around him are the alienated fruit of his own labor. But they should not be, should they, Andrei? After all, *he* created them with his own sweat and blood and labor power. *He* gave them life. *He* is their creator. But it is only because of capitalism and its alienating effects on the worker that the things that are rightfully his become foreign to him and his life."

Andrei offers me a piece of the pretzel, but I am too excited to accept it.

"Your art, Andrei, is a revolt against the alienation of the objects that are rightfully the worker's. Your art says that these things, which you capitalists have tried to take from me, are really mine. These objects, which surround me, are not my masters or my enemies, but my possessions, my servants. Your art liberates the worker, Andrei. It defies capitalism and heralds socialism!"

"Yeah? Fab. Have a pretzel."

"*Exactly*, Andrei! Those are my sentiments as well. You know what, Andrei? I shall write an article about you. The story of an American working class artist and son of Ukraine." I take a sip of water.

"Are you of working class background, Andrei?"

"My father was, uh, a house mover. In Pittsburgh."

"A house mover?" I ask. "What is a house mover?"

"He moved, uh, houses," Andrei says. "He and his friends had this, uh, technique. I don't know what, but they had this, uh, technique for moving, uh, houses. I mean, like, they moved houses."

"Then he was a worker!"

"Yeah, I guess so."

"And Pittsburgh is the home of the American working class, is it not? The production of steel is its central economic activity. I have seen photographs—the powerful steel mills, the smokestacks, and a river, yes? The exploitation of proletarian labor must have been extreme, even by American capitalist standards."

"The place stank," Andrei says. "We lived in this slum down, uh, near the river. Then we, uh, moved up the hill. We had our own, uh, house. And a yard." Andrei squeezes his nose. "It still smelled."

"Like New York," I say, "the financial citadel of world capitalism."

"Worse." Andrei releases his nose and turns his eyes upward.

"Like capitalism, Andrei. The system is dying, just as Karl Marx said it would. And the patient is beginning to smell."

"Uh, yeah," he says in eager assent. "I wonder where the waiter is."

"The Soviet Union," I continue, "smells of sweat—the sweat of living, working human beings."

"Sweat?" Andrei says. "Don't you have, uh, deodorant?"

The waiter comes and turns to Andrei, "The usual, sir?"

Andrei nods and says, "Make it two. I, uh, ordered Schnitzel for you. It's fab here. Want another drink?" I nod, and the waiter scribbles our order on his pad and hurries away.

"I grew up in Kyiv," I say, "the capital of Soviet Ukraine."

"Uh-huh."

"My father was a worker in the Bolshevik Factory, one of the largest in the Soviet Union. But that was after the Great Patriotic War was over and we came back from Kazakhstan."

"What kind of, uh, war?" Andrei asks.

"The Great Patriotic War. It is what you Americans call the Second World War."

"I was in, uh, high school then."

"I was hungry all the time," I say. "I was just a small child."

"Yeah," he says, "high school really sucked."

Our Schnitzels arrive—two enormous breaded cutlets, like flattened pieces of Chicken Kiev. They are accompanied by a creamy potato salad and a cucumber salad. A small wedge of lemon lies next to the Schnitzel, and I watch Andrei squeeze it gently over the cutlet and place it on the side of the plate.

"*Smachnoho*,"[14] he says, his mouth full of Schnitzel.

"*Smachnoho*," I reply. So he speaks enough Ukrainian to be able to wish me a good meal! I am intrigued. I slice my Schnitzel and marvel at having met a fellow Ukrainian worker in the bastion of American imperialism. I decide to try Russian first.

"*Vy govorite po ukrainski?*"[15]

"Uh," he says—and I can see that he understands—"a little. We spoke, uh, *po nashemu* at home."[16]

Of course, I think, the Ukrainians in that border region still had an undeveloped national consciousness and preferred to say they were "our own kind" and spoke "our own."

"You spoke *po nashemu* with your parents?"

"Uh, yeah. I still do. With, uh, Mama."

"So you grew up speaking *po nashemu*?"

"Uh-huh."

"When did you first learn English, Andrei?"

"The kids, uh, we all spoke *po nashemu* and then, uh, we all spoke English. We'd speak *po nashemu* when, uh, we'd leave the neighborhood."

"*Po nashemu* is a dialect of the Ukrainian language, Andrei," I say. "I heard it when I vacationed once in the Carpathians. I understood every word." I am momentarily distracted by Andrei's unusually vigorous chewing. "They are hardworking people. They suffered terribly from the Polish and Hungarian landlords. When Soviet power came in 1939, they greeted us with bread and salt."

"Yeah," he says as he balances a large piece of potato

---

14   Ukrainian: *Bon appétit*. It is unclear from the text whether Andrei actually spoke Ukrainian or whether Sasha simply provided the Ukrainian equivalent of Rusyn.

15   Russian: Do you speak Ukrainian?

16   Ukrainian: our own [language].

on his fork, "we used to do that, uh, the thing with the, uh, salt and bread. In Pittsburgh." The potato falls into the cucumber salad. "In church."

"I am an atheist," I declare. "I hope that does not shock you, Andrei, but every Communist is an atheist. Religion, as Marx taught, is the opiate of the people."

"Uh, I used to do amphetamines," he says. "Candy's my thing now."

"That was a wise decision, Andrei. Drugs are also an opiate. The vanguard must always be clear-headed."

"I, uh, like church," he says. "I just *adore* icons."

"That is an aesthetic reason, Andrei. In that sense, I also like churches—as architecture, as art. But only as architecture and art that testify to the working people's creative genius."

Andrei pushes away his plate. "God," he says, "I'm stuffed. Have you ever seen my, uh, Marilyn?"

"Your wife?"

"No way, uh-uh. Monroe."

"Ah, the actress!"

"My, uh, painting."

"A painting? Yours?"

"It's, like, iconic." He chuckles. "That's what the, uh, critics said."

"You painted an icon of Marilyn Monroe?"

"There's, uh, lots of gold paint and her face is in, uh, the middle of the canvas." Andrei places his knife and fork carefully on the plate.

"Done?" He reaches for a toothpick and begins rising from the table. "It's on me."

The only thing on Andrei is his smile, but, despite my

momentary confusion, I say nothing and follow him to the exit.

This so-called icon of Marilyn Monroe, the Hollywood actress who committed suicide, mystifies me. Why would a socialist realist artist paint a tawdry movie star? A woman who played in exploitative Hollywood films? A blonde bomb, as they say, with nothing in her head but men and seduction? Such a painting would be unthinkable in the Soviet Union. A Soviet painter would paint a portrait of a Soviet actress or present a genuine heroine of the class struggle in an objectively positive light. Icons have traditionally been of Jesus, his putative mother, or the so-called saints. They have been of gods or of holy people, and were intended to represent windows to heaven, through which the miserable sinners could see the other world. But an icon of an empty-headed actress like this Monroe? What is Andrei up to? Is he religious? A believer? But even if he is, surely he does not consider this Marilyn to be holy or a goddess. After all, she was just a poor woman whom the capitalist machine exploited and killed. And then it strikes me in the eyes. Andrei is trying to say that Marilyn Monroe was a victim of capitalism—a *martyr* crucified on the cross of capitalist relations of production!

This Andrei Warhol is, I begin to realize, an exceedingly clever man. He is a socialist realist through and through, but one who has succeeded in transposing this art form to capitalist conditions. And, in the process, he has subverted capitalism. He speaks little, and he seems to have little to say, but I am beginning to appreciate that there is far more to this seemingly naïve painter than meets the eye. Beneath the placid surface is a revolutionary soul committed to struggle and liberation. The Americans say that still waters run deep. A more accurate statement, at least in Andrei's case, would be that still waters hide turbulent currents and strong undertows.

At Party headquarters. Jim and several comrades are working at their desks or speaking in muffled tones on telephones. I open a file, the one I prepared on the Negro revolution, and realize that the neatly ordered papers have been rearranged. Has Jim been looking through my files? Vigilance is a good attribute of every Communist, but surely he trusts me. After all, I trust him. Then again, he did warn me a few days ago. Did the other comrades look at my papers? But I have nothing to hide, and they know who I am.

Has Jim been instructed to inform on me? I doubt that he would have looked through my things without an explicit order to do so. He is too good a Leninist to have acted on his own. So who could have ordered him? Gus Hall or some other nachalnik within the American Party? But why would Comrade Gus have any doubts about me? He knows exactly who I am. He has been told, explicitly, to provide me with all the assistance I need. And I cannot imagine that he would violate our orders. Besides, if anyone is above suspicion, it is the good Comrade Gus Hall. Perhaps one of his subordinates acted without his knowledge? Possibly, but unlikely. There is discipline in the Party. But if the American comrades are not responsible, who is? Our comrades? But they know, even better than the Americans, just who I am. They have never attempted to pry into my work in the past. (Or have they?) I recall no similar incidents from my many travels to other parts of the world. So why now? Or is it the Americans? The CIA? The FBI? That would make sense, but that would also mean that the imperialists have infiltrated the ranks of the Party. Comrade Jim as an American spy? The thought is preposterous.

At home. I calm my nerves by reading Comrade Gus's analysis of imperialist rivalries. What a mighty intellect! This Russian bear thinks and writes like Lenin.

I leave the hotel early in the morning and take the "A" train to Harlem. My small if respectful tribute to the profound humanity of Negro music. A long ride, and all around me are the tired black faces of Negro workers. Many are sleeping; some stare at me. Of course, they do not know who I am, and to them I am a symbol of capitalist racism and oppression. I think for a moment that I should strike up a conversation with one of them, that I could begin to explain the position of the Soviet Union and the international Communist movement on the Negro question, but then decide against it. That is a job for our American comrades. They know best how to speak the language of the Negro working class. And my spontaneous desire to promote socialism could objectively hurt the cause of socialism. It is important to remember—I must always remind myself of this—that Communism is more important than any one Communist. Iron discipline and complete dedication, passion and vigilance—these are, and always will be, my watchwords.

A meeting with a group calling itself the Panthers. My

contact, a lanky youth named Bimbo, is waiting for me near the token booth in the metro station at One Hundred Twenty-Fifth Street. The smell of urine is pervasive. He is dressed in basketball shoes and red pants and carries a large radio on his shoulder. A good disguise. I would never have guessed that this was a comrade had we not agreed that he would carry a copy of *The Daily Worker* under his right arm. We exchange prearranged pleasantries—I say, "You read that Communist stuff?" and he responds, "All the time, man, all the time"—and then he leads the way and I follow at a distance of about ten meters. I am shocked by what I see as I emerge from the metro. The outside is just as depressing as the inside of the station. Barely standing brick houses, uneven streets, crumbling sidewalks, dirt and filth all around, and, worst of all, unemployed and visibly demoralized Negro toilers gathered on street corners, leaning against boarded-up storefronts, asking passersby for money, their gnarled hands stretched out. It strikes me in the eyes that Harlem resembles Kyiv after its liberation from the Nazi hordes.

We scurry down a narrow alley strewn with colored glass, rusty cans, and yellowing newspapers, walk to the back of a yard that is overgrown with weeds and littered with stained mattresses, and slip down a staircase to a small room. A yellow light bulb hangs nervously from the ceiling, and the dark gray walls are covered with dog-eared posters—mostly of Negroes, but also, I note with satisfaction, of Cuban workers and peasants. My guide exchanges a few words with the three young Negroes in the room. They speak a dialect I do not understand, and all have enormous heads of perfectly rounded hair. One of them, evidently the leader, indicates with a rapid movement of his head that I should sit down on a backless chair. I do. He asks me what I want to know. I reply that I am researching the revolutionary struggle of the Negro working class, that the Soviet workers and peasants support their cause wholeheartedly, and that I would be grateful if he could tell me more about their plans. Would there be a revolution? When? What was their position on the nationality question? Would they expropriate the capitalists? Would they distribute the land to the peasants?

"Like, man, dig it," he says, and then proceeds to tell me, with great fervor, how the struggle arose, who its leaders are, what the attitude of the working class is, and how the revisionists and splittists threaten to destroy the movement. The man is a superb agitator and propagandist.

"But how will you conduct the struggle?" I ask.

"We're gonna smash whitey," he declares.

"You must smash the state. That is what Lenin taught."

"We're gonna smash the machine, man."

"How will the masses be involved?"

"Things are gonna burn, baby, burn."

"The things of the ruling class?"

"Everything, man, it's all gonna burn." He is sweating, as if from the intense heat of the expected conflagration.

I resolve to ask him a hard question: "What is your position on the Jewish question?"

He knits his brow and peers at his comrades. "We gotta split, man," he says, "the pigs are everywhere." (A pig is, I later learn, a colorful metaphor for capitalist police!)

As the three Negroes get ready to leave, their leader shows me his handgun.

"You ever offed a pig, white boy?"

I know that I should say nothing and therefore remain silent.

A few minutes later, my guide and I follow. He turns off the light and locks the door. We retrace our steps through the alley, and, after walking briskly for several blocks, he brings me to a park located on the side of a steep hill.

"That's Columbia, man," he says, pointing to the imposing buildings above, "that's where whitey rules."

"Power to the people, Comrade Bimbo," I say and raise my right fist. Then I nod good-bye and climb the uneven stone stairs.

The unemployed are everywhere, huddled on the benches, standing in groups and drinking. At the top of the hill is a different world. I have read of the social contradictions that afflict capitalism but, once again, am shocked to see that poverty and wealth can co-exist this close together. Below are the racially oppressed Negroes; above are their racist oppressors. All that separates them is a hill and a park, and most of the slope seems to belong to the Negro workers anyway. And yet, at the crest there is a boundary, not physical, but real nonetheless. The Negroes know that to cross that boundary risks their being lynched by a racist mob. And the imperialists dare to criticize our wall of peace in Berlin!

I have been instructed to call Seymour and do so from a public telephone on One Hundred Eighteenth Street and Amsterdam Avenue. A man's voice answers, and after I introduce myself as a friend of "Karl," I am told to go to the steps of a church—St. John's Cathedral—several blocks away. The irony of Seymour's choice of meeting place appeals to me. I am certain that I will like him.

"But how will I recognize you?" I ask.

"Don't worry, man, you will," he says.

And I do. As I approach the church, I see a young man with long hair and an American army jacket leaning against a handrail and reading a book. The cover is easy to see, and I immediately recognize my own *Report from the Land of the Mahatma*! Progress Press had told me that the book would be distributed throughout the world, but I am pleasantly surprised to see that even American students can read Soviet writers. That is a good sign. Seymour is likely to be well versed ideologically. As much as I admire the enthusiasm of my newly found revolutionary Negro friends, I am disturbed by their lack of ideological sophistication. That is understandable, I know—as with Ukrainians and Russians, centuries of serfdom and exploitation have left their mark—but I fear that their class enemy will outflank them ideologically, especially if they fail to develop adequate means of expressing the objectively real interests of the working class. But this Jewish proletarian radical, Seymour, seems to be a very different political animal.

"Aleksandr," he says as he approaches me. "I knew it was you, because you're the only person to have noticed this book."

"Sasha," I say casually. "Please call me Sasha."

We shake hands and he points to a Hungarian café across the street. "We can talk there," he says. His choice of venue is obviously a signal that we are comrades. After we occupy a corner table and order two black coffees, Seymour points to the book.

"Have you also written about China?" he asks while flipping through the pages. "That's where the revolution is happening, man."

"No," I say politely but firmly, "that is where the revolution has been betrayed. Mao Zedong is a revisionist. I hope you are not a Maoist, my young friend."

"Relax, Alex," he says, "I'm just playing with your head." (Another colorful Americanism that means to confuse someone. In this case, the head represents a football, and to play with it is equivalent to dribbling a ball and outmaneuvering an opponent.)

"The revolution," he continues, "is in Cuba."

"Exactly."

"And here," he adds.

"That is why I have come to New York," I say. "Are the workers ready?" Our coffees arrive, and I watch Seymour add three spoonfuls of sugar.

"It's the students, man." He takes a long sip. "*We* are the revolution."

"But there can be no revolution without the working class!"

"Why not?" he shoots back. "Just look around you, Sasha. Here, Berkeley, Berlin, Paris, Rome—all over, man. It's the students who are leading the struggle."

"Perhaps," I say, "but at some point the workers must join you for your efforts to succeed. A student insurrection cannot overthrow capitalist relations of production."

"Think so?" he says. He stirs his coffee. Then he smiles enigmatically. "Just wait and see, man."

Seymour is stubbornly resistant to "seeing more," but I have to admire his commitment to and faith in the revolution.

"And what of the Communist Party?" I ask.

"What of it? They're OK, but they don't get us. Know what I mean?"

I shake my head.

"I mean, like, look, man. They say they're the vanguard. We know we're in charge. We can't both be right, right?" He takes another sip and says, "Hell, now it's too sweet."

"But, Seymour, why not form a popular front? An alliance of all progressive forces?"

"That's cool with us," Seymour says. "I'm not so sure about them. But hey, man, tell me about Russia. I've never been there. I *should* go, but Cuba tops my list."

"Are your ancestors from Russia?"

"Yeah, my grandparents escaped the pogroms."

"The Jewish question has been solved," I say with as little arrogance as possible, "and Jews, like all Soviet nations and nationalities, are now active builders of mature socialism. Our experience could be useful to you."

"Maybe." He adds some water to his coffee. "I like your position on Vietnam. And you're right-on about capitalism and imperialism."

"You have read the great Karl Marx?" I ask hopefully.

"Of course, man, we all read him. And Lenin and Stalin and Trotsky. Hey, man, we're students."

"And Mao Zedong?"

"The little red book, cover to cover."

"Whom do you admire most?" I ask with trepidation.

"None of the above, man. Well, maybe Trotsky. No, Marcuse. Definitely Marcuse. He's right-on, man, *absolutely* right-on."

I see that Seymour belongs heart and soul to the so-called New Left. Time, and bitter experience, will teach him that he is wrong, but I know that there is no point engaging him, just now anyway, in an ideological debate. That can wait. I must be patient with the Americans. After all, even if a misguided revolutionary, he is still a revolutionary and can, if nothing else, prepare the ground for the final assault by the Party. I decide to change the subject.

"How many students are there in the revolutionary movement?"

"Thousands, man, all of them. They all support us."

"May I meet your comrades?"

"Sure," he says. "Next week, Tuesday. At the West End. I think you'll find it interesting. They've got beer, too." Again, he smiles enigmatically.

I think of Seymour's infantile views as I ride the metro to my hotel. Unlike the hippies, he has well-developed political positions. But like the hippies, he is subjectively wrongheaded and objectively wrong. If his comrades are like him, it may be impossible for the Party to find a common language with the students. In any case, the task will be exceptionally difficult.

Once inside my room, I have a hundred grams and dine luxuriously on the bread, cheese, tomatoes, cucumbers, and "polska kielbasa" I bought. When I close my eyes and inhale, I am reminded of home. Would not our Party group have had its meeting today? I believe so. I indulge in a sweet reverie. The discussion ends, the votes are tabulated, and out come the bottles, our good peasant bread, and our Soviet sausage! And then the joking and laughing begin, until some comrade sighs, "All good things must end," and we head for home. This room, this city, even Party headquarters—they are not my home.

That thought reminds me of how my papers were

inspected. Might there be a bug in my room? I search everywhere and, just at the point of thinking that all is well, that perhaps I have just been paranoid, I discover a small listening device in the mouth of the telephone. American, not ours. Would the comrades have done this? Possibly. Would the American security services? Probably. I conclude that I am also being followed. I will have to be careful, or more careful. That will not be difficult, and I should have expected as much from the imperialists. The ideological struggle continues. Indeed, it has even intensified as Communism has begun making serious inroads into the former colonies of the imperialists. And capital, wounded, cornered, and desperate, is fighting back. Well, we shall fight back, too! We shall win, for the future belongs to us, not to them.

Once again, I dream of the man who jumped in the hotel. Curiously, all of us accept his death matter-of-factly, despite the shrieks and panic. Even so, I awake exhausted. Worse, the listening device troubles me. If the Americans planted it, I do not care. I would expect nothing less of them. But what if they did not? What if some intrigue within the American Party has produced subversive forces committed to promoting divisions, creating splits and diversions, and undermining the revolution? This would not be the first time that ideological enemies had infiltrated Communist ranks and done us harm. How many such wreckers have I alone uncovered? And this will not be the last such infiltrator. So why am I disturbed? Why can I not sleep? Because the effort to spy on me has been done so clumsily and obviously. This means that either (1) the person behind this is a rank amateur (but where would an amateur get a bug? Perhaps that is possible in this country?) or (2) the person behind this is a very clever professional who either wants me to think that this is really the work of an amateur or is trying to intimidate me, to send me a signal. The first option strikes me as unlikely. I am, to be honest, too important to attract the attention of amateurs. Then it must be the second possibility—professionals sending me a signal. But why would they think I could be so easily intimidated? They know who I am. They must know my background. In that case, it is simply a signal. They are telling me that they know I am here and that they are watching me. But did I not know that? Of course, I did. So what do I know? Nothing. Even with dialectical reasoning, I am no closer to figuring out this puzzle.

The American procurator general, Robert Kennedy—the Americans affectionately call him "Bobby"—has announced his candidacy for president of the United States. He is the brother of the assassinated John F. Kennedy. Both are the sons of a rich capitalist who made his millions importing illegal alcohol into the United States. The comrades are mildly enthused by his candidacy. At least he is not a conservative right-wing warmonger, one of them says. I learn that he is a so-called liberal Democrat and opposes the war against the Vietnamese people. That makes him objectively anti-imperialist. If he is elected, the United States may withdraw and the Vietnamese Revolution will triumph. The important point is this: The capitalist ruling elite is divided. They will not be able to respond with one voice to the revolutionary struggle of students, workers, and Negroes. Lenin promised peace, bread, and land to the toiling masses in 1917. This Kennedy promises peace. It will be up to the Party to deliver on bread and land.

One day, as I am sitting at my desk, Comrade Arnold steps in with a large-eared comrade. He resembles a former instructor of mine at the Institute of Journalism, a Jewish comrade, Vyacheslav Solomonovich Ginzberg. A good teacher who, as I recall, hated Zionism as much as he loved Communism.

"Sasha," Comrade Arnold says, "I want you to meet the linchpin of the Party, Comrade Morris Childs." Comrade Morris takes my outstretched hand and pumps it enthusiastically.

"Comrade Gus Hall spoke of your devotion to the cause," I say. "It is a great honor to meet a true revolutionary, Comrade Morris."

"The pleasure's mine, Sasha. Call me Morris, OK?"

"We call Morris our secretary of state," says Comrade Arnold. "He's just come back from Prague and Moscow. Your neck of the woods."

"Is the situation in Czechoslovakia really as worrisome as it seems?" I ask.

"The deviationists have the upper hand," says Morris, "but we are hopeful that the correlation of forces will turn in our favor. The Czech and Slovak working class has not been fooled by Mister Dubček.[17] Only some intellectuals appear to have lost their way." I take full note of the "Mister."

"American propaganda?"

"Radio Free Europe," he says. "As you know, Munich isn't far from Prague."

---

17   Slovak Communist leader who led the deviationist movement for
        so-called reform in Czechoslovakia known as the Prague Spring.

"The CIA's dirty hand is everywhere," I sigh.

"And so is"—Morris nods his head solemnly—"the FBI's." He casts a glance at Arnold, who slips out of the office and silently closes the door. "Be careful, Sasha. I'm sure they're tailing you. They tail all of us."

"That," I shrug, "is the price of revolutionary struggle."

"But these are American imperialists," he says. "They're capable of anything. I know I don't have to tell you, Sasha, but be vigilant." How strange, I think, that he should repeat Jim's warning, almost verbatim.

"Your advice is appreciated," I say. "And it will not go unheeded."

"Perhaps we could have a longer talk some day?" he says. "I was very impressed by the USSR's visible progress in socialist construction. Your analysis of mature socialism would interest me greatly. So would your views on capitalist contradictions and the current correlation of forces. Personally, I think the non-aligned movement will grow in importance—and tip the balance."

"I spent several years in New Delhi," I say. "I know the Indian working class."

"I know," he replies. "India could swing the cause of socialism irreversibly in our favor. The future belongs to—"

"—us." I nod in assent. "The future belongs to Soviet power. There is no doubt about it."

I explore New York City. It truly is, as they say, a "melting cauldron." I leave the hotel in the morning and walk south down Eighth Avenue. Tiny Puerto Rican restaurants and shops occupy both sides of the avenue. I had not been fully aware of how close I lived to poverty.

South of Fourteenth Street the atmosphere is different. I am in the famous artistic Bohéme—Greenwich Village. The buildings are smaller and more manicured, windows have curtains or shutters, streets are narrower and no longer go only north to south or east to west, cafés and bars appear with great frequency. Most striking are the people. North of Fourteenth Street they are shabbily dressed immigrants. South of Fourteenth they are either affluent or artistic in appearance. The political sentiments are visibly more left wing. Anti-war posters adorn fences and lampposts. Young people wear buttons proclaiming their opposition to imperialism and capitalism. Invariably, they wear their hair long, the men and the women. Here, more so even than on Union Square, I have difficulty distinguishing males from females. And they are great animal lovers: Every second man I see on the street appears to have a dog, often a small poodle.

I make my way down the notorious Eighth Street, the center of the hippie movement. Small stores sell drug-related paraphernalia—pipes, water pipes, tweezers, and the like. Every few meters, some young man approaches me with an offer to sell narcotics. I hope, as I observe these miserable people, that they have not penetrated the revolution.

A theatre is advertising "Films by Warhol." So Andrei is also a director! Back home he would be in both the Artists' Union and the Cinematographers' Union—an accomplishment worthy of the Order of Lenin. A surfeit of talent! I buy a ticket and find a seat in the back of the almost empty theatre. The lights go out and a flickering black-and-white image of a handsome young man appears.

He is leaning against a brick wall obviously meant to symbolize his working class status. There is no sound in this hopelessly alienated world. Instead, he stands, doing *absolutely nothing*. The reference to mass unemployment is perfect. He fidgets, he leans back his head, he grimaces, he closes his eyes. He is tortured. The film comes to an end, and his miserable condition remains unchanged. There is no color, no sound, no life in this awful capitalist world. There is only a brick wall and his tortured self. The film moves me to tears. I cannot stand to see my fellow workers suffer in this way and run out. As the cold air restores my sense of balance, I marvel, yet again, at Andrei's proletarian genius and human compassion. This man loves humanity. And the brilliance of the title, which so neatly captures the humiliating nature of labor in a capitalist system. *Below Job* even translates well into Russian. I shall have to speak to Andrei about showing the film in Moscow.

In Washington Square. I witness an anti-war demonstration. Several hundred people, mostly young, all with long hair and in dirty blue jeans, are in attendance. Mounted policemen, most sporting hefty paunches, weave their way through the crowd. They appear eager to provoke a violent response, but the demonstrators are peaceful. I listen to some of the speakers. They demand an immediate withdrawal of American occupation forces from Vietnam. They denounce American imperialism. The crowd cheers. They support this Kennedy. But I notice that many are there to socialize. Many are smoking what I take to be marihuana. Many are kissing. Alas, adolescent utopian socialists will never make a revolution.

I buy a map of New York in an enormous bookstore,

named, curiously enough, after the German philosopher
Brentano. As I pass the section with books of photography,
I notice two boys furtively leafing through an oversized
volume with shots of nudes. They are visibly embarrassed as
I stare disapprovingly at them. Is this what the capitalists
call freedom?

Then a long march along one of the most depressing
streets I have ever seen—the Bowery. There is nothing
here, for block after block, but cheap bars, cheap hotels,
and hundreds, perhaps thousands, of drunks and derelicts.
Welcome to America! Most of these pathetic men are too
weak to lift themselves from the sidewalk and ask me for
money. I go into one of the pubs. The drunks sit at the
tables and on stools, coddling shot glasses with both hands.
They lift them slowly, carefully, to their quivering lips,
take small sips, and gently place them on the shiny surface
before them. I find an empty stool between two tired men
and order a vodka "on rocks." My neighbors look at me with
surprise.

"And for my comrades, too," I add. This is a small way
of showing proletarian solidarity, but let these miserable
Americans experience the generosity of Soviet man.

"Thanks, pal," says one. His voice is raspy and his
breath smells of New York's streets.

"Do not mention it, friend."

"Can I have another?" says his companion. He has
gulped down the drink and is looking at me with pleading
soft eyes.

"Of course, comrade."

"Hey, how about me?" says the first.

A socialist competition! I feel a tap on my shoulder. Two unshaven men in soiled white shirts and stained suits are standing behind me.

"Hey, buddy, can you spare a few bucks? We've been on a binge. Gotta get home."

I give them five dollars. Another man joins them. I see that I shall soon be out of money. I quickly pay the bartender and run out.

I have just enough dollars for a modest dinner in the Chinatown area of Manhattan. I find a small, brightly lit proletarian restaurant at the bottom of a flight of stone stairs. I take a seat at a corner table. All around me are poor Chinese workers, mechanically maneuvering food with chopsticks into their hungry mouths. I do not understand the waiter and he does not understand me. After several minutes of negotiation, he goes away and shortly returns with an enormous roast duck. I am certain I did not order it, but decide not to send it back. The worker could lose his job, and it is not his fault that he is trapped in this exploitative machine. The fork is dirty, so I try to eat the duck with the chopsticks. Eventually, I abandon the struggle and use my hands—as at home! Will I be able to pay for the duck, or has my proletarian heart gotten the better of me again? I am one dollar short. I try to explain that I never ordered so large a duck, but the waiter loses his temper and begins to shout—in Chinese. I understand only one word—"police." Mindful of the Negro term "pig," I leave what money I have on the table and, for the second time today, run. Outside, the waiter continues with his expletives, but I dash down an alley and, after several minutes of stumbling about dark streets, finally find the metro. But, as I plunge my hand into my pocket, I find that I have no tokens!

As I am about to exit the station, a familiar voice rings out, "Sasha!" What a stroke of luck! It is Morris.

"Short of change, comrade?" He smiles as he hands me a token. "Lucky for you that I happen to have been here on Party business. It's a long walk to Twenty-Third." This time, I pump his hand enthusiastically. What a wonderful comrade!

A letter from Kelebek awaits me at the hotel. My good friend misses me; so does Kolibri. Leningrad is cold, and the short days are depressing. There is growing concern within the Party about the emerging crisis in Czechoslovakia. Revisionist elements within the fraternal party are trying to seize control and return Czechoslovakia to capitalism. There is, apparently, even talk of leaving the Warsaw Pact and joining the imperialist NATO alliance. Kolibri has been sent on a mission to Prague. Kelebek has run into Katyusha at a reception at the Journalists' Union. She looked sad, he writes. I cheer myself up by reading Brezhnev's speeches.

Whom do I see in the lobby of the hotel but Andrei? He is sitting on the sofa, dressed in a black suit and shirt, smiling as a young woman is talking loudly and chopping the air with both hands. I admire his composure. As I approach them, he notices me and says, "Uh, Sasha."

"A pleasure to see you, Andrei," I beam. And I am genuinely pleased by this wonderful coincidence. "And who is this charming lady?" Her hands lie in her lap and she looks at me with clenched teeth. I can see that I am an unwelcome intrusion on her exposition.

"This is, uh, Valerie. Uh, Solanas."

"I am honored to make your acquaintance, madam," I say and bow slightly. She turns away with unnecessary rudeness. "Your friend does not seem to like me, Andrei."

"Valerie's like that with, uh, everybody. Aren't you, Val?" For reasons that I cannot fathom, Andrei appears to be enjoying our discomfort.

"Oh, fuck off, Andy," Valeria says. "Where the hell is my script?" She abruptly rises from the sofa and, without saying a word to either of us, storms out of the hotel.

"Uh, sit down," Andrei says quietly.

"Thank you, Andrei," I say. "So who is this Lithuanian woman, Valeria Solanas?"

Andrei smiles. "Nobody. Wants to be a superstar."

"Like your Marilyn?"

"Uh-uh. Wants to star in my, uh, films. Like, uh, Veeva."

"You know, Andrei, I saw one of your films recently."

"Uh-huh."

"It was a devastating portrait of an anguished worker."

"Uh-huh."

"I was moved to tears, Andrei."

He crosses his arms and leans back.

"I like the sound the, uh, camera makes."

I laugh at his joke.

"Uh, really."

"But Andrei," I protest, "that film was bursting with emotion and love of man. Surely that passion came from you!"

"The actors, uh, do their thing, and the camera, uh, does its thing."

"Are you saying they improvise?"

"Uh, yeah."

"So the camera is just there to record?"

"Uh-huh."

"No montage? No plot?"

"What's that?" He smiles.

"Pure film?" And then it strikes me in the eyes. "That is genius, Andrei, pure genius. You do nothing to interfere in the camera's recording of material existence."

"Uh—"

"*That* is a radically proletarian position, Andrei. You remove all traces of bourgeois ideology and hierarchy from the interaction of the camera and the working class."

"Uh—"

"And you let the workers speak for themselves. Andrei, not even Eisenstein or Dovzhenko[18] did that!"

As I finish speaking, a wiry man with short hair and sunken eyes approaches us. I have seen such types in the Caucasus. Andrei invites him to sit down, and he does. I half-expect him to try to involve us in some blackmarketeering scheme.

"Sasha, Lou."

The man extends a bony hand and we shake.

"Lou Reed," he says. His voice is surprisingly gruff, like an army sergeant's.

"Sasha Ivanov," I reply. "Are you a painter like Andrei?"

"No, man, I play guitar."

"Lou sings," says Andrei.

"Like *Dean* Reed!" I exclaim.

"Like *who*?"

---

18   Sergei Eisenstein, a world-famous Soviet Russian filmmaker; Alexander
          Dovzhenko, a world-famous Soviet Ukrainian filmmaker.

"Dean Reed," I say emphatically, "is one of the world's most *famous* American singers. He joined the revolution and is now living in the German Democratic Republic." Dean Reed's namesake looks puzzled. "He performs in the Soviet Union, Cuba, and many other socialist countries. Dean Reed is a great man, a true revolutionary, a real friend of the global proletariat. I have met him on several occasions. He is also an excellent actor. His anti-imperialist Westerns are very popular."

An inspired thought crosses my mind. "Andrei, perhaps you would like to use him in one of your—"

"Hey, man," says Dean Reed's namesake, "that's really great. Look, I gotta run."

"Good-bye," I say to him. "Are you and Dean Reed related?" Unfortunately, the other Reed does not hear me.

Once again, Andrei is smiling.

"You're a trip," he says.

"Thank you, Andrei," I reply. "I have traveled much and I know the world. But tell me, what are you doing here?"

"We're shooting."

I raise my eyebrows.

"A movie," he says.

"Ah!" I cry. "Here in the hotel? But where are the camera crews?"

"Don't need them."

"Ah, yes, of course, you only need the camera."

"Want to, uh, watch?" he says and tightly grasps my fingers.

We take the lift to the eleventh floor and walk down the hallway to the right. At the far end of the corridor stand several longhaired men and unusually blonde women in tight skirts and extravagant make-up. The door to one of the rooms is open and a tripod is positioned in the doorway. The camera is running, and I hear loud female voices coming from the room. They appear to be arguing. Andrei approaches the camera and looks through the lens. I peer into the dark room and am shocked to see that the voices I hear are from a film. The room is empty, save for a flickering screen and a projector. I see three women: two are sitting on an unmade bed, a third is on the floor. One of the women on the bed—beautiful, dark-haired, and with a strong face—is shouting at the others. The other woman on the bed appears to be crying, and the third is silently writhing on the floor. I do not understand what is going on, but I am enthralled by the power of the dark-haired woman. Suddenly, she refers to herself as "Hanoi Hannah" and I begin to realize just what is taking place. The symbolism is effective, especially as this Hanoi Hannah has, without being Oriental, slightly slanted eyes. I see before me a cinematic representation of the imperialist war in Vietnam! But *this* war is being fought in the bedrooms of the capitalists. In Andrei's version, the war is not some distant event. The Vietnamese people are fighting the imperialists in their very homes. The war is in America. The war—it strikes me in the eyes—*is* America! But one thing still mystifies me.

"Andrei," I ask, "why are you filming a film?"[19]

"It's the, uh, Chelsea girls," he says.

"But these Chelsea girls have already been filmed."

"Yeah, but we never filmed, uh, a film," he says. "It's fab. Take a look."

"I am not a cinematographer, Andrei. I am not qualified to take a look."

19   This film of a film appears to have been lost.

"No sweat," he says and steps away from the camera.

The experience is exhilarating. I watch Hanoi Hannah go on the attack! The imperialists cringe. What a shame that Kelebek and Kolibri cannot witness her victory.

"Zoom in and out," Andrei says.

"May I?" But before he answers, I focus on Hanoi Hannah's beautiful face. What a heroine, I think. You deserve the Lenin Prize, Comrade Hannah. With you in the vanguard, the proletariat will triumph, even in America.

"Thank you, Andrei," I say, my palms and forehead wet with sweat. "You have opened new vistas for me. Truly, there are no limits to the forms that proletarian struggle can take."

"Hey, Andy," some man yells, "who the hell is this guy?"

"No sweat, Paul," Andrei says. "He's a pal. Sasha."

"We're filming, Andy"—I can see that he is close to losing his temper—"and your pal's in the fucking way."

"Uh, yeah," Andrei responds, "no problem."

"My apologies, Mister Paul," I say.

"We're making a film, pal, and you're not part of the crew."

"Uh, calm down, Paul," Andrei says firmly. "It's my film."

"Yeah, like fucking *Lonesome Cowboys* was your film."

"Uh, Paul—"

"Fuck, Andy, this is no joke. The fucking Feds are after us because of you."

Andrei says nothing.

"They're gonna fuck us over," the man says, "really fuck us over. No fooling around, OK? We need to talk. Got a minute?"

"Uh-oh," Andrei says as he turns to me. "Drop by at the Factory, Sash. Tonight."

"A-Okay," I say and realize that this is the first time I have used this colloquial expression without feeling self-conscious. As I walk away, I see that Andrei and Paul have gone to the far end of the corridor. Andrei is leaning against the wall, his arms crossed, his face impassive. His friend Paul is making karate-like motions with his hands and talking excitedly. Hanoi Hannah is still shouting, so I cannot hear what Paul is saying. But I am not really listening. My thoughts are focused on the unusual nature of Andrei's creative activity. *He is filming his own film.* What can that possibly mean? And then, as I enter the lobby of the hotel, it strikes me in the eyes. I am reminded of Plato's parable of the cave. Andrei can only mean to show the vast extent of bourgeois alienation. My friend Andrei is saying that capitalist reality is as real as a film of a film! He instinctively knows that the only true reality is socialist. I must remember to speak to him about his philosophy one of these days.

At Party headquarters. As I sit at my desk and look at the papers and files scattered about, it strikes me in the eyes that I have been here for several weeks and have yet to produce anything of substance. This is unusual, as writing comes easily to me. Yes, I have written a few reports (though I doubt that the comrades in Moscow learned anything they did not know already), but it is high time that I justified my wage and wrote an article for the press. A "Letter from America" is one possibility. "Revolution in the Bastion of Imperialism"? "Socialist Realism in America"?

A letter from Katyusha. She misses me, etc., etc., but everything is A-Okay. I realize that I have not written to her as well and immediately compose a brief letter.

Comrade Jim and I have a discussion over coffee and sandwiches. We sit at the large table that Jim uses for stuffing envelopes and stacking leaflets. He asks me how my meetings in Harlem and at Columbia University went. I tell him that I am impressed by the profound revolutionary enthusiasm of my interlocutors, but am somewhat worried by their lack of ideological sophistication. There is much work for the Party, I say. Jim says that the Party is active among Negroes and students, but that there are objective constraints and subjective difficulties. The Negroes mistrust whites, even when they speak of civil rights and social justice, and most leading members of the Party are white. An accident of history, he surmises, but there is nothing to be done about it now. Worse, he says, many Party members are Jewish, and the Negroes associate Jews with landlords. Your nationality question, I remark, reminds me of conditions in tsarist Russia. Jim says that the students, though far more receptive to left-wing ideology, also have a highly developed anarchist streak and that is dangerous. They mistrust all organizations and claim to be opposed to all vanguards. And then there are the subjective barriers. Many comrades are fearful of traveling to Harlem, and many simply do not understand the students. Their long hair, their crazy clothes, their use of drugs—which Jim also thinks are impediments to the revolutionary struggle—arouse the contempt or lack of understanding of many comrades. I say I understand. I also say that perhaps the American comrades should

study the Soviet experience more closely. How did Lenin
and the Bolsheviks manage to win over the peasantry in
1917? How did they solve the Jewish question? How did
they recruit the students of Petersburg and Moscow? There
are important lessons to be gleaned from their example.
Comrade Jim agrees wholeheartedly.

I then ask him what he thinks of the ongoing revolution
in America. Where would it go? How would it change
capitalism? Would it be successful? He says that, without
the Communist Party at its head, it could not succeed, and
that is why resolving the problem of the Party's relations
with Negroes and students is so fundamental. I agree.
But then he says that, even if the revolutionary struggle
fails this time, it would still have a progressive impact on
American society. The young were becoming anti-capitalist,
and that was significant. Negroes were rejecting the system
as well, although they did not yet fully comprehend that
racism could never be eradicated in a capitalist society. I
interject with a comment about the Soviet Union's solution
of the nationality question, and Jim agrees that the Soviet
experience is valuable and could serve as a model for
America as well.

"According to Lenin," I say, "every nation, especially
a subordinate one, has the right to self-determination
up to and including separation. That was the American
Party's line in the past, but it no longer seems to speak
of self-determination with as much forcefulness. Why not,
Comrade Jim?"

"Because," he says, "the Negro workin' class is still
unsure of its own powers and don't fully 'ppreciate that
self-determination would be the solution to its problems."

"Subjective barriers?"

"Yeah," he says, "a whole lot of 'em here."

"Are you saying that the superstructure is autonomous in the United States?"

"No way, man," he says, "the material base determines the sup'structure, even in America. But the sup'structure's a real bitch here, Sasha. America's history is the reason. So the Party had to do what it had to do."

I agree that this was a wise course of action. I then ask Jim about Andrei.

"That white-haired weirdo?"

"Yes," I say, "he is out of the ordinary, but I believe he is a deeply proletarian artist."

"You're kiddin', ain't you?" Jim says. "The guy wears a fuckin' wig. He's a fruit."

"A what?"

"A fruitcake," he says, "y'know, a faggot."

"His nationality, Jim, is American," I correct him, "and like all Americans he suffers from the deformities of this society. Have you seen his art, Jim? It is the purest socialist realism. He depicts the objectification of labor and its fruits—as well as the exploitation of labor, and the fruits of that objectification—far more subtly and persuasively than any artist in the Soviet Union. How is it possible that this, as you say, weirdo has managed to express himself in so proletarian a manner?"

"You're kiddin', Sasha, ain't you?"

"No, Jim," I reply, "I am dead serious. I grant you that Andrei and his entourage are reflective of the illness of American society—after all, how could anyone, even you, not be affected by capitalist social pathologies?—but this son of a Ukrainian worker from the steel city of Pittsburgh is a proletarian at heart, and his subtle understanding of the exploitation of the working class, while implicit and perhaps unconscious, is clearly evident in his paintings."

"A Ukrainian worker?" Jim says solemnly. "Didn't know that, man."

"That is right, Jim," I say. "He and I are very much alike. We are both the progeny of the Ukrainian working class. I chose socialism and revolution consciously, because I had the good fortune to grow up in the Soviet Union. Andrei has chosen socialism unconsciously. His working class origins, his cultural background, are responsible for that choice. Ukrainians are a nation of peasants and workers, Jim. There has never been a large Ukrainian bourgeoisie. Capitalism is culturally foreign to Ukrainians. I do not mean to say that they are natural socialists, but I do believe that socialism is 'naturally' close to their hearts."

"The triumph of the sup'structure?" Jim asks.

"In this case, the superstructure and the base are identical. As with your Negroes," I add. "They have no choice but to be socialists, because socialism is the answer to their class oppression as workers and to their racial oppression as black people. They may not know it, and neither does Andrei. But just like Andrei, their actions are intrinsically socialist. After all, Jim, Andrei's studio is called the Factory. Do you think that is an accident?"

"No shit?"

In the evening, I go to that very same Factory, as I had agreed to do. No one but Andrei is there, and upon seeing me he says that his mother has just called and that he has to rush home. Would I like to go with him? See his house?

Meet his mother? I am delighted at the opportunity to see an American working-class home and immediately say yes. He locks the doors of the Factory and we go outside.

"Shall we take the metro, Andrei?"

"Uh, no," he says, and raises his hand, slowly, to hail a taxi. I climb into the back and Andrei follows. The seat sags—I am reminded of Soviet taxis—and, as we tilt inwards, our elbows touch.

"My apologies," I say. "It is very tight here."

"Tight's OK," Andrei replies.

We drive north, and after a few minutes I realize that we have passed the Soviet Mission to the United Nations somewhere on our right. We turn right in the nineties and then the driver stops the vehicle in front of a stone building on a busy thoroughfare, Lexington Avenue. I climb out and Andrei pays the worker for his services. As Andrei exits the taxi, he extends his arm and I grab his hand and pull him out.

"Wow," he says, "you're *super* strong, Sash."

"My army training," I say. "It made me into a man."

"I can tell. It's fab."

"Mama!" Andrei shouts. "Mama, I'm home!"

A small gray-haired woman, as Ukrainian in her features as one can possibly imagine, appears at the bottom of a staircase below the ground floor.

"Andiku," she says quietly, "I was sleeping." How touching, I think, that she should call him by the diminutive.

Andrei rushes down the stairs and, suddenly speaking a dialect of Ukrainian, asks her if she is well.

"*Dobre, dobre*,"[20] she nods. "I felt weak before and I knew that only seeing my Andik would make me well." Andrei takes her in his arms and plants a soft kiss on her gray head.

"OK, OK, Mama," he says, "OK, OK." He then leads her up the stairs and introduces me to her.

"*Vy hovoryte po nashemu?*"[21] she asks.

"Of course I speak your language," I reply.

"Oh, my God!" she cries, her hands raised to her open mouth. "You're one of us!"

"Yes, I am, Pani[22] Warhola. The same blood runs in our veins."

"Oh, Andiku, finally a friend who is one of our own!"

I take her wrinkled hand and kiss it delicately.

"Oh, Sashenka," she smiles, with girlish bashfulness. "Andiku, see? You should be a gentleman, too."

"Mama," he says impatiently, "enough. Please."

"Stop rolling your eyes, Andiku," she says, and draws closer to Andrei. "Come inside, boys, come inside. I baked a walnut cake, Andik's favorite." Andrei looks at me and smiles. I can see that he loves his mother. What Ukrainian boy would not?

We enter the kitchen—where else?—and sit down. Andrei washes his hands in the sink and then hands me the soap and towel. I do the same. How strange it is, I think, to be in a proletarian household somewhere in Manhattan. The table is cluttered with familiar things—a salt shaker, a pepper shaker, a small pot of honey, a little jar of sugar cubes, a plate full of candy, a piece of chocolate, a butter

---

20　　　Ukrainian: Good, good.
21　　　Ukrainian: Do you speak our own? It is unclear whether Andrei's mother spoke Ukrainian or whether Sasha simply provided the Ukrainian equivalent of Rusyn.
22　　　Ukrainian: Mrs.

knife, a folded newspaper, a few letters with Czechoslovak stamps, and some string. While Andrei and I sit down, his mother opens the refrigerator and removes, first an enormous cake, and then a bottle of vodka.

"Pour yourself some, while I make the tea. And pour me some, too," she adds slyly. She lights the stove and returns to us.

"My sweet boys," she sighs, and we raise our glasses and drink the vodka. Andrei and his mother down theirs immediately, and I smile inwardly. Ukrainians will always be Ukrainians, wherever fate may cast them. Andrei's mother places the kettle on the table and gives the two of us a tea bag. She sits down and crosses herself. As she does, I see that Andrei casts a glance at me.

"How long have you lived in America?" I ask.

"Oh my God, oh my God. How long has it been, Andiku? Your father came here before the war, and then he brought me here after the war."

"The second war?" I ask and immediately realize that my question is incorrect.

"No, no," she smiles gently, "the first. The soldiers kept coming and going. They took everything. America was a paradise. We had a house and the boys could go to school. And there was no war in Pittsburgh." Then she adds, almost as an afterthought. "War is a terrible, terrible thing, my dear Sasha."

"Kyiv was destroyed in the war," I say. "We played in the rubble, but I remember how my mother cried whenever she looked at the ruins."

We fall silent for a few seconds, and then Pani Warhola says, "Let's have some cake." She proceeds to cut two

enormous pieces for Andrei and me. "My Andik loves cake.
He always has, haven't you, Andiku?" Andrei is too busy
eating to reply. But he does look at me and roll his eyes
again.

"Tell me about Pittsburgh, Pani Warhola."

"Oh, it was *such* a smelly city—"

"No kidding, Mama."

"—but so many of our people lived there. It was good,
Sashenka. There were neighbors, we knew them all, we
would visit each other all the time. And we would always
sing. My God, how we sang! All the time"—she nods her
head dreamily—"all the time. Here, in New York, no one
sings, except"—she looks severely at Andrei—"Andik's
crazy friends."

"Uh, leave my, uh, friends out of this, Mama."

"OK, OK, Andiku, OK, OK." Then she smiles and looks
at me again. "Andik's father had such a voice. Oh, how he
used to sing! Especially on our Christmas.[23] When all the
Americans would be working, and we would gather in our
house or at my sister's, the whole family would gather, and
we would eat and sing and eat and sing. Those were such
good times."

"Mama forgets the, uh, bad times," Andrei says to me.

"That is understandable," I say. "I too have forgotten
the hunger we felt after the war."

"I'm glad I, uh, left Pittsburgh," Andrei says.

"When was that?"

"After, uh, college. In 1949."

"Oh, Sasha," Andrei's mother gushes, "my Andik was
such a talented artist. He won prizes!"

---

23   January 7th.

"New York was a new, uh, world for me," Andrei says. "It was just fab."

"Andik's father was a house mover, Sashenka, and Andik was always ashamed of that. But his father was a good man. He worked so hard, all his life. All his life, but then he died. Well"—she crosses herself—"that's God's will."

"New York was fab, *simply* fab. I could be, uh, myself here."

"And my Andik became a famous designer, did you know that, Sasha? For all the big ladies' magazines. Shoes, magazines, everything, he designed everything. And he even published books, did you know that, Sasha? And"—she glows proudly—"I wrote the words to them."

"About cats. They were about, uh, cats."

"And now my Andik is a famous painter, Sasha. An artist! And people buy his paintings, and they pay hundreds of dollars for them. Isn't that right, Andiku? Would you like another piece of cake, boys?" Andrei pushes his plate away, but I say yes, even though I cannot eat another bite. "Oh, please, Andiku, have a small piece. Join Sasha. He can't eat alone. Sashenka"—she turns to me conspiratorially—"would you like to see our family albums?"

"Uh, Mama," Andrei says, "don't."

"It is A-Okay, Andrei," I say, "I enjoy looking at old photographs."

She rushes off to some other room and returns with two albums. The hand-carved wooden covers are decorated with colored patterns, exactly like ones I have seen in Ukraine.

"Look, my dear Sasha, here is Andik at the age of one." She turns the page. "And here is Andik on his first day of school. Remember, Andiku, how you cried when I left you there? And here is Andik...."

And so she continues for the next hour. After several minutes, Andrei leaves and says that he would be upstairs. I see why looking at old photographs embarrasses and bores him, but I am fascinated by this glimpse into Andrei's working-class background. The faces on the photographs are all visibly Slavic, the hands visibly those of workers and peasants, the dress visibly that of the poor. Andrei's mother babbles on and on, and she is clearly elated, but I feel such sadness for the fate of my people. Oh, how you have suffered! At least, now, you can rest in the Land of the Soviets.

After she closes the second album, she turns to me and, with a gleam in her eye, says, "Another vodka, Sashenka? Andik doesn't like it when I drink. OK, OK?"

"OK, OK," I nod.

We drink to Andrei's health, and then she says, "OK, OK, Sashenka, now go to Andik. Up the stairs. Hear the music? That means Andik's working. Andik is always working. Too much, maybe." She pauses. "Just like his father." She kisses me on the forehead and retreats down the stairs.

I knock on Andrei's door and walk in. Contemporary American music is playing at an ear-splitting volume, and Andrei is bent over a canvas, a paintbrush in his hand. Variously sized canvases are stacked against the walls, which are covered with drawings, prints, and paintings. I notice a religious icon in the corner. Andrei's? Or his mother's?

Andrei says something to me, but I cannot hear him.

"What?" I say, and he points with the paintbrush at a chair. "No," I say with raised voice, "I will just look around, if you do not mind."

He nods and returns to his work. Poised above the canvas, Andrei resembles a black cat. He extends one leg in order to view something from one angle. He extends the other leg to view it from some other angle. He crouches, he gets on all fours, sometimes he just kneels and rotates his head slowly. I steal a look at the canvas and see that it, like the one in the Factory, is of enormous flowers. Ukrainian folk art immediately comes to mind. This Andrei Warhol is just a Carpathian craftsman, I think, probably like his ancestors.

I walk along the walls and look at the objects adorning them. There are curious sketches of shoes and cats—is this what his mother was alluding to?—there are small drawings of naked little boys and girls, and there are, in addition to a few large paintings of capitalist commodities, sections of newspapers and magazines: headlines, photographs of car crashes, advertisements, and other printed items. Andrei, evidently, is a close observer of bourgeois society. I see that his socialist realist art is rooted in an intimate familiarity with the bourgeois superstructure and its alienating phenomena.

Andrei approaches me, his face smudged, his mouth sucking on a candy.

"I'm, uh, sorry about Mama," he says. "She can be crazy."

"Not at all, Andrei, I found your family photographs to be quite moving. I would like to reproduce some of them in the Soviet press." And suddenly it strikes me in the eyes. "Andrei, I will write an article about your art! Your art and your life. Is that A-Okay with you?"

"Uh, yeah," he says, "sure."

"Then I will leave you to your work, Andrei. You will be a hero in the Soviet Union!"

"Uh, yeah, sure," he says, "fab."

As I open the front door, Andrei's mother appears at the bottom of the staircase.

"You're going, Sashenka?" she says. "Already? Come again." Her eyes are twinkling. "You are good for my Andik."

And then a strange thing happens. As I shut the door behind me and step onto the sidewalk, I hear a woman's voice shout "Hey!" I turn in the direction of the voice and see that it belongs to Valeria, who is leaning against a lamppost and smoking a cigarette.

"Miss Solanas! What are you doing here?"

"Just watching," she replies and flicks the cigarette into the gutter. "Where're you going?"

There is, though it is already late, much traffic in the street. I look around, with a confused expression on my face, and say, "I am looking for the metro."

"The fucking subway?" she says as she takes me by the arm.

We walk silently for a few meters and I look at her face out of the corner of my eyes. She is a small woman, with nervous, penetrating eyes, a tight mouth, and a hungry, gaunt face. Like many young American women in New York, she wears jeans and a bulky old jacket. Her hair is cut short. Most American women her age wear it long and uncombed, or seemingly uncombed, as a sign, I assume, of protest against bourgeois norms of dress. Atop her head sits a Lenin-style worker's cap. This Valeria could be a Bolshevik agitator in revolutionary Petrograd.

"You're close to Andy," she states.

"Not very," I respond, "not yet, but I like him very much." She looks at me quizzically. "I think he is a proletarian genius."

"No fucking shit?" she says. I notice a tone of heavy irony bordering on sarcasm in her voice.

"Andrei is a remarkable exemplar of the creative intelligentsia."

"Where d'you get this Andrei shit? And what the fuck's an exemplar?"

"That is his real name. He is Ukrainian. Like me."

"He's a fucking man," she says with finality. "And he's gonna get fucked one of these days. The bastard stole my script."

Fortunately, we reach the metro entrance at just that moment, and I am spared the necessity of replying to or commenting on something I do not fully understand. We part, I walk downstairs, while Valeria turns back up the avenue. Is she spying on Andrei? Evidently. But why? I do not know enough of his life and work to be able to guess knowledgeably, but it is clear that she believes Andrei offended her deeply. A stolen film script? Why would Andrei steal a script when his films are improvised? She appears to be a hard woman—though her eyes suggest that she has a feminine core, which would be natural. Or perhaps she is unusually sensitive? Perhaps that tough outside image is just that—an image? I know such women in Leningrad: hard as nails on the outside, but merely women on the inside.

I take the metro to Twenty-Third Street and, much to my discomfort, discover that my hotel is several blocks away. I pass a park on my right in which "bums" lie, sleeping or drinking, on the benches. Then, on my left, I walk past a beautiful building shaped like a narrow wedge. I was here, I realize, on my second day in New York. The rest of the street—the blocks are unusually long—is empty, except for occasional drug addicts and prostitutes. Several look at me and say hello or hi.

A thought-provoking speech by Leonid Illich[24] on the nationality question. I think I shall quote sections in my article on Andrei.

I spend the whole day writing. My report and the article about Andrei. A pleasant surprise at lunchtime. Morris appears in my door with sandwiches and coffee. As we begin eating, he asks me how I have been doing.

"Very well, I have been making great progress in my research."

"Excellent," he says. "And no problems, otherwise? All's well? I got you ham and cheese."

"All is quite well, Morris."

"Let me be direct, Sasha," he says in a whisper. "Have the Americans tried contacting you?"

"No." I then decide to be fully frank. If the Politburo trusts Morris, then so shall I. "But—"

"But what, Sasha?"

---

24   Leonid Illich Brezhnev, of course, the world-famous Soviet
        Communist leader.

"There was a listening device in my hotel telephone."

"Was?"

"I removed it."

"You should've told me, Sasha. We need to know what the class enemy is up to."

How can I tell Morris that I was not quite sure that the device was the work of the American intelligence services?

"The office," he says, "we're always on the lookout for bugs here."

"Have there been any?"

"No. Well, we don't think so. We can never be quite sure, you know."

"I understand," I say. "I have friends at the Mission.[25] They could help."

"We've spoken with them. They've checked. Found nothing." Morris finishes his sandwich and tosses the wrapper into the wastepaper basket. "Two points!" he exclaims. "Want my pickle?" Then he turns to me with a serious expression on his face. "But you must be careful, Sasha. I'm sure they're after you. Be on your guard. The FBI's been known to use every underhanded trick—"

"That is the nature of the class struggle," I say calmly.

"Be vigilant, Sasha, be very, very vigilant. You are in the bastion of imperialism. Nothing, absolutely nothing, is what it seems like." He pauses to take a long sip of coffee. "Terrible stuff," he grins. "Have you ever read *Alice in Wonderland*, Sasha?"

I nod.

"Well, this is Wonderland. You, my dear friend, are little Alice. And little Alice has fallen into a deep, deep hole."

---

25   The Soviet Mission to the United Nations on East 67th Street.

A meeting with Comrade X. My instructions are contained on a slip of paper shoved under my hotel door: an intersection and a phone number. I walk to the corner of Thirty-Second Street and Broadway and find the designated public telephone. We agree to meet on a boat that departs from a pier on West 42nd Street at noon. I decide to walk and see what the famous Times Square is like. Glittering cinema marquees, little restaurants selling pizza and greasy sausages, and everywhere—drug addicts, bums, prostitutes, policemen. A microcosm of capitalist society: the shine and the money side-by-side with the dirt and the poverty, and all are supervised by the forces of coercion. The neon signs and flashing light bulbs hurt my eyes. The rest of Forty-Second Street is even worse. The lights disappear, and all that remains is dilapidated buildings, jagged windows, garbage, and the human refuse of capitalism. Comrade X and I meet, as agreed, on the boat and spend three hours talking. The view of Manhattan, as we circumnavigate the island, is breathtaking. Seen from afar, of course, capitalist society appears to be without faults. Look at it more closely and what you thought was a hill turns out to be a garbage dump.

Times Square, I learn, is called "seedy"—meaning that it is decayed and degenerate. How curious that such a terrible condition should be derived from a word, seed, that spells birth, hope, joy, and renewal. But why should that surprise me? Capitalism perverts everything it touches. Under its malignant influence, even seeds produce death and become "seedy."

At the office. Work on the article. And a letter to

Katyusha. She has written to me several times since my last letter, and I have yet to respond. But I assume that she has heard from the comrades that all is well with me. I tell her about this and that, and I spend several paragraphs describing New York. At noon, I leave the office to have lunch, but while passing the door to the Factory decide to step inside. Andrei's irascible filmmaker friend, Paul, is sitting at a desk, shouting obscenities into a telephone. The thin brunette I saw in the lobby of the hotel is sitting on the couch, smoking a cigarette, her legs crossed, her bony knees provocatively displayed.

"Who the hell are you?" she asks, a bored expression on her powdery face.

"Aleksandr Ivanov, a Communist and a journalist," I say. "And a friend of Andrei Warhol."

"A *friend*?" She arches an eyebrow. "I didn't think Andy had any friends. I'm Veeva."

"Ah, so you must be the famous superstar."

"Damned right, Al."

"Sasha," I say, "please call me Sasha."

She smiles again. "You lonesome, cowboy? Wanna sashay with Veeva, Sasha?"

"I am a journalist, Miss Veeva," I say with proletarian pride, "*not* a cowboy."

She lifts her skirt, and I feel myself reddening as I see that she is wearing no underpants.

"Too bad," she says as she lowers her skirt. "And don't forget Andy's mine. Got that, cowboy?"

I walk hurriedly toward the back and hear Gerald and Andrei talking. They are crouched over some paintings. Gerald is holding a large screen in his hands. Andrei is holding a can of paint.

Gerald sees me first and says, "Hey, man."

"Hello, Gerald," I say, "hello, Andrei. I hope I am not disturbing you. I was going to have lunch."

"Have a seat," says Gerald, "we'll be done in a second."

I have observed painters in their studios in Leningrad and Kyiv. This is the first time that I see the creative process unfold outside the Soviet Union. I watch Gerald place the screen on the canvas. Andrei steps back and thinks. He hands Gerald the can of paint. Gerald dips a large paintbrush into the can and smears the paint across the screen. The process is new to me, and as I am trying to comprehend just what they are doing, it strikes me in the eyes that the most remarkable aspect of this process is that they—two men—are doing it together, simultaneously, cooperatively, collaboratively. It is not quite like an assembly line in a genuine factory—or, for that matter, even in a pizza restaurant—because Andrei and Gerald take turns, consult, pause, and so on. That kind of activity would be impossible in a factory, where every worker must perform a precise pre-assigned task. Before and after the productive process, our workers consult, debate, argue, and decide in a democratic fashion just what they will produce and how, and how much and for whom. In *this* Factory, production and deliberation are fused in the same process. There are no three discrete phases, as in a factory, of deliberation, production, and evaluation. Here, deliberation, production, and evaluation take place simultaneously, involving both artists to the exact same degree, all the time, from beginning to end.

This is Andrei's studio and Andrei is the artist with the famous reputation, but it is clear from watching the two work that Gerald has as much to say about every stage of the creative process as does Andrei. So much so that it is valid to ask who the real artist is— Andrei or Gerald? Of course, the question is absurd. It makes sense only in a bourgeois context that places undue monetary value on authorship and innovation. In a socialist society, in a society of workers, the question of authorship is irrelevant. All workers objectively contribute to the process at all times. But, even in the Soviet Union, workers contribute only in the first and third stages of the creative process. Production itself still entails use of the assembly-line technique invented and perfected by none other than that arch-capitalist Henry Ford. Here, in Andrei's Factory, the creative process is completely anti-capitalist and completely socialist. The collective—Andrei and Gerald—work on everything at all times, equally.

It strikes me in the eyes that Andrei's cinema-tographic technique is identical. I had originally thought that improvisation was at the core of Andrei's films, but that is only true from a bourgeois perspective. Seen in a different light—that of socialist realism, of course— Andrei's filmmaking is really a collective enterprise, in which the director, cameraman, and actors play equally important roles. There is no nachalnik, no authority, no domination or subordination in the process. This is not to say it is anarchic—Andrei Warhol is definitely no Nestor Makhno[26]—because all the workers of the film agree on the kind of film they want to make and the way in which it will be made. So a kind of democratic centralism prevails, but it is a democratic centralism that is not imposed on the collective by a director with the power to ruin people's

---

26   World-famous Ukrainian anarchist, active during the Revolution and known for his ideologically incorrect views.

lives, but by the collective itself. The cinematic workers all contribute equally.

I am reminded of the beautiful woman who played Hanoi Hannah. It was clear to me even then that she was a proud and forceful individual who would not submit to Andrei's iron will. But these thoughts bring me back to Andrei, who has, perhaps unwittingly, perhaps wittingly, developed a truly socialist form of creation. What he has done is reproduce under modern conditions the way of work that the toiling masses of all countries and all times had pursued until capitalist industrialization atomized them and alienated their labor. Andrei has reunited the collective with its work. He has effectively overcome the alienation of labor produced by capitalist conditions. He is a proletarian giant, all the more impressive because of his modesty and self-effacing nature.

"Hey, man," says Gerald, "can you help us with this thing?"

I rise and proudly contribute my own labor power to the creative process. My contribution is small: I help Gerald move the screen. But, I think, it is a contribution nonetheless. Would something like this be possible in a capitalist art studio?

But then something terrible happens (or so I thought at first). As I try to lift the screen, I raise its left side higher than its right and some paint runs down one side and drips onto the canvas. I am aghast, I freeze, and, as I am about to apologize, a wondrous thing occurs.

"Hey, man, no sweat," Gerald says. "Hey, Andy, take a look at this."

Andrei casts a long glance at the canvas: The paint

has fallen onto one of the delicately wrought flower petals, to my unschooled mind ruining the composition. Instead of displaying anger, however, Andrei produces a barely audible "huh" and taps me gently on the back.

"Nice going, Sasha," he says.

"But Andrei," I stammer, thinking that he is being ironic, "I apologize deeply."

"Uh, why? It's fab now."

"Yeah, man," says Gerald, "something was missing, and you found it."

I am dumbstruck. And then I realize that I have just witnessed a historic moment in the development of socialism. Andrei and Gerald have not only included me in their collective, but they have also shown me just how initiative and spontaneity can be combined with forethought and planning. We struggle with these questions all the time, and, as I know, they have not yet been satisfactorily answered in the Soviet Union. There is either too much planning, and then workers' initiative suffers; or there is too much initiative, and then planning suffers. I suspect that even our artists, with their meticulous concern for detail and exactitude, suffer from the same problems.

But here, in Andrei's Factory, on Trade Union Square, that question has been resolved. A mistake, I see, need not be a mistake. If interpreted correctly—creatively and from the perspective of workers' true interests—a mistake can actually promote the productive, and creative, process. That is to say, a mistake is not necessarily a mistake. By the same token, a correct move may turn out to be incorrect. There is no way of knowing exactly which is which beforehand. In that sense, planning and initiative are two sides of one coin.

There cannot be just one; each side needs the other in order to result in maximum effectiveness and productivity.

Andrei and Gerald may have also shown me just how that theoretical consideration can be translated into reality. All the workers must be involved in deliberation, production, and evaluation all the time, and deliberation, production, and evaluation must be merged into one creative process. Can this be reconciled with central planning? Of course! But only if the Party, as the collective representative of the working class, is actively involved in every stage of planning and production. The Party must incorporate the workers and the Party must, as a kind of collective worker, deliberate, produce, and evaluate continually—so that these three stages become, over time, one.

Gerald interrupts my reverie. "Hey, man," he says, "I'm fucking starved. Let's get some pizza."

As we sit around a small table, my first encounter with this Italian food comes to mind and, inwardly, I laugh at my own clumsiness. This time I have no difficulties. A black-haired Italian boy brings us the pizzas on red plastic trays. Each of us has two slices. Like Gerald and Andrei, I order a Coca-Cola, which comes in a small cup brimming with ice. I would normally remove the ice, but decide not to, as it does not seem to bother my two comrades. We are creative workers eating the food of the poor and drinking the elixir of the capitalists! The thought amuses me, but why not? When America experiences its own socialist revolution, why should it not continue drinking this so-called Coke? The workers will decide that question on their own. They will determine how they want to live, what they will produce, and how they will create. Gerald and Andrei sprinkle some spices on their pizza, and so do I. Long live the revolution!

As we part, Andrei says, "Mama says you should, uh, come to dinner."

"I would love to, Andrei."

"Uh, tomorrow," he says, "OK, OK?"

Back in the office, I incorporate these ideas into my article about Andrei. I am inspired and work without pause until the early evening. I suddenly notice that everyone but Jim has left and that he is also getting ready to go.

"You gonna stay late, Sasha?" he asks. "Wanna join me fo' a drink?"

I place my papers in a neat pile and say yes.

"Let's go to Third," Jim says.

It is only after several blocks that I realize he means Third Avenue. To the left of a small theatre, called the Variety, is our goal. Typically, the inside is dark, and there is a long bar with stools on the left. On the right are compartments with rectangular tables and benches. Scruffy men in crumpled suits are sitting, silently, on the stools, their empty eyes fixated on the beer glasses, bottles, and small shot glasses before them. A large smoky mirror adorns the length of the wall on the left. In front of the mirror, on several levels, are arrayed variously shaped bottles. They remind me of the presidium at the May Day Parade on Red Square. The bartender is a large man, with thick wavy hair, bushy eyebrows, and a broad chest—a veritable Cossack. He paces up and down the bar, pouring drinks, refilling beer glasses, and engaging the men in short conversations.

"How you doin', John?" says Jim to the bartender.

"Good to see you, Jimbo. The usual?"

"Yeah." replies Jim. "This here's Sasha, my pal from Russia."

"Russia?" says John. "Never been there. Heard it's cold as hell. So what's your pleasure, pal? It's on the house."

"*Which* house?" I ask.

John and Jim exchange a hearty laugh.

"The drink, Sasha," Jim says. "That means the drink's free." They laugh again.

"What'll it be, fella?" says John.

"Vodka," I say. "On rocks!"

Again, they laugh heartily at my use of this Americanism. I join in the pure and simple laughter of two men who share a deep proletarian bond.

We sit down in a compartment. Jim places our drinks on the table and points to a bowl.

"Have some nuts, Sasha."

"They are on the table, but are they on the house?" I ask, and he bursts out laughing. I like this Jim.

I raise my drink and propose a toast. "To the revolution!"

Jim raises his glass and replies, "Yeah, to the revolution." We down our vodkas and, almost simultaneously, reach for the beer mugs and empty them in several gulps. Jim motions to John. He lifts his arm, points at me and himself, and then twirls his hand. John replies, "Coming up, Jimbo."

"I like to unwind here, Sash," Jim says. This is the first time he has dropped the *a* at the end of my name. Like Slavs, Americans, I notice, also prefer the diminutive to the full name.

"You work very hard," I say. "Anyone can see that you are completely dedicated to the Party."

Jim lowers his head and appears to be looking into his empty shot glass. Then he smiles, but just barely. "Yeah, Sash, the Party means a lot to me. Used to be my whole life."

"But?" I ask warily.

"But somethin's missin'," he says. "Used to love the Party, like it was a woman. Know what I mean? Now, somethin's missin'." He shakes his head. "Somethin's missin'. Hey, here come the drinks."

"Then let us drink to you, my dear friend," I say. "May you burn with revolutionary fervor once again!"

"How 'bout you, Sash?" he says. "Don't you ever feel tired?" Jim leans toward me, as if we were two revolutionary conspirators. "I'll level with you, Sash. I don't think there's gonna be a revolution. Don't get me wrong. I wanna revolution. America needs a revolution. But is there gonna be one? We gonna lead it?" Jim strikes the table with his hand. "Fat chance."

"But if the chance is fat, Jim, then there must be cause for optimism." I know that my attempt at wordplay is weak.

"No way," he says emphatically. "No fuckin' way."

"Jim," I say gently, "I cannot agree with your pessimistic assessment. I have been to Harlem. I have been to Columbia University. I have met with Negro revolutionaries and with student revolutionaries. They are absolutely committed to the revolution. They are confident of victory, and I am inclined to agree with their optimism."

"Aw, c'mon, Sash! Those guys think they're makin' revolution, but they wouldn't know a revolution if it bit 'em in the ass. And they sure as hell ain't no Communists."

"Yes," I reply, "that is true. They are not Communists. I am not even sure they are Marxists. But they *are* revolutionaries, Jim, and, if enough of them push, the capitalist system could collapse."

"And then what? You think them capitalists are just gonna let 'em? You think they're just gonna let a revolution take place? No fuckin' way, Sash."

"But the people—"

"What 'bout the people?"

"The people will support them." I feel, as I speak, that I do not quite believe what I have just said.

"The people don't even know them guys exist! I mean, look, Sash. You ever see how regular people look at 'em students? They hate 'em. They hate the way they look and what they do and everythin' they stand for. The people will be on the capitalists' side, Sash. You ever see how black folk look at 'em radicals? Same thing, Sash, same thing."

"Trade union consciousness," I remark, "that has always been the major problem afflicting the proletariat. That is why we have the Party. It must lead, it must be the vanguard. You know that, Jim. You, as a Party member of so many years—"

"Twenty."

"—you know that."

"Uhhh," he almost moans, "that's even mo' depressin'." He looks me in the eyes. "We off the record, Sash?"

"I am afraid I do not understand what—"

"We just talkin' like two friends? Or we talkin' like Party members?"

"Ah, I see. Yes, Jim, of course. Our conversation will not leave this bar."

"OK, then, so listen up, Sash. The Party's infiltrated. Don't know who, don't know when, but I do know the FBI, the CIA, and"—he chortles—"probably you guys have penetrated us. Nothin' stays secret in the Party. Nothin's what it looks like. No one knows who's really runnin' the show, Gus or Morris or the Central Committee or the Party Congress, or, maybe it's really Washington. Or"—he pauses—"Moscow. We're puppets, Sash, and no one knows who's pullin' the strings. No fuckin' way are puppets gonna lead a revolution, if you know what I mean."

I am silent. I know that our people have penetrated the American Party, but that is nothing new. And I have always assumed that the American security services would have tried to penetrate it as well. But I am shocked by the depth of Jim's despondence.

"Nothin' gets done, Sash. We debate until we're hoarse, but that's it. We're bein' sabotaged from inside, Sash. We ain't that dumb, Sash, we're even pretty smart. We know how the world works. We know this country. We know the people. But nothin', absolutely nothin', we do works."

"Jim," I say, "now it is my turn to speak to you in confidence. I have discovered a listening device in my telephone in the hotel. And my papers at Party headquarters have been tampered with." I know that I may be committing a security breach by divulging this information to Jim, but this would be a small price to pay for winning his confidence and getting better insight into the affairs of the American comrades.

"No shit?" he says.

"None at all."

"I ain't fuckin' surprised. See what I mean? Someone's

pullin' this shit on you, and I ain't got a clue who. *Damn*. Let's have 'nother drink."

"I thought it might be the FBI."

"Could be, but you know what that means, Sash. They've got access to the office, that's what it means. Probably have a fuckin' key to the fuckin' front door," he says in disgust.

"Could it be the Party's own security apparatus?"

"*Nyet*, Sash. You were vetted before you came here. Besides, you're from the fuckin' Soviet Union. If that don't make you one of us, what the hell does? I mean, it *could* be the security guys, hell, it could be *anyone*, but they sure as hell ain't doin' this for the Party. Fuck, Sash, if they're eavesdroppin' on you, what's that say 'bout our, uh, *vanguard* organization?"

"Yes," I say, "I share your concern."

"It ain't just concern, Sash. It's *way* past concern. I dunno what I'm doin' here. See what I'm tryin' to say? I don't fuckin' know what the hell I'm doin' in the Party no mo'."

"But a Communist does not resign, Jim," I plead. "Our commitment to the revolution is forever."

"Aw c'mon, Sash, you gonna lecture me, too? I'm fuckin' tired of bein' told what to do. *Fuck!*" Jim pounds the table with his fist. "Fuck, Sash. I thought I could trust you."

"My apologies, Jim," I say. "I am not lecturing you. It is an old habit of mine, to speak of Party discipline. Do not take it personally."

Jim still has an anguished expression on his face. I try to soothe my friend.

"I understand what you are going through. Jim, I became a Party member just as the cult of personality was exposed. That was a terrible shock for me. I had grown up worshipping Comrade Stalin. He had won the war. He had built socialism. My parents worshipped him, too. And then, one day, to be told that all your beliefs were false, that the man you thought was a hero was actually a wrecker—that was difficult, Jim, very, very difficult."

"Yeah," he says, "I get you, Sash." I can see that my friend's rage has passed.

"And a few years later Comrade Khrushchev—the man who had exposed the cult—resigned, and *he* was denounced as hare-brained."

"Hey, that Khrushchev was awright. I remember that shoe poundin' of his at the UN. What a pisser!" A broad smile spreads across Jim's black face.

"My point, Jim, my point is that these leaders we have, whether in the Soviet Union or here, well, these leaders they come and go. Sometimes they are right and sometimes they are wrong, but mostly, if they pursue policies within the framework of the Party, mostly they are right. And they do, somehow, promote the cause of Communism."

"That's what you *believe*, man. You *know* that fo' a fact?"

"I do not, Jim. You are right, I do not. But I believe it. And if I were to stop believing it, Jim, what would my life be worth? Could *you* live without Communism? I could not."

"That's my problem, Sash. I'm thinkin' I could."

"In that case, my friend, let us have another drink," I say and twirl my hand at the Cossack bartender.

It is almost midnight when we leave the bar, and Jim is completely drunk—Russian drunk. He is happy, and he has forgotten his worries, but he is incapable of walking a straight line or, for that matter, even walking. I take him by the arm and tell him that I shall walk him home. That, he tells me, is at the easternmost end of Fourteenth Street. After one block of struggling with his weight, I realize that I will have to find a taxi. Several empty ones speed past us, but finally one stops. I load Jim into the backseat and sidle up next to him. I close the door with some difficulty and tell the Negro driver to take us to Avenue C. We are there in a few minutes, but the quality of the neighborhood is noticeably worse than the abominable conditions of Union Square. All the garbage cans are battered, many are lying on their sides, their foul-smelling refuse is spilling out. The sidewalks and streets are littered with newspapers, bottles, cans, cigarettes, wrappers, and dog droppings. Tough looking boys stand in groups of three or four near the lampposts or sit on the stairs leading up to the buildings. They are all Negro or Puerto Rican, and their tattoos remind me of the Soviet criminal element. Radios are playing loudly; their cacophonous shrieks violate the stillness of the night. As we emerge from the taxi, I notice that girls wearing tight shorts and sporting large round earrings are consorting with the boys. The taxi departs immediately, and Jim and I are left standing in front of his building, a brick structure with the crisscrossing fire escapes typical of New York.

"Hey, Jimmy!" One of the boys dances up to us. "You been havin' a good time?" He and his friends break out in laughter.

"Jimmy, my man," says another, also twisting his hips and snapping his fingers. "Slip me five!" They laugh again.

Jim stands, swaying slightly, holding my wrist.

"What you kids doin' out so late?" He laughs and points at them. "Ain't you supposed to be in bed? What yo' Mama gonna say?"

"What *yo'* Mama gonna say?" one of them responds.

Another boy dances up to Jim and raises his hand, and Jim strikes it. "Power to the people," he says.

"Power to *me!*" the boy cries. "Fuck the people."

We enter a long, dimly lit corridor that reeks of some chemical disinfectant.

"Six B, Sash," Jim says, "that's my place."

I hear contemporary music in every apartment that we pass. Sometimes I hear loud voices, both male and female, engaged in arguments. We are in a New York slum, it occurs to me, and my friend Jim is a true Communist, whatever his doubts, living with the very people he is hoping to help. He shares in their material conditions of life; he suffers their privations. And, as I could see from the brief exchange outside the building, he is on good terms even with the young hooligans. I am saddened as I think these thoughts. Why is it that the best Communists suffer most?

We climb the cramped staircase to the sixth floor. Jim is getting heavy and, after I manage to open the door—there are three or four locks, and it takes me several minutes to figure out which key goes into which lock—I turn on the light and dump him on a small couch situated to my left. Jim falls like a sack of potatoes and emits a slight groan.

"Thanks, man," he says and extends his hand. "How 'bout a nightcap? The beer's in the fridge."

It is then that I realize that Jim lives in one room. A

refrigerator, stove, and sink are clustered in one corner. Next to the sink is what appears to be a bathtub covered with a dented metal plate. There is a small table with three rickety chairs in the middle of the room; newspapers and documents cover it, so there is no room even for a cup. The couch Jim is sitting on must also serve as his bed. A desk and two bookshelves occupy another corner. I am ashamed, I realize, to think that my own apartment in Leningrad consists of five rooms. True, I am married. True, I have many books. That is all true and that is all irrelevant. The only real issue is: Who is true to the ideals of Lenin, the ideals of Communism? Me or Jim? I know the answer, alas.

"Very well, Jim, let us have this nightcap."

I open the cans and we drink the beer straight from them. Jim smacks his lips.

"Long live the revolution!" He raises the beer can. "Power to the people!" I know that he is being both sincere and ironical.

I look around the room and see framed photographs hanging above his desk. They show a younger Jim and a small Negro woman with large eyes and a long neck.

"Your wife?"

"Dead," he says. "Died ten years 'go."

"She was young."

"Yeah. Now she's just dead."

"Children?"

"Nope."

"Brothers? Sisters?"

"Nope," he smiles, "just l'il ol' me." Then he laughs. "Just l'il ol' me and the ree-vo-lu-shun!"

I do not know when we fall asleep, but in the morning, when I awake in a sitting position on the couch—my neck and back muscles aching and my mouth tasting of straw—I notice that over ten cans lie at our feet. Jim is still asleep in his corner of the couch, so I decide not to wake him. I wash my face in the sink, rinse my mouth with cold water, and quietly leave the apartment. Fourteenth Street is empty except for some sanitation trucks. The rising sun hurts my eyes, so I avert them and rush home.

Dinner with Pani Julia and Andrei. I bring a large bottle of Czechoslovak slivovitz for her and a bag of candy for him. Both are delighted as I hand them the gifts. They are like children, oohing and aahing excitedly, almost as if they had never seen such splendid things before. They usher me into the living room, where I see that I am not the only dinner guest. Gerald is sitting on the couch, which is covered with a shiny plastic sheet, like a commodity waiting to be unwrapped. He is examining some book, his tousled hair falling in cascades above the pages. Only his Roman nose is visible. I am struck, yet again, by this young man's physical beauty. He is, as usual, wearing a sports shirt and jeans. Standing near the fireplace is a tall thin man with thick eyeglasses and a perfectly tailored blue suit. Pani Julia takes me by the hand and leads me in his direction.

Gerald says, "Hi, man," and I nod in response.

Pani Julia stands me in front of the tall man. "Sashenka, this is my very, very, very dear friend, Pavel. From the old country, Sashenka, from home!" She is speaking her combination of Ukrainian and Rusyn. Pavel smiles and extends his hand, accompanied by a slight bow.

"Good evening," he says to me in perfect Russian.

"And Pavel," she continues, "this is our dear, dear Sashenka." We shake and Pani Julia takes us by our hands and leads us to the couch.

"Sit, boys, sit," she says. "Andiku!" she calls. "Andiku, bring the glasses and the slivovitz!" Andrei catches my glance and rolls his eyes. But I can see that he is happy to see his mother in such good spirits.

As Pani Julia raises her glass and speaks, I examine Pavel more closely. His suit, his excellent Russian, his cuff links, his silk tie, and, most of all, his air of confidence and self-control tell me that Pavel is no mere peasant from Pani Julia's Carpathian village. I know the type very well. I suspect he is a captain. But why would a high-ranking member of the Czechoslovak security services be here in New York, having dinner with Pani Julia and Andrei and Gerald and me? Once the toasting ends, we sit down and Pani Julia rushes off to the kitchen. Andrei and Gerald are looking at a catalogue of Andrei's artworks, pointing at passages and giggling. I turn to Pavel. I can see from the expression in his eyes that each of us knows exactly who the other is.

"*Stranno, da?*"[27] I say.

"Strange, indeed," he murmurs in response.

But I wonder whether the coincidence is not too coincidental. We rise with our glasses in our hands and walk to the hearth, where a small fire is burning. On the mantle above the fireplace are black and white and brown faded photographs of Andrei, Julia, and a man who must be Andrei's father. In some of the photographs, Julia and some

27   Russian: Strange, yes?

women are dressed in traditional folk costumes, standing stiffly with taut faces, pressed lips, and large eyes.

"So you are from Pani Julia's village?"

"Yes," Pavel responds, "Julia Zavacka was a very pretty girl."

"From the Carpathians to New York. That is quite a great leap forward."

"Indeed." He smiles in acknowledgement of my pun. "I owe my advancement to the Party, of course."

"Of course."

"And you?"

"I am a journalist," I say, though I suspect Pavel knows my biography quite well.

"Writing about the great Andy Warhol?"

"No, about the revolution."

"Ah, the revolution!" he exclaims. "And how goes the revolution?"

"I should be asking you." I take a sip of the slivovitz.

"We are building socialism with a human face," he says, seriously and without a trace of irony. "Comrade Dubček has the support of the working class and peasantry."

"But his commitment to proletarian internationalism appears to be less than complete." I wait for the whole import of my statement to sink in. "*That* is a grievous mistake, as you must know."

"The Czech and Slovak nations are eternally grateful to the Soviet Union for bringing socialism to them. Their love is, as you know, undying."

I find Pavel's irony to be tiresome and decide to change the subject.

"Have you seen Andrei's art? He is a proletarian genius."

"He is," Pavel counters, "a man of the people, a *Ukrainian* genius. His art embodies all the virtues of the Ukrainian nation. It is simple, direct, and it revels in color."

I am glad to see that Pavel has exposed his deviationist beliefs with that one comment. My suspicions are confirmed. He is an exponent of Dubček's anti-socialist course. Worse, he is a bourgeois nationalist who places the nation above class. Czechoslovakia's revisionist tendencies are, I see, far more serious than I had thought. When even highly placed members of the security services, veteran *chekists*[28] such as Pavel, have succumbed to bourgeois nationalist blandishments, then what hope can there be for the country as a whole? Why is Pavel here? I had thought he was interested in me, but that, I now realize, cannot be true. He is here to recruit Andrei for what he calls socialism with a human face. He will fail. I will see to that. The ideological struggle continues, even in Pani Julia's living room.

At that moment, she emerges from the kitchen and tells us to sit down at the dining room table. She takes Pavel and me by our hands. The table is round and I place myself between Gerald and Andrei. Pavel seats himself next to Gerald, and the seat between Pavel and Andrei is reserved for Pani Julia. An enormous plate of steaming plump dumplings sits in the middle of the table. Bowls of sour cream, fried onions smothered in molten butter, and two bottles of cold vodka complete the picture.

Pavel exclaims, "Ah, varenyky!" and rubs his hands.

"Hey, Andy," Gerald says, "we should do a painting of these ravioli some day."

"Uh, yeah, maybe," Andrei replies. Like a good Ukrainian peasant, he is wholly preoccupied with the food.

---

28   Popular term for heroic members of the Communist security service.

Pani Julia is, as I can see from her glowing eyes, in seventh heaven. We eat and drink in silence; only Gerald, the Italian, seems uncomfortable with our east European village ways. He makes occasional comments about the food, but no one responds. Andrei—amazingly—has piled perhaps twenty varenyky onto his plate and smothered them with heaps of onions and sour cream.

Pani Julia looks up from her plate and says, "Eat, boys, eat." When we are finished, Andrei helps her collect the plates. As they exit the room, he kisses her gray head and she smiles, almost imperceptibly.

Pavel sits back and looks me in the eyes. "Socialism with a human face is inevitable," he says matter-of-factly. "The will of the people cannot be stopped."

"I agree," I say, "but what is the will of the people?"

"Our public opinion surveys show that we have the support of the majority of the population."

"Perhaps, but the majority can easily be wrong."

"Trade union consciousness? Is that what Lenin called it?"

"Precisely."

"So who knows best what the people want? The Party?"

"Exactly," I reply, "the Party."

"The Communist Party of Czechoslovakia is in full agreement with the majority of the people."

"This does not mean that *your* Party is right. You *have* heard of left-wing infantilism?"

At this point, a visibly agitated Gerald, until then preoccupied with twisting his napkin, loudly interjects, "What the *fuck* are you guys talking about? This is *New York*, man, the greatest city in the world, and you guys are talking like you're still living in the fucking nineteenth century."

"Not quite, Gerald, the lives of millions of workers and peasants hang in the balance."

"*Fuck* your workers and peasants!" he says. "Those pierogis we just stuffed our faces with, *they're* the real thing. The Factory, *that's* the real thing. All of this"—he waves his hand at me and Pavel—"is just fucking bullshit crap. I mean, like, you two guys wouldn't know a worker or a peasant if he crapped on your face. You ever been up to the Bronx? You wanna see some *real* workers and peasants? They'd beat the shit out of you."

"Not our Czech and Slovak workers and peasants," says Pavel. "They are with us. You are wrong, Mister Gerald." I cannot suppress a smile at that locution, "Mister Gerald."

"Oh, fuck," says Gerald. "Don't you guys get it? Art, man, *that's* real. Poetry, *that's* real. Sex, *that's* real. You guys live in some fantasy world. You're like some fucking Mickey Mouse in fucking Disneyland!"

At that, both Pavel and I burst out laughing.

"Very well, Gerald, let us talk about ... what? What should we talk about? Sex? Come, comrade," I wink, "let us show our friend Gerald how questions are asked."

Pavel winks back. We know that, despite our ideological differences, we are birds of a feather.

"Now you're talking!" exclaims the unsuspecting Italian.

"Tell us about your women," says Pavel in a tone that brooks no dissent.

"What the fuck for?" Gerald asks.

"Just tell us about your women."

"What's to say? They left, I stayed."

"*You* never left them?" I ask.

"Only when I couldn't breathe anymore."

"*They* never felt suffocated? Only *you?*"

"How the hell should I know?"

"You never asked them?"

"Hell, no."

"They never hinted at anything?"

Gerald shrugs his shoulders.

"Ah," says Pavel, "our friend Gerald is a man of action and few words. I suspect he never said anything until after he decided to leave."

"Yeah," Gerald says. "There was nothing to say."

"But you could have said you were suffocating," I say.

"What the hell for?"

"It might have made a difference. It might have saved—"

"Why would I wanna save something I didn't wanna save? You guys don't get it, do you?" Gerald pours himself another vodka.

"So you wanted these liaisons to end?"

Gerald nods.

"And you wanted them to end *before* you felt you were suffocating?"

"Fucking right."

"That does not make sense," I say. "Why would you want to end a liaison before it even began?"

"I knew I'd suffocate."

"Then why did you begin it in the first place?"

"I wanted a woman."

"So you want to have it both ways," Pavel says.

I notice that Andrei is smiling. Pani Julia is in the kitchen, singing.

"No way," he counters. "I want it until I can't breathe. I don't want it after I can't breathe. What's your problem, man?"

"You are being Jesuitical," I say.

"Hell no," he grins, "just smart."

"Tell us about one of your women," Pavel commands.

"Which one?"

"Uh, tell them about, uh, Benedetta," Andrei interjects.

"An Italian?" Pavel says admiringly. "No doubt an artiste, like you."

"She was a fucking model."

"Ah," Pavel exclaims, "an intellectual!"

"Yeah, well, no," says Gerald, seemingly oblivious of Pavel's irony. "I don't know. She was gorgeous."

"Gerald followed her to Rooo-ma," Andrei says. "As in, uh, romance."

"Lay off, Andy," Gerald growls, "just fucking lay off."

"Uh, sorry," Andrei says.

"Well, Gerald, so how did you meet?" I ask.

"Some party. Where else?"

"Was it love at first sight?"

"Are you kidding? She had a great ass."

"Did you say that to her?"

"Are you guys tripping?"

"Did you make love?" Pavel asks.

"What do you think?"

"I think you have doubts about your sexuality," Pavel says without batting an eyelash. I am speechless. Such talk is unheard of in Communist society, and it is indicative of the degree to which Pavel has deviated from Leninism. Andrei, I notice, is giggling.

"Fuck you, man," Gerald cries, "fuck you up the ass!"

Andrei is giggling furiously, his hand across his mouth.

"So then you followed her to Rome." Pavel's change of tone, and pace, is perfect.

"Fuck you, man," Gerald says. After a second, he continues, almost contritely. "Yeah, I followed her to Rome."

"She left you," Pavel continues, "and you followed her. Heroic behavior, Mister Gerald."

"It was a kick. I hardly remembered her."

"Her way of talking?"

"No, *her*. Her face, her body—*her*."

"So why did you go to Rome?"

"What would *you* do if some chick says she gets wet thinking about you?"

"Weren't you starting to suffocate?" Pavel asks. "Wasn't it time to go?"

"Would *you* have ended it? Fuck, let's stop this shit."

"When did you see her in Rome?" Pavel is relentless in his pursuit.

"A few months ago. I went there after Cannes."

"The film festival?" I ask.

"Yeah, we were supposed to show *Chelsea Girls*, but it was a bust."

"That's a lie, Gerald," Andrei hisses.

"So you went to Rome. And then?" Pavel ignores Andrei's surprisingly ill-mannered intervention.

"Yeah, we spent several days screwing in some fleabag."

"And what did her boyfriend have to say about it?"

"Boyfriend? She had no boyfriend," Gerald says. "How the fuck should I know?"

"Every model has at least one boyfriend," Pavel says, "even in Czechoslovakia." Notwithstanding his deviations from the Party line, I must admit that his technique is masterful.

"That was, like, really weird, man," Gerald says quietly.

"She told him. She actually told him. She said she couldn't lie."

"Did you believe her?"

"Are you kidding? She was fucked up. She obviously wanted—"

"—to get back at him."

"Fucking right. What are you guys, a bunch of shrinks?"

"But still you continued?"

"No chance of suffocation, right?"

"But there was a good chance you'd be beaten."

"No way," Gerald says. "That's why she told him. She knew he'd respond in this fucking passive way. She could have her kicks and screw him and I could have my kicks, too."

"So you just stayed in Rome, with your model and her boyfriend?"

"We went to Capri." He pauses. "It was far out, man."

"Ah, so you fell in love."

"Yeah, that sucked."

"You hadn't planned on it, and you hadn't wanted to."

"No way, José."

"Did you feel suffocated?"

"Didn't have time. She decided to end it as soon as we stepped off the ferry."

"But you couldn't, could you?"

"It's, like, crazy, you know?"

"*You* became the supplicant."

"Let's end this shit."

"She took you back."

"Yeah."

"You embraced the suffocation."

"Yeah."

"So that was that?"

"We broke up again and got together again."

"A *perpetuum mobile*! How long did that go on? A few more months?"

"Yeah, and then it just kind of died."

"It is always sad when relationships wither away."

Gerald is suddenly agitated. "Fuck! What are you, the fucking Gestapo?"

Pavel and I smile in response. We hear the sound of hands clapping. It is Andrei, who is standing in the doorway. He is grinning impishly. As Gerald says, "What the fuck!", Andrei steps aside to reveal a film camera.

"That was, uh, fab," he says, "*really* fab."

"You were filming us, Andrei?" I ask, feeling slightly alarmed. What is happening to my instincts? I have always been able to tell when I was being secretly photographed. I am befuddled, but I console myself with the fact that Pavel also failed to see anything.

"Yeah, Mama helped me set up." Pani Julia pokes her head from behind the door. "You guys are, uh, superstars."

"Yeah," cries Gerald, "Ondine'll[29] go crazy when he finds out!"

Andrei chortles.

"Who is Ondine?" I say.

"The Pope," Gerald says. "Don't you know the Pope?"

"I am a Communist."

Andrei and Gerald break out in laughter. Pavel is seething with anger.

"Those are police methods," he says, his face red, his

---

29   One of Warhol's world-famous male superstars, who referred to himself as the Pope in *Chelsea Girls*.

eyes bulging, and his nostrils flaring. "Do you always spy on people?"

"No, uh, yeah," says Andrei. "It's the camera. It just films stuff."

"Yeah," says Gerald, "like the Empire State Building. Or"—he giggles—"Taylor's ass."[30]

"This is nonsense," says Pavel. "You are eavesdropping, you are violating our privacy. This is no laughing matter, gentlemen."

"Uh, no," says Andrei, and promptly laughs. Gerald joins him. After a few seconds so do I, though I do not fully understand why the situation is funny. But their laughter is infectious, and the sight of Pavel, the self-righteous socialist with a human face, sputtering is too absurd.

"I think I understand all too well," he says, slamming his fist against the table and shoving his chair away. "Good night," he says peremptorily and heads for the door. Pani Julia catches him by the sleeve, but he is unmoved. Before he leaves, however, they embrace and he whispers something in her ear and she smiles.

"*Nu*," Pani Julia says in her heavily accented English, "who want tea?"

"Andrei," I say, "the camera is still running?"

"Uh-huh."

"Yeah, man," says Gerald, "now it's your fucking turn."

"Gerald!" Pani Julia cries sharply.

"Sorry," he responds, almost sheepishly. "It's your turn in the hot seat, man."

"But the camera is filming!"

---

30   Taylor Mead, a world-famous New York poet who starred in an experimental Warhol film, *Taylor Mead's Ass*.

"Forget the fu– stupid camera!" Gerald explodes. Pani Julia smiles. "Just talk, for chrissakes," he says, "just talk."

Very well, I think, since the solidarity of our collective is at stake, I will go along with Gerald's request. I decide to start with the most important facts.

"My father and mother were Communists all their lives."

"Hey, man, it runs in the family!"

"Shhh!" Pani Julia casts a severe glance at Gerald.

"My grandparents were not. They supported the anti-Bolshevik government during the Revolution."

Gerald yawns loudly.

"Shhh, Shhh," says Pani Julia again. "Ignore brat, Sashenka."

"They were peasants. From the same village near Kyiv."

"Like *my* parents and grandparents!" she cries.

"But mine left the village, Pani Julia."

"When, Sashenka? During collectivization?"

"What the hell is collectization?" asks Gerald.

"That, you stupid boy, is when Communists took land from peasants and peasants starved."

"It was necessary," I say. "Industrialization was the order of the day, and the rich peasants were hiding grain from the working class."

"What're you talking about, man?" asks Gerald.

"It's OK, Sasha," says Andrei. "This is far out. Go on."

"My maternal grandparents did die in a famine. In 1933," I say. "I do not even know where they are buried."

"Where *you* want be buried, Sashenka?" says Pani Julia. "We have plots near Pittsburgh."

"In Kyiv, of course."

"They say where one buried is home."

"Kyiv is home," I say. "And Pittsburgh?"

"No, no, of course no. But Czechoslovakia is too far."

"*I* want to be buried in Pittsburgh," Andrei says.

"In that dump?" Gerald exclaims. "Why the hell would you wanna do that?"

"That's where my, uh, family is."

"It only home we have, Sashenka," Pani Julia adds. "Where else we go?"

She fills our glasses with vodka and we drink silently.

"Hey, Sash," Gerald interjects, "I wanted to ask you something. When did you become a Commie?"

"When I entered the Institute of Journalism. But I always knew I would join the Party."

"I'm not a joiner," Gerald says defiantly. "I need elbow room."

"The Party is my family, Gerald."

"Your fu–"—he glances swiftly at Pani Julia—"your *family*?" He laughs. "I couldn't wait to leave my family."

"The Communist Party is not that kind of family, Gerald."

"Know what, Sash? I think your head's messed up. You've never grown up. That's your problem."

"Because the Party is my family?"

"Fu–"—again the penitent look—"damned right."

"But it *is*," I insist.

"You're off your rocker, man."

"Excuse me?"

"You're crazy, man, totally crazy. Is everyone like you in Russia?"

"Of course," I say proudly. "My best friends love the Party as much as I do."

"Then you're all messed up."

"We are building Communism, Gerald. Can you understand that? Only a disciplined collective, led by the Party, can do that."

"Your Communism's a drag, man."

"I beg your pardon?"

"It's a drag, Sa-shen-ka. It's a downer. Who needs it?"

"Mankind," I say, simply and with dignity.

I am shocked by my own frankness. Andrei is watching me, his face impassive, his eyes barely twinkling, his lips slightly curled. The only way I can explain my openness is in terms of his mesmerizing influence. The more passive he is, the more one feels the need to speak. What a curious power. In that sense, he is completely unlike the great Lenin, who moved all who listened with his passionate oratory. Lenin spoke, and the masses followed. Andrei remains silent—and the masses follow. What a curious power he has inside him. Outside he appears weak and malleable. Inside he is like steel.

"Is the camera still running?" I ask.

Andrei gets up to look.

"Uh-oh," he says, "we've run out of, uh, film. Yeah, uh, I don't know if we, uh, got that."

"Oh, that's too much!" cries Gerald. "That's just too much. But hey, man," he says turning to me, "that was one helluva story! That was one helluva story!"

As Andrei attaches a spool of fresh film to the camera, I see that Gerald is beginning to look uncomfortable again.

He knows that he is next. I hear a click and immediately turn to him.

"Tell us about another disastrous affair, *Mister* Gerald. There must have been others," I say with undisguised malice.

"Yeah," says Andrei, "tell us about Jean."

Gerald groans. "Not her." But he is grinning.

"Yes, her," I say.

"Couldn't I just jump off a bridge?"

"Didn't you, uh, push her? Into the river?" Andrei asks.

"Almost," Gerald laughs. "That was the closest I ever came to murder."

"She must have angered you," I say.

"She infuriated me. She was the most unreasonable bitch I ever met. Sorry, Missus Julia."

"But you fell head over heels for her, did you not?"

"I was an asshole," he says. "Uh, sorry."

"She was married," Andrei says.

"Yeah, but this broad had been collecting lovers for years."

"Was that why she was unreasonable?" I ask.

"Nothing satisfied her. I never knew where I stood. I never knew where she stood."

"Did you tell her?"

"Yeah, but then she'd roll her eyes and say *I* was infuriating. Or she'd smile and say she's a woman." Gerald leans forward, palms pressed on the table, as if ready to pounce. "That would drive me crazy. You mean *all* women are stupid? You mean they're *all* difficult? I asked her that, and she'd say *I* was infuriating."

"You *can* be infuriating," I say. "That is clear to me even though we barely know each other."

"She was a psycho."

"But you kept on seeing her. For how long?"

"Almost two years."

"So who was the *real* psychotic, Gerald?"

"I was in love." He jerks his head back melodramatically and presses the back of his hand to his forehead.

"Again!" I cry. "And with a psychotic!"

"Yeah, that sucked."

I resolve to adopt Pavel's frontal tactics. "Was she a good lover?"

"Hell, no!"

"But still you stayed with her for two years."

"Nineteen months."

"What did you talk about?"

"Nothing."

"Nothing at all? That is impossible."

"The love talk lasted a few months. The rest of the time, we argued. About everything."

"So why did you not leave her sooner?"

"I did. A few times. Once I almost pushed her off a dock." Andrei laughs.

"She couldn't have pressed charges," Gerald says. "The last thing she wanted was for her husband to find out she'd screwed a million guys."

"You kissed and made up after every break-up." I can almost hear Pavel asking the questions.

"We'd talk, and everything seemed perfect." The expression on Gerald's face turns sad. "But nothing ever changed. She *wanted* those fights."

"Did they energize you, too?"

"No," he says, turning pensive. "It was like visiting a sick friend. Every time you see him, he's closer to death."

"My wonderful friend Kolibri," I say, "had a liaison that ended over and over again, and after each ending, it revived, but always a little less. After five or six such dyings, it finally died. You feel sorrow, he said, so you persist, you keep visiting the patient. Would you just stop visiting a dying man? Kolibri said the same is true of a liaison. How can you leave it, if it is so terrible? Why would you leave it, if it is so good? People are always dying, hospitals are always full of patients, the dying must always be visited, and who are you to stop this circle from turning, to refuse to visit the dying?"

"Right on, man, right on," says Gerald, "absolutely, fucking right on."

Andrei stands up from the table and walks over to the camera and turns it off.

"That was, uh, really good," he says. "Really, uh, dramatic."

"Andrei," I say, "now it is *your* turn."

"Uh"—he smiles at me—"I have, uh, nothing to say."

"Quite the contrary, Andrei, you have everything to say. Just look at your paintings, your art, your films!"

"Uh, yeah, well—uh, no. That's my, uh, outside. Not my inside."

"How can you say that, Andrei?"

"He's right, man," Gerald says. "Andy's all surface."

"Like, uh," Andrei says, "like my, uh, paintings."

"But, Andrei"—I feel like taking him by his shirt and

shaking him—"I have told you that your paintings are masterpieces of socialist realism. They are extraordinary critiques of capitalism! I have never seen anything like them in my own country. I am certain—"

"That's jive, man," says Gerald. "Andy's just Andy. He may be an asshole, but he's just Andy."

"Andrei belongs to the working class, Gerald. He belongs to the revolution."

"Like I said, man, that's jive, pure and simple."

"Uh," Andrei asks, "the working class, huh?"

"Yes, Andrei, the working class—the toilers of the world."

"And the, uh, what? The revolution?"

"Yes, Andrei, that too."

"Cool."

"*See?*" I turn triumphantly to Gerald. "*See?* Andrei says it is *cool.*"

"Jive, man," Gerald says, "pure fucking jive."

"Gerald! Sasha!" Pani Julia exclaims. "Please leave my Andik in quiet. And you, Gerald, wash mouth with soap, or I wash it you."

As we drink, shot after shot accompanied by increasingly nonsensical toasts to art and peace and friendship, it strikes me in the eyes that I have never in my life been witness to such outpourings of intimate personal details as today. Gerald told us about two of his affairs. I—who never speak of private matters in public—related my life story. And we revealed ourselves on *film*. As the camera was rolling, we undressed. Only Pavel took offense and would not, despite his self-professed love of human faces, submit to such a procedure.

Two more things strike me in the eyes. First, our revelations were made during what can only be called interrogations. I have conducted interrogations, and I have witnessed many more than I have conducted, and I cannot fail to be impressed by how first Pavel and I, then Gerald and Andrei, elicited information. We prodded Gerald with questions, and he felt powerless not to answer. Even more amazing is my own willingness to relate such personal family details to a roomful of spectators. I am, after all, trained not to talk of things that could be turned against me. And yet—despite knowing that the camera was recording my every word and gesture—I spoke. I revealed facts that these people have no need to know. But not only do they now know these facts, anyone who watches the film will know them, too.

Second, while all of us bared our souls, or at least tried to, Andrei pointedly did not. He stayed silent throughout. He appears to have been absent from the room for most of Pavel's and my interrogation of Gerald, and he was only minimally present, as it were, silently sitting in the background during the subsequent revelations. And yet— it strikes me in the eyes again that, despite his seeming absence, Andrei was actually the *spiritus movens* of the whole evening. He hovered above us. His silence prodded us to speak. His silence and his seeming absence *compelled* us to speak.

Andrei claims to have no inside, to be all surface. That is, I now see, just a subterfuge. His paintings ostensibly only depict capitalist objects, but in reality they subject them to a savage proletarian critique. So, too, Andrei insists he is nothing more than half-smiles and vague gestures, but in reality he is imposing his will on the world and on us. Andrei, I suddenly realize, is an American Lenin, a revolutionary with an iron will and a clear vision of the world. Like Vladimir Illich, Andrei knows exactly what he wants, who he is, and what the world is like. Like Vladimir Illich, Andrei is committed to a revolutionary transformation of the material—and spiritual—conditions of existence. I am in the presence not just of a socialist realist genius, an artist without peers in the socialist world. I am in the presence of a great revolutionary leader.

Small wonder that Andrei has a Factory peopled with willing collaborators committed to realizing his vision of the world. Who would not follow this second Lenin?

It is well past midnight, and Pani Julia says that it is time to go to bed. I make to go, but she indicates with a quick wave of her crooked hand that I should remain sitting.

"We have room, yes, Andiku? You can sleep here, Sashenka. And you also, Gerald."

"Uh, yeah, Mama, OK, OK," Andrei says. "That would be fab."

I am too tired to say no. Having spent yesterday sleeping at Jim's, I am reluctant to sleep in a strange bed again, but I feel enervated by the evening's experiences and know that I have no strength to return to the hotel. Pani Julia rushes off to fetch the bedding, while the three of us sit silently at the table. Gerald pours himself a slivovitz, while Andrei just sits motionless, with an enigmatic smile on his lips. I am fighting sleep and struggle to keep my eyes open.

"Come, boys," says Pani Julia, who, astonishingly,

appears to be wholly unaffected by the food and drink and confessions. She takes Gerald and me by our hands and leads us to guestrooms on an upper floor of the house.

As Gerald closes the door behind him, he whispers to me, "If you want company, Sash, you know where I am." I smile and let Pani Julia take me to my room. She leads me to the bed, and, after I sit down, she proceeds to remove my shoes.

"Pani Julia!" I cry. "Please, it is not—"

"Sleep, Sashenka," she whispers and leaves the room as silently as a cat.

I awake in the morning with the vague, but uneasy recollection of having dreamed of Valeria. Why and how she should have occupied my sleep I do not know. We had not talked of her that evening, I have not thought of her since the last time I met her outside Andrei's, and yet, the whole night my dreams focused on her and only on her. And—I am almost ashamed to write this—my dreams were explicitly amorous. I recall vaguely our making love, and I recall thinking that she had the most voluptuous and desirable body that I have ever seen. What extraordinary notions! In reality, Valeria is a thin and mousy Lithuanian woman, and her body is anything but voluptuous. Still, it must be true that I find her desirable. Why else would my dreams center so obsessively on her? Did I tell her I loved her in my dream? I think I did, but am not sure.

Why Valeria? Why not the lascivious Veeva? Valeria is the only woman with whom I have had anything like a real conversation in New York. Is that why she entered my dreams? Not because I have feelings for her, but because she was the vehicle for other, erotic desires? But where did these desires come from? Did the whole evening—the confessions by Gerald, my own revelations, and my realization that Andrei exerts some mysterious force over the people in his surroundings—have this effect on me?

I do not know. That is the one thing I do know. No, there is something else I know. I have entered a strange world. The world of imperialism and capitalism is strange enough to a Soviet man like me. Its ways have confused, intrigued, and repelled me from the day I first set foot here. The world of American Communism is also strange—so familiar, and yet so unlike anything I have experienced at home. The world of American radicalism—the Negroes, the students—is also something I have never before encountered. And then, to top it all off, I have fallen into the magical world of Andrei Warhol. It is a socialist world, a socialist realist world, a proletarian world, a Leninist world—and yet it is also a world in which the forces of motion, the dynamics that inspire it, are very different from those I know. There is no gravity here, and I am weightless. Morris warned me. He was right.

As if these thoughts were not enough, as soon as I leave Andrei's house my confusion deepens. For who should be there, standing on the other side of the street, if not Valeria? She runs across the street, and I see that there is absolutely nothing voluptuous about her. She is wearing, like so many American women who fancy themselves radical, a miniskirt, an olive green United States Army jacket, and a cap. The effect is to hide her figure and annihilate all traces of her femininity. She should meet our Soviet women, I think, in

order to learn how emancipation from capitalist oppression
can be combined with the eternally feminine. And her long
and hungry face is anything but attractive. And yet—as I
watch her, my heart leaps.

"That must've been some party," she says as she steps
lightly onto the sidewalk.

"We talked," I say, "endlessly."

"That fuck! I bet you did all the talking."

"Why, yes," I stutter.

"The fucking manipulative fuck! That's fucking Andy
Warhol for you."

"No, Valeria—"

"The name is Va-le-rie."

"Very well—Va-le-rie. You are quite wrong about
Andrei. He is—"

"Like hell I am. He's a fucking manipulative fuck."

"—a genius."

"For fuck's sake," she cries, "Malanga does all the work.
Fucking Warhol just watches. And who do you think makes
the films? Fucking Morrissey, that's who."

"They collaborate, Valeria—"

"It's fucking Valerie!"

"My apologies, Va-le-rie. They collaborate. Andrei works
best in a collective. He is a collectivist. Like all proletarian
artists."

"He fucking takes the fucking credit for their fucking
work!"

"No, Va-le-rie. He inspires them, he directs them. He is
like the Party, and Gerald and that Paul you mention, they
are like the masses."

"Oh, for fuck's sake, what the fuck are you talking
about?"

"Come," I say, "come have coffee with me."

We walk to Eighty-Sixth Street and enter a café called Leo's. It occurs to me that for the first time Valeria and I will be alone. I laugh inwardly, as I realize that we are on what the Americans call a "date." It is an odd time to have such an assignation—eight in the morning—but it is no more odd than all the other adventures I have had in the last two days. I wonder where Jim is and what he is doing.

We walk toward the back of the café and occupy a booth. The tired waiter comes, we place our orders, and he returns with two cups of coffee. The coffee, I notice, has spilled into the saucers, and after he drops the cups onto the table with a clatter, I place paper napkins on the saucers.

"That is better," I say. "Now we can drink."

"You're fucking weird."

"Perhaps," I say as I take a sip of the coffee, "but perhaps that is the price of proletarian culture."

"Like I said, man, you're fucking weird."

I smile at her, almost condescendingly. "Why do you hate Andrei? He is a decent man, even if he is not the brilliant artist I think he is."

"He's a fucking manipulative sonofabitch."

"All artists are, Valeria—excuse me, Valerie."

"He's fucking with me." Fortunately, I understand the semantic difference the preposition "with" makes in this locution.

"Why would he do that?"

"I'm a star, and the bastard knows it." She stirs her coffee. "And that bitch Veeva kisses his ass."

"*That* disturbs you?"

"The asshole stole my manuscript."

"Andrei," I say, quietly but firmly, "is innocent."

"What are you—fucked up? He jerks me around. One day he wants me in his films. The next day he doesn't. Who the fuck does he think he is, the fucking manipulative fuck?"

"Do you *want* to be in Andrei's films, Valeria?"

"I just wanna cut his balls off."

"That measure seems extreme," I say, "and most unnecessary."

"He's a fucking male chauvinist pig."

"Andrei could *never* be a policeman!"

"He hates women, the fuck. He wants to dominate us."

"Andrei?" I ask incredulously. "Andrei lives for his art, Valeria. He loves his art. Women or for that matter men— they are the material for his art."

"He's a domineering sonofabitch."

"But Valeria, *we* submit to what we think his will is. It is almost as if we submitted to a domination we ourselves created. It is not Andrei's fault, or even his doing."

"You're fucking crazy. He's fucked up your head completely."

"Besides, I do not think you are a woman of violence."

"Huh!" she snorts in response. "You think you know me, don't you? Typical fucking man."

"Am I also a pig?"

"You're a man, and that makes you a pig."

"No," I counter gently, "the contradictions between the sexes are the product of capitalism. They are not intrinsic to the sexes. Exploitation is the essence of capitalism, Valeria, and the exploitation of the proletariat by the bourgeoisie carries over into all spheres of the superstructure—culture, race, the nationality question, and relations between men and women. If you want to rid the world of that contradiction, Valeria, you should struggle to achieve socialism." I end my lecture with an addendum: "In the Soviet Union, men and women are completely equal."

"I still think he's a fuck, and that you're fucked up."

"Well, perhaps," I try to laugh, "but is it not better to struggle for true liberation than to seek revenge on an artist who loves his mother too much? You should visit me at Party headquarters sometime. Marx and Lenin and Gus Hall will change your life."

"Let's blow," she says and, after dropping a few wrinkled dollars on the table, rises to go.

"Very well," I say, "let us blow."

Once outside, she turns to me and says, "Let's go to the park." I nod, and we walk, in silence, down Eighty-Sixth Street to Central Park.

"Let's get some beer," she says and steps into a small gastronom. She reappears a few minutes later with a paper bag in her hand.

"Let's go to the Needle," she says.

I raise my eyebrows.

"Cleopatra's Needle. Where all the high school kids go to drink."

Another adventure! This time I shall be drinking American beer in the early morning near an ancient Egyptian monument frequented by American adolescents desirous of getting drunk. The Needle turns out to be an obelisk. Bespattered benches surround it, and the whole circular area is hidden from the surrounding pathways by tall bushes and trees. The ground is littered with crushed beer cans and broken bottles.

We find a place on the cleanest bench and Valeria opens the bag and takes out two cans. She opens both with a can opener and hands me one. I have barely raised it to my lips when I notice that she is well on the way to finishing hers. A socialist competition, I think. Very well, Comrade Solanas, we shall see who will win, a Ukrainian journalist or a Lithuanian actress. I drink my can and reach for the second. We finish at the same time. I finish the third a split second before Valeria.

"A tie!" I cry. "You are an excellent drinker, Valeria. A Soviet woman through and through."

"Fuck you," she smiles. I believe this is the first time I have seen her smile, and the effect is charming, almost feminine.

"No," she says, "I've got a better idea. Fuck me." And before I can say anything, she fumbles at my zipper, lifts her skirt, and mounts me.

"I hate men," she says slowly and deliberately, "*all* fucking men."

At Party headquarters a note from Seymour, reminding me of the meeting of student radicals. I had, I realize shamefacedly, completely forgotten but decide to go. My desk is a mess. Newspapers and books have piled up on it, and my own papers have been pushed into a corner. A paper coffee cup with cigarette butts inside stands forlornly amid this *balahan*.[31] I throw it into the wastepaper basket.

Jim appears in the doorway, holding a mug of what I assume is coffee.

---

31   Ukrainian: mess.

"Hey, where you been, man?" he says. "You ain't been here fo' days." He looks at me closely. "You look like a wreck, man."

I have not shaved or bathed, and my clothes are rumpled. I feel ashamed to tell him about my adventures at Andrei's, and even more about Valeria. Worse, I know that Jim would be astonished to learn that a Soviet journalist had committed such an egregious breach of security. I have not revealed any state secrets, I know, but I also know that I have been all too willing to talk freely about myself. As to Valeria, what can I say? I am a man. This is hardly my first indiscretion, but what worries me, slightly, is that this particular liaison may have exceeded the bounds of the purely physical. What if she falls in love with me? What will I do then? She is Lithuanian, I am Ukrainian. This would not be the first time that the friendship of peoples would have assumed such an intimate form.

"I have been writing," I say. "I have more meetings this evening."

"Been meetin' with 'em students?"

"Yes." This is the first time that I have lied to Jim.

"Still think they're gonna start a revolution, Sash?"

"Ah." I pause. "That is less clear now."

"Told you so. How 'bout them black radicals?"

"You may be right about them, too."

Jim smiles. "Y'know, Sash, Gus's been lookin' for you."

"Do you know why, Jim?"

"No idea."

"And you, my friend? Still despondent?"

"I'm quittin', Sash. Don't tell no one. I still ain't a hundred pe'cent sure, but I think I'm gonna do it."

"What will you do?"

"What others do. Get a job, maybe get married."

"And leave the revolution."

"Sorry, Sash. The revolution left me a long time ago. I told you."

"Yes," I say wearily, "yes, you did, Jim."

"Sorry, Sash."

"No need to apologize, Jim. I understand. If only everyone had struggled so hard and so long as you."

"I'm tired, Sash. I can't go on."

"I know."

"Don't you ever get tired?"

"Sometimes. Yes, sometimes."

"You ever think 'bout quittin'?"

"That is not an option for me, Jim."

"Well, if you ever change your mind," he laughs, "we could start a commune in Newark."

I clean my desk. The mounds of paper remind me that it is high time to write a letter to Katyusha. When did I last write? One or two weeks ago? How many times have I written in all? Too few. Katyusha understands, of course. This is not the first time I have been abroad, and my letter writing always drops off. But it has never dropped off quite this much. I have always managed at least one letter a week.

As I think these thoughts, it strikes me in the eyes that I have been in New York for over one month now. The time has passed far too quickly. And what have I to show for my stay? I have written several reports for Moscow; at least that part of my activity has remained unchanged. I have read a great deal about the student and Negro radicals. I have had only one meeting with them. I have written a few clumsy articles about America for the Soviet press. I have still to keep my promise to Arnold and write something for *The Daily Worker.*

My record is shameful, though not completely so. I have come to know Andrei's strange yet familiar world. Should I write a book about him? At the very least, I should finish that article. What else? My knowledge of the English language has improved immeasurably. I must laugh as I recall my first awkward steps. Now, I can even converse with and comprehend most Negroes. And I have a far better understanding of the peoples of the United States and the mechanics of capitalist oppression. In fact, I have almost become an insider. Our propaganda depicts that oppression as based on violence and force. That is true, but not fully true. There is also a willful acceptance of capitalism here. Or perhaps it would be better to call it indifference? Naturally, that acceptance, that indifference, is the product of capitalist propaganda. But not only. Someone like Valeria cannot see beyond male oppression of women. For her that is everything. At home, we call that a petty bourgeois deviation that mistakes superstructural phenomena for the objectively real. And it *is* a deviation, I have no doubt of that. And yet, I also have no doubt that Valeria truly believes in what she says. She is no mere puppet of the bourgeoisie. Something else is at work here.

Even the superficial Gerald, with his women and vulgarities, is not just a puppet of capitalism. He does not have an iota of Andrei's genius, and he would be completely incapable, on his own, of the kind of devastating critique of capitalist relations and alienation that permeates Andrei's works. And yet, Gerald is not just a servant of Andrei. He is his collaborator and partner, and I know that he is indispensable to Andrei. There must be, even in Gerald, a latent understanding of the nature of capitalist exploitation—although his appearance and behavior suggest that he is blissfully unaware of the kind of world he lives in. Even Andrei's radicalism and revolutionary spirit are expressed only through and in his art. He is not an orator like Lenin. Indeed, he is not even the best of conversationalists, although his silence does produce a response that almost amounts to a dialogue.

Things here are not quite what they appear to be. In Soviet society, the outside and the inside correspond to, reflect, and complement each other. In capitalist society, the outside, although a product of the inside, serves to conceal it. But with Valeria, Gerald, and Andrei—perhaps even with Jim—the outside and the inside appear to be unrelated. How can that be?

I hear Jim coughing. "Sash," he says, "Gus's here. In his office. Got a minute?"

Comrade Hall rises from his desk, hand outstretched, as I walk in. Jim quietly closes the door. Morris is also in the room, a book in his hands.

"Sit down, comrade, sit down," Gus says.

"Coffee?" Morris asks. He closes the book, blows off the dust, and places it on a shelf.

"Thank you," I say, "no."

"So," Gus says, "have you spent your time productively?" He pauses and smiles. "Excuse me, the question is ridiculous. Of course you've spent your time productively."

"Yes, Comrade Hall, I have been learning firsthand about the nature of capitalism and imperialism."

"Call me Gus," he says. "Remember, I'm Gus and you're Sasha. And that's Morris."

"My apologies." How could I have forgotten this simple man's earlier suggestion? Morris smiles, sensing that I am embarrassed.

"Then let's get down to business, Sasha." I smile involuntarily, as I hear Gus use the capitalist expression.

"You're right to find my use of that word amusing, Sasha. That's testimony to how deeply capitalism has penetrated our minds." Gus takes a deep breath. "Sasha, you must have noticed that our working class suffers from trade union mentality."

"As we know from Lenin," I say, "all it takes to start a revolution is a spark."

"An *iskra*," murmurs Morris.

"I couldn't agree with you more, Sasha," Gus says. "Our responsibility, the *Party's* responsibility, is enormous. And our leadership is indispensable."

"Exactly," I say.

"I keep telling Gus that our Party's up to the job," interjects Morris, "but he remains the eternal skeptic."

"The eternal *perfectionist*," Gus corrects him. "Things can always be better."

Gus rises from his chair and walks to the front of the desk. Morris and I watch him as he removes his jacket and loosens his tie.

"Sasha," he says as he sits on the desk, "the Party is like a living organism. All the organs have to be healthy for it to function properly. And the general secretary is like a doctor."

"An excellent analogy."

"*This* doctor"—Gus points to himself—"is worried."

"See what I mean?" Morris adds mournfully.

"About what, if I may ask?"

"I'll be straight with you, Sasha. Morris and I know we can trust you. " Gus looks me in the eyes. "Sasha, I believe the Party has been infiltrated."

I look from Gus to Morris and back to Gus.

"I believe, Sasha"—Gus raises both arms in the style of a general secretary delivering an address at a Party congress—"I believe that an American agent has wormed his way into the Party organism. A virus weakens the Party and harms the revolution."

For several seconds I am speechless. Finally, Morris breaks the silence by clearing his throat.

"I don't know, Gus," he says, shaking his head, "I just don't know."

"Dammit, Morris," Gus explodes, "we have a mole. I *know* it!"

"How long have you had these suspicions?" I ask.

"They're not suspicions, Sasha. They're certainties." Gus leans back and crosses his legs. He appears to have regained his equilibrium. "For several months."

"I disagree, Gus." Morris speaks quietly, but with a resolve that reminds me of Pavel. "The Party is healthy. Sasha, you've been here a while. Tell Gus what you think."

"What evidence do you have, Gus?" I am determined not to take sides, at least not immediately.

"The police, the FBI, they anticipate our every move." Gus begins pacing nervously. "We decide to hold a strike in some small factory in some small town in the middle of nowhere. What happens? Our people are arrested on bogus charges the day before the strike. We march against the war, and our placards are destroyed. We decide to sell *The Daily Worker* on some university, and campus security is beefed up. I could go on and on, Sasha. I know the imperialists believe we're a mortal threat to their beloved capitalist order. And I know they're smart and effective. But *this* smart? *This* effective? *Impossible!*"

"Gus," Morris explains, "they follow us. They tap our phones. Of course they know what we're up to." Both men are right, of course, but I decide to err on the side of caution.

"Perhaps Gus has a point, Morris. Such efficiency does seem too accidental to be an accident." As I speak, I think of my conversation with Jim. "How can the Soviet Union help the Party, Gus?"

Gus smiles. "The real question, Sasha, is how *you* can help us."

"I am a journalist, Gus."

"I know."

"I am not in the security services."

"Of course you're not."

"Then how can a Soviet journalist help you?"

"Morris and I need an ally, Sasha, someone we can trust completely. The one thing we know for certain is that you're not the mole."

"I could not be."

"Exactly. I want to lay a trap for this mole, Sasha. It has to be someone in the Politburo, someone with direct access to our highest decision-making process."

"How many people would that be?"

"Ten. With me and Morris, twelve."

"What should I do, Gus?"

"First of all, be our eyes and ears."

"I understand. And second?"

"Speak to the members of the Politburo. Find out who they are, what they're thinking. You've been in the Party all your life, Sasha. You know good apples, and you know bad apples. Help me find the bad apple. I know Morris thinks I'm exaggerating, but—"

"We can never be too secure, Gus," Morris says solemnly. "You know what I think about this mole business, but I'm with you all the way. Always have been, always will be."

"Should I attend meetings of the Politburo?" I ask.

"Of course," Gus replies. "We'll say that you're writing a series of newspaper articles about the Party. You'll be able to interview everyone. You'll collect your impressions, and then we can meet again."

"Do you suspect anyone?"

"Why, Morris, of course!" He lets out a booming laugh. Morris and I join in.

"Very well, then, comrades." I rise from my chair. "We shall find this mole. We shall extirpate this virus."

"Thank you, Sasha."

"Thank the Party," I say, "and Soviet power."

"I do," Gus says, "every minute of every day."

"As do I," Morris sighs, "as do I."

I return to my desk and decide that the wisest course of action is to speak with my comrades at the Soviet Mission. I dial the agreed-upon telephone number and ask for "Nick."

In turn, I am told that I have called a wrong number. The meeting will be in two hours. It gives me just enough time to attend the student meeting at the West End. Seymour actually came through—something I confess not to have expected—and I know that my credibility with him and his comrades will depend on my showing up.

Comrade X is waiting for me at a little brick stand near an artificial pond in Central Park. Cleopatra's notorious needle cannot be far from here, I think. He is eating a sausage and moves off in the direction of a terrace as soon as he sees me. I buy myself a sausage as well and follow him. Comrade X is seated on a bench, and he is visibly upset that bright yellow mustard has spilled on his black coat.

"A great inconvenience," I say and offer him a napkin.

"Oh, thank you," he says, "but I cannot imagine eating a hot dog without mustard."

I sit down near him and begin munching on mine. The sausage is edible, but the slightly moist roll cannot compare with our good Ukrainian black bread.

"Excellent," I say with a smile on my face.

"*Bon appétit*," he replies.

When I am done eating, Comrade X laughs. "We really should change our routine. Let's take a walk. There's a lovely fountain not far from here. We can talk there."

We stroll for some five minutes and then come upon a red-brick plaza adjoining a lake. The fountain is located at the foot of broad stone stairs. Here, too, I see only bums.

"You have been indiscreet, comrade," Comrade X says. Can he have Valeria in mind?

"How so, comrade?"

"You should not call from the Party office. Their phones are tapped. By the Americans."

"And by us, evidently."

"Yes, and by us."

"The matter could not wait, comrade."

"Ah," he says, his forefinger raised to the tip of his nose, "the question of the mole!"

"Yes," I say with some surprise. "How did you know?"

"It is an old story. An obsession of our dear friend, Gus Hall."

"You sound doubtful."

"Not at all," he says. "We know that the American Party is thoroughly penetrated. It always has been, and there's no reason to think that it no longer is."

"So Gus, I mean Comrade Hall, is correct in his suspicions."

"Of course."

"But you—we—prefer that things remain as they are."

He says nothing.

"So we *want* the Party to be penetrated." And then it strikes me in the eyes. "Of course," I cry out, "the Americans think they have penetrated and neutralized the American Party, but in reality we are using their mole to provide them with false information." I pause. "Do we know who the mole is?"

"We have our suspicions," Comrade X says, "but it doesn't matter. We know that whatever we pass on to Comrade Hall will, eventually, reach the mole—"

"—and the Americans."

"Exactly."

"Very clever, but is the price not too high? That means accepting the American Party's ineffectiveness and the failure of revolution in America."

"That *would* be too high a price," he says, "*if* the Party could ever be effective and *if* the revolution could ever succeed here. But look around you, Comrade Ivanov. Our propaganda insists that the victory of Communism is inevitable in capitalist societies. But no one really believes that, least of all the security organs. Do *you*?"

"So sacrificing the Party is really a small price."

"That would appear to be the objective reality."

"Especially if that sacrifice enables us to confuse the imperialist secret services."

"Comrade Hall probably told you how the American police always anticipate Party actions, didn't he?"

I nod.

"We know that. We have always known that. But consider what that means from our point of view. The American intelligence agencies are being diverted from the real threats to their system."

"Our people."

"Of course. So let them burn *The Daily Worker*. No one reads it anyway. Let them break up demonstrations. While the imperialists are expending their resources on such minor diversions, our agents are able to—"

"Yes, I understand." I feel sad. "Poor Gus. How deluded he is. I do not think he has any idea of what is going on."

"None at all. Gus Hall is a good Communist. He executes all his orders faithfully and unquestioningly."

"We are using him."

"Of course. The Party uses all of us. We are cogs."

"Poor, poor Gus. He wants so much to be a revolutionary leader."

"We all want things we can never attain."

"So what should I do? He wants me to investigate the members of the Politburo and tell him who the mole is."

"Do as he says."

"And if I find the mole?"

"Oh, we shall let the mole carry on. You'll have to identify someone else as the culprit."

"He will be purged."

"This is not Maoist China, comrade. He'll be purged and blacklisted and then he'll find a job and buy himself a small house with a white fence and a big dog."

"Then I know who the mole is. A Negro, Jim. He is disillusioned and is planning to leave the Party."

"Excellent."

"But wait," I say. "He is not on the Politburo."

"This Jim, isn't he the chief administrator at the Party office?"

"Yes."

"Then he has access to all Party documents and decisions."

"It is settled," I say and keep walking as Comrade X stops to look at a lanky girl on roller skates.

I cross Central Park to the western side of New York and board the subway for Columbia University. The café where the students are meeting is a few blocks south of the station. The West End is shabby and poorly lit. A large square-shaped bar is situated in the middle and small booths line the walls on the right and left. Sitting on the barstools and occupying the booths are young people, mostly longhaired boys in jeans and longhaired girls in either very short or very long skirts. I see no student radicals and, for a moment, I am uncertain what to do—until I hear yelling in a back room. It is the students, seated around a long wooden table with Seymour at the head. Like the students at the bar, the radicals are drinking beer.

Seymour sees me and flicks his wrist at the chair next to him. I think he will introduce me, but he does not. Instead, he says, "Here, have some beer." Then he shouts into my ear, "We're discussing our next demo."

The meeting is chaotic, unlike anything I have ever seen or experienced before. Seymour is the chairman, I assume, but he does nothing to guide the discussion. Students interrupt one another continually. No thought is expressed fully. No sentence appears to be finished. Curses fly with abandon. I see why Jim is so skeptical about these students' ability to communicate with the masses.

"Like, fuck, let's seize—"

"Fuck seize, we gotta off the pigs!"

"That's suicide, man, they're gonna—"

"Do fucking what? They're weak, man, they're—"

"—pigs, man, they're pigs."

"And pigs have guns and—"

"So fucking what?"

And on and on it goes like this, with the temperature of the discussion rising with each interrupted thought and each gulp of beer.

"What do you think?" Seymour turns to me. He is obviously expecting a positive evaluation, but I decide to be honest.

"The discussion is confusing."

"Hey, man, *this* is democracy."

"Well, yes, but you *must* reach a resolution. You *must* make a decision and embark on some action."

"This *is* action, man."

"It is talk," I say.

"This is democracy, man, this is people's power. We're the action faction, man."

"But will you hold a demonstration? That is the only important question."

"Sure we will. Eventually. After everyone settles down, we'll make a decision. It always works that way."

"How do you expect the working class to follow?"

"Fuck the working class, man. We're gonna make the revolution without it." Is Seymour inebriated? Can he be serious?

"But that is impossible!"

"We're doing it, man. So are the French. And the Germans. Don't tell me it's impossible when we're doing it."

"But you will fail!"

"Sasha," he turns to me with what looks like exasperation, "have you ever read Marcuse?"

"No." I sense my resolve is wavering.

"Read him. Then we'll talk about what's impossible."

I smile at Seymour. I see that this conversation can only go nowhere. I also see that the student revolutionaries, if they are all like this collective, will fail. With or without this Marcuse.

Their incoherent discussion continues, and pitchers of beer are brought and consumed with growing intensity. The beer has no foam and is tasteless, good only for getting drunk. A boy and girl seated in a corner are kissing, and his hands are wandering freely over her body. She responds by wrapping her leg around his thigh. No one seems to mind this public display of intimacy. At the same time, my encounter with Valeria comes to mind, and I feel embarrassed. More students wander in; there are now about thirty in the room and the debate has degenerated into a bazaar-like cacophony. I smile involuntarily, as I think that this is just what Lenin had in mind when he wrote of left-wing infantilism.

Suddenly, a voice booms above the chaos, "Let's liberate the fucking University!"

"Yeah, yeah!" other voices chime in, until, for no obvious reason, the voices merge into a chorus of agreement. I am amazed by this transformation of chaos into order, although I remain no less skeptical of the ability of these boys and girls to execute revolutionary action.

"Why," I turn to Seymour, "do you want to seize the University?"

"To protest the fucking war, man."

"The Vietnam War?"

"Yeah!"

"But what does Columbia University have to do with the national-liberation struggle of the Vietnamese people?"

"It's part of the system, man."

"But the war is being led by your Pentagon and the military-industrial complex. How do you expect to help the Vietnamese workers and peasants by seizing a university?"

"Fuck, Sasha, Columbia's part of the fucking system. It's all the ruling apparatus, man, the power elite. It's, like, about hegemony, man. Get it?"

"But, Seymour"—I sense that I am beginning to plead—"the University is not bombing Vietnam. The *Pentagon* is.

The *military* is. The arms-producing militarist corporations are. Seizing the University will only distract the workers from the *real* struggle, which is against capitalism and the military-industrial complex."

"You're fucked up, man."

"Then tell me," I persist, "how will seizing the University stop the war? Or promote revolution?"

"Students *are* the revolution, man. Get it? *Students are the fucking revolution!*"

"You will fail without the working class."

"Oh, fuck, Sasha, read—"

"—Marcuse. I know."

"Oh, for fuck's sake," Seymour cries. "It's not just Marcuse, Sasha. Have you read Gramsci? Or Habermas? Or Barthes? Or Adorno? Or Horkheimer? Or Benjamin? Have you read *any* of them? Until you do, man, maybe you'd better leave the action to the action faction and just shut up."

I say nothing. Seymour's outburst depresses me, and I resolve to leave. They are children, well-meaning children perhaps, but children nonetheless. There is no point talking to them anymore; there is no point writing about the "student revolution." There will be no revolution until they grow up. In the meantime, they will drink beer, grope, kiss, argue—and believe that that is revolution. Very well, let them do what they want to do. I say good-bye to Seymour, who merely nods in response. I do not ask him about their next meeting, and he feels no need to tell me.

As I walk past the bar, a bearded man smiles at me. My first thought is that he is a pederast.

"I see you've been meeting with our students."

"Yes," I say bitterly, "they are very passionate."

"But their logic is often faulty, isn't it?" He looks at me inquisitively. "You're Russian, aren't you?"

"Did my accent betray me that easily?"

"I have a good ear. The name is Dante." He places a booklet on the bar and extends his hand. "I teach philosophy."

"Sasha. I am a journalist from the Soviet Union."

As we shake, I notice that the cover depicts none other than Andrei.

"I know that man," I say proudly.

"Who? Andy Warhol? *You* know Andy Warhol?"

"Yes, we are friends. And comrades. I think he is a genius."

"So do I!" exclaims Dante.

"Really?" I am amazed to hear that my views are shared by a member of the American intelligentsia.

"He has redefined the nature of art," Dante says. "His *Brillo Box*, for instance, is—"

"I think you mean *socialist realist* art," I say quietly, fearful of dampening this American Dante's childlike enthusiasm.

"No, no, he's redefined *art*. Look at this," he says as he thumbs through the booklet. "That's an exact replica of a Brillo box, yet Andy's *Brillo Box* is art and a regular Brillo box isn't. Why?"

"Excuse me," I say, "but what is Brillo?"

"What difference does it make?

"Please, Professor Dante, answer my question."

"A cleanser."

"All is clear, then," I say, "Andrei—"

"Who is Andrei?"

"Andrei Warhol. He is a Ukrainian."

"I didn't know."

"There are many things you do not know, my dear Professor Dante. Such as that Andrei's art liberates the objects of labor from capital and returns them to their rightful owners—the working class. Tell me, Professor Dante, who uses this Brillo?"

"People," he says.

"Do *you* use it?"

"Why, no."

"Do rich capitalists use it?"

"I suppose not."

"So who uses it, Mister Dante? Workers use it, that is who."

He grins weakly and nods his head slowly.

"It was a pleasure meeting you," I say.

"Perhaps you'd like to address one of my seminars?" he asks timidly.

"You can find me at the Chelsea Hotel. Sasha Ivanov. Good-bye." As we shake hands, I notice that his grip has gone limp.

It has rained and Broadway is glistening with the colors of neon. I walk south, toward the subway. As soon as I reach One Hundred Tenth Street, however, I decide to keep walking. My head is too full of too many impressions, and I need exercise to clear it. It takes me three hours to walk to my hotel, but I am glad to have done so. Broadway, I notice, is a microcosm of New York, perhaps even of capitalist society. I cross One Hundred Tenth and immediately enter a different world—one inhabited by poor people of various nationalities. The stores look shabbier, the restaurants are dirtier. Small groups of men huddle in doorways or on street corners, drinking and playing radios. I could be someplace in the non-aligned world. By the time I reach Ninetieth Street, I am back in capitalist America. Whites predominate, they are well dressed, the stores and restaurants and bars are more elegant. I pass Lincoln Center and see women in long gowns and men in tuxedoes. And then I reach the theatre district, where bright lights and huge advertisements illuminate the wet streets, and prostitutes and junkies and bums mingle freely with matronly theatregoers and policemen. At Times Square, I decide to walk beneath the rows of marquees lining Forty-Second Street. Garish light bulbs pulsate nervously, the smell of greasy food permeates the air, policemen on horseback patrol the street, and hungry men and women prowl the trashcans. My senses are overwhelmed, and my head begins to ache. *This* is capitalism. I turn left at Eighth Avenue and walk amid hulking dark buildings until I reach an enormous post office and sports arena. From there until Twenty-Third Street the avenue is lined with grubby bars, and more bums, prostitutes, and junkies. Welcome to America, I think, a country that desperately needs a revolution and a country that may never have a revolution.

There is a letter from Katyusha. I read it in the lift. All is well at home. Once in my room, I read one of Leonid Illich's less inspired speeches and a marvelous chapter from Gus's book and fall asleep almost immediately.

In the morning, I reread Katyusha's letter. All is well, but I think I notice a certain distance in her tone. And her usually perfect penmanship is blurred, suggesting she was distracted or in a hurry. I decide to write back immediately, two pages of detailed descriptions of New York, my work, my comrades. I say nothing about Andrei or the students.

As I enter the lobby, I see, sitting on a sofa and reading a newspaper, Valeria. Is she waiting for me? I am both excited and apprehensive to see her.

"Hello, asshole," she says.

"Valeria, my Lithuanian mouse, what are you doing here?"

"Haven't seen you in a while, scumbag."

"I have been very busy."

"That's what all men say."

"It is true, Valeria."

"I need to use your bathroom."

"Very well." I know she is lying. "Come upstairs."

I arrive at the Party office, and Jim greets me. I ask him if Comrade Gus is in and he nods yes. I knock on Gus's door and enter.

"Good morning, Gus," I say, "good morning, Morris."

"Sasha!" Gus seems unusually pleased to see me. "Come in, my friend, have a seat."

"Comrades," I continue without sitting down, "I have pursued some inquiries. With friends who have excellent information."

"Ah, I thought you would!" Gus wags his forefinger. "And what, dear Sasha, did your excellent friends have to say?"

"They know who"—I turn around to see whether the door is closed—"the mole is."

"Didn't I tell you so, Morris?"

"You are a clever man, Gus," I smile. "You have used me."

"But you don't mind, Sasha. I know you don't."

"I would have done the same."

"Exactly. We are Communists." Gus shifts his glance expectantly from me to Morris and back to me. "So who is it?"

I write Jim's name on a piece of paper and hand it to Gus. He raises his eyebrows and frowns. Morris laughs and says nothing.

"Impossible," Gus says. "He's loyal. I know that for a fact."

"Perhaps he once was," I say quietly. "But now he is not."

"Impossible." Gus shakes his head. "Absolutely impossible."

"He is planning to leave the Party," I say. "He told me so himself. And my friends have proof of his treason."

"Why didn't they ever show it to me?"

"Everything is under control, Gus."

"But I'm the goddam general secretary of the goddam Party!"

"And the American Party is an ally of the Communist Party of the Soviet Union. My friends assured me you would know where your loyalties lie—or should lie." How I detest having to convey a threat to this good comrade.

Gus falls silent. Then he mumbles, "And the proof is incontrovertible?"

"Yes."

"What should we do?"

"Let him resign."

"I agree," says Morris, "let's just cut him loose."

"But," Gus says, "why would a successful mole resign? He's a valuable asset for the Americans."

"Because he knows he's been uncovered," Morris says. "That's obvious, Gus."

Gus lowers himself into his chair and shakes his head in disbelief.

"How long has this been going on, Sasha?" he asks. I am beginning to feel profoundly sorry and embarrassed for this honest Russian bear.

"At least five years."

"Five years!" Gus whistles. "So all my work has been useless."

"No, Gus," I say soothingly, "my friends say that you have been invaluable. Jim may be a mole within the Party, but the Party is a mole within capitalist society. Those are their exact words."

"Precisely!" Morris adds.

"Did he say when he'd resign?"

"Soon," I say. "But I shall encourage him to do so immediately."

"Thank you, Sasha," Gus says, "and thank your friends. From the bottom of my heart." I see before me a broken man.

"Do not worry, comrades, Soviet power will protect you." My statement sounds empty, but what else can I say?

"This is a sad day for American Communism," Gus says. Morris places a hand on his shoulder.

I say nothing. I know Gus is right.

I need to calm my soul and decide to pay a brief visit to Andrei. I walk downstairs, holding on to the curved banister and carefully negotiating the steep steps. The door to the Factory is slightly ajar and I walk in without bothering to knock. Gerald is sitting at the front desk, his outstretched legs resting on a pile of photographs. His head is thrown back and he is holding a coffee cup on his stomach. A cigarette is burning in the ashtray. He tilts his head forward and opens one eye.

"Man," he says, "have I got a fucking hangover."

"Then you should have some vodka, my Italian friend, not coffee."

"Ain't got any," he groans.

"You must have some alcohol here." I cast my eyes around and espy a bottle of wine on a windowsill. It is open and the wine is probably tasteless, but it will do.

"Drink this," I order.

"Fuck," he sputters, "it tastes like shit!"

"Drink it," I say, "all of it." He does.

"Do you feel better?"

"Yeah," he mutters, "it's beginning to work. You're a fucking hangover doctor, Sash."

"An old trick. Every Russian knows it."

He looks at me carefully, one eye still closed.

"You know," he says slowly, "you and that other guy really gave me the once-over. What are you, fucking cops?"

"I am a journalist, Gerald, but the Czech was from the security services."

"A fucking spy?"

"Yes."

"Well, you made some team. Do *all* Russian journalists talk like cops?"

"I was interviewing you, Gerald. *He* was interrogating you."

"Felt fucking the same."

"Perhaps," I say. "But I am only a journalist."

"You gave me the fucking third degree, man. What the fuck for?"

"I ask myself the same question, Gerald. It was as if we were in church. And suddenly we all began confessing."

"Fuck! And Andy was the priest!"

"Have some more wine, Gerald." He extends the coffee cup and I fill it. "The two of you have been together for a long time." That evening, and my own indiscretions, are topics I prefer not to pursue.

"About seven years," says Gerald, "maybe eight. I knew Andy when he had his studio in an old firehouse on Eighty-Seventh."

"A remarkable collaboration."

"Used to be, Sash. We had some great times. Now Andy treats me like shit."

"But you paint together. You were his guest."

"Yeah," says Gerald, "but he's become a sonofabitch. And not just toward me, Sash. Andy's messing with everyone. I don't know what's gotten into him."

"I have met Valeria Solanas—"

"That crazy dyke?"

"—and she has expressed herself critically about Andrei as well. You know, Gerald, Andrei is a genius, and all geniuses are difficult. Dostoevsky, for instance—"

"I'm thinking of leaving the Factory," Gerald declares.

"Do my own thing." I am stunned, but not too surprised by this latest revelation.

"Perhaps that is for the best. Perhaps you can start a new life. Have you ever thought of getting married, Gerald?"

"For fuck's sake, why? The pussy's free, and it's everywhere. Hey, Sasha, are you messing with me again?"

I smile. "My apologies, it is an old journalist's incurable habit to ask questions."

"Now *you* tell me something, Sash. You ever go the other way?"

"Other women? Of course."

"Oh, fuck it, Sash, I mean men."

"No," I say, "I have normal drives." He opens his other eye.

"Fucking normal? You know about Andy, don't you?"

"He is shy, and he is attached to his mother."

"Fuck!" he bursts out laughing. "He's a fucking fruit!"

I have no idea how to respond.

"A fruit! A fag! For fuck's sake, Sash, he likes *boys*."

"Andrei?"

"Yeah, your fucking *Ahn-dray*."

"But, how can you know?"

"Fuck, Sash, it takes one to know one."

"Excuse me?"

"I do too, Sash. *That's* why."

"Excuse me, Gerald," I mumble and rush off.

I run down the stairs and bolt outside. Like Lenin's after the seizure of the Winter Palace, my head is spinning, and I need fresh air. I am breathing heavily, and my heart is pounding. I feel stunned and shocked and embarrassed at being stunned and shocked. Perversion is commonplace in the capitalist West. I know that. I have read about it, I have seen it, I have been told about it. So why am I shocked? Because it is Andrei, that is why. Of course, now that I think about it, I see that Gerald is right. Andrei has all the earmarks of a pederast. His shyness, his love of his mother, his gentle mannerisms, his uncertain voice—the signs were all there for me to see. So why did I not see them? The answer seems obvious. Because I have been blinded by his artistic genius, by his proletarian origins.

I enter the park. Bums lie asleep on the benches, ragged junkies stand near the entrance, long-legged Negro prostitutes preen as if they were on some Black Sea promenade. And then I realize what I have known all the time. I have entered a perverted world—a capitalist world that destroys human life and forces normal human beings to act in abnormal ways. These bums and addicts and prostitutes were not born that way. They were made by the world, by the social conditions in which they live. Why should Gerald, why should Andrei be exceptions? The wonder is that, despite these irresistible pressures to conform to capitalist perversions, Andrei has managed to remain true to his healthy proletarian roots and develop an art form that promotes the interests of the toiling masses.

What would I be like if I had had the misfortune to be born here? It is my happy fate to have been raised in material and class conditions that develop all of man's true potential—as a worker and as a man. And I have done well: I am in the Party, I struggle for Communism, I serve the Soviet state. But Andrei had none of these advantages— and he too, even if less than fully consciously, struggles for Communism and Soviet power. I realize as well how important Pani Julia is to Andrei's class consciousness. This simple peasant woman embodies all the good qualities of toilers everywhere. Andrei's excessive dependence on her is, I see, a blessing in disguise. She keeps him connected to his proletarian roots. And to his nationality. Something as simple as a plate of varenyky reminds Andrei of who he is and of what his obligations to the revolution are. Very well, Andrei lacks full consciousness of his class position. Even so, he is objectively at the forefront of the world proletariat's struggle for a new and better life.

I give several panhandlers money, evade a car while crossing the street, and enter the building. As I do so, I feel a gentle touch upon my right shoulder and a whispered "Sasha." I turn around and, feeling almost as if I have had a confrontation with fate, see Andrei—smiling his slightly crooked smile, his eyes shielded by sunglasses.

"You were, uh, so into yourself. Uh, you didn't even, uh, hear me."

"I was deep in thought," I say.

"Girl trouble?"

"No," I respond all too quickly. Does Andrei suspect something about my liaison with Valeria?

"Not, uh, *boy* trouble?"

"Oh no, Andrei." And suddenly it strikes me in the eyes just how blind I have been about Andrei. He is who he is. It is *I* who have mistaken wishes for reality.

"Uh, come upstairs. I want to, uh, show you something."

As we enter the Factory, we find Gerald sleeping in the same position as before. Andrei shakes his head and takes my hand. We go to one of the back rooms. Andrei turns on the light and removes a roll of paper from his satchel. He unrolls it on the table in the center of the room and smoothes it out, repeatedly and delicately, with his hands.

"I've, uh, been drawing."

I look through the sheets and am mesmerized by what I see. Each is a charcoal drawing, executed quickly and almost carelessly, of the hammer and sickle. Sometimes of both, sometimes only of the hammer, sometimes of the sickle. This is my first encounter with Andrei's drawings, and I cannot fail to notice a striking difference in style. His paintings are carefully executed. Even those that have intentionally blurred lines and seeming mistakes have a meticulous, methodical quality about them. These drawings, in contrast, are spontaneous, free, and unencumbered by preconceptions of any kind. But the style is not the only thing that strikes me in the eyes and takes my breath away. The content—beautifully rendered images of the glorious symbols of Communism—is no less astounding.

"These are remarkable, Andrei." The words come slowly, almost hesitatingly, to me. "I have never—I have *never* seen anything like this."

"You, uh, like them?"

They are magnificent, Andrei, I want to shout from rooftops. Do you not see that you have accomplished what generations of Soviet artists have failed to do? Do you not see that you have managed the perfect synthesis of form and content? Do you not see that the simplicity of your drawings is the perfect complement to the power of Communism? Do you not see that you have succeeded in conveying with a few strokes of charcoal the beauty, strength, clarity, and inevitability of Communism? Do you not see that you are a genius? A proletarian genius, a Communist genius, a revolutionary genius?

"They are," I say quietly, "the most powerful and persuasive expression of Communism I have ever seen."

"I did them after, uh, you left."

"After that dinner with Pavel?"

"Uh-huh. I thought, hell, if this Communism stuff means, uh, so much to you and that Pavel guy, maybe I should, uh, find out what's the big deal."

"Do you have the Soviet flag at home?" I say hopefully.

"Mama has a book. She helped me. Oh, just remembered," he says while groping for something in his bag. "These are for you. From, uh, Mama."

I take a plastic container and open it. Varenyky! I break out laughing.

"I will have one," I say, "may I?"

"Uh, sure," he smiles, "they're yours."

"Have one, too."

And, suddenly, there we are, two Ukrainian workers, two revolutionaries, two Communists—munching on potato dumplings in the famous American artist Andy Warhol's Factory studio!

"You must visit me in the Soviet Union, Andrei," I say. We have managed to eat all the dumplings and are now wiping our greasy hands on a paint-covered rag.

"Uh, sure."

"There is so much for you, as an artist, to see."

"Uh, tell me, Sasha, is Red Square really, uh, red?"

"You mean Communist?"

"No, red. Is it painted, uh, red?"

"Why, no," I say.

"Let's do it, Sasha. Let's, uh, paint it red." In his childlike enthusiasm, Andrei squeezes my knee.

"Ah, my dear friend, that would be very complex."

"All we need, uh, all we need is paint."

"And the permission of the Moscow City authorities. Perhaps even of the Kremlin."

"*You* can do it, Sasha."

"It *would* be a magnificent gesture," I say dreamily. "The fiftieth anniversary of the revolution was last year. That would have been the perfect time."

"We can do it, uh, anytime."

"How much paint would we need?"

"Thousands of gallons."

"Would we also paint the Kremlin walls?"

"Uh, just the square."

"You are right. It is *Red* Square, after all." I am getting dizzy with—anticipation.

"We'll film it," he says. "The whole, uh, square."

"Yes, yes"—I can barely contain my enthusiasm—"every brick, we can film every brick turning red!"

Andrei smiles. "It's Mama's pierogis," he says. "They're better than, uh, amphetamines."

At the office. I sit at my desk with my eyes closed and a smile on my face. Once again, that sly Little Russian has sucked me into his world and made me a slave to his will. He is a magician. The idea of painting Red Square red now strikes me as silly—and completely unrealistic. But perhaps that is because I am not, like Andrei, an artist and a pathbreaker. I cannot imagine overcoming the bureaucratic hurdles before such a project. And so, I abandon it before I have even tried. Andrei, in contrast, proceeds from the imaginable and assumes that it must be doable. Perhaps he is wrong. But at least he may succeed. I will certainly fail. The comparison with Lenin again strikes me as apt. However different the two men are, they share this one quality—of accomplishing the impossible, simply by setting their will to it. There is much that I can learn from these giants.

My thoughts are interrupted by a knock. It is Jim—and I suddenly remember that I have promised Gus to engage in a terrible subterfuge against this honest comrade.

"Can I come in?" he asks. "Gotta talk to you 'bout somethin'."

"Of course, my friend." I speak casually, but inwardly I am full of trepidation.

"What you been up to, Sash?"

"I am still investigating the American revolution." I cannot resist smiling at the irony.

"No shit?"

"My sentiments precisely," I say. "And I have come to appreciate just how wise a man you are, Jim."

"Yeah? So how's this fo' wisdom?" he asks. "I *ain't* quittin'. What the hell, I've been in this goddam party all my life. Where'd I go?"

My fears have been realized. I sensed that something was amiss when Jim knocked on my door, and I was right. I see that I am now in the exceptionally awkward position of having to convince Jim to *leave* the Party. If he does not, the Party will be forced to rid itself of an infiltrator, and although I know that the days of the cult of personality are long gone, I cannot say for sure that Jim will not come to some harm. I might have been indifferent to such a fate before I knew him personally, but, now that I count him among my friends, I know I have no choice but to persuade Jim that his original resolution, to leave and lead a "normal" life, was correct.

"It is your choice, dear Jim, but if you are here to ask for my opinion, I shall be frank with you—frank as a friend and frank as a comrade."

"Sash, you know you're the only person I can talk to 'bout this."

"Then, my friend, I think you are making a mistake."

"Huh? I thought you'd be glad."

"I *am* glad that the Party has such a strong hold on you. That proves that the cause of Communism will be victorious. But I am not glad that you see the Party as a refuge, a second-best alternative. Jim"—I look reassuringly into his troubled eyes—"the Party needs activists. The Party needs revolutionary cadres. It does not need fellow travelers or tired and disillusioned comrades who have devoted their lives to the cause and now deserve rest."

"Like l'il ol' me, huh?"

"Jim," I continue, "I have become acquainted with the American Party these last few weeks and months. You have many good comrades, but they appear to be in the minority. Most of the comrades I have met strike me as somewhat"—I sense that I cannot find the right word—"*distant* from the working class and the proletarian cause. The Party needs to be rejuvenated, and I am not even sure that Gus is the right man for the task. But"—I see that Jim does not look surprised by what I have just said—"*that* is another issue. I am certain, Jim, that the Party definitely does not need another distant comrade."

"But I can help."

"Can you, Jim? Can you really? If you do not believe in the cause anymore, then the Party necessarily becomes a *job* for you."

"Sash, it ain't never been just a job. You know that."

"Not in the past, Jim, but now? And in the future? If you do not believe—deeply believe—you will become a cynical bureaucrat. I know that kind of comrade. We have enough of them in the Soviet Union."

"How d'you handle 'em?"

"We are large, Jim, and our society is Communist. If the Party becomes bureaucratic, the proletariat will always force it to fix its ways. And we are always getting new cadres—fresh, young, energetic comrades who want to build a Communist future."

"Yeah, all of us in the Party, we're all gettin' old."

"So make way for the young, Jim. Give them a chance to build Communism."

"I dunno." He shakes his head. "What'm I gonna do outside the Party?"

"You told me yourself. Were you not going to get a job? Get married? Why should any of that change? And besides, Jim, do you think that your work as a Communist stops just because you are no longer a member? Americans suffer from trade union consciousness. You know that better than I do. A revolutionary among the workers can make an enormous difference."

"What's Gus gonna say? And the others? What'm I supposed to tell 'em?"

"Tell them what you told me. The real Communists will understand. And those who are just bureaucrats—do you really care what they think?"

"Can I visit you in Leningrad, Sash?"

"My home will always be open to you, my dear friend."

I feel proud. I have successfully averted a crisis within the Party. Jim will now resign, Gus will accept his resignation, the mole will remain untouched, and Comrade X will continue to use him to penetrate American intelligence. And I will retain a good friend in this kindhearted Negro.

Later in the day, as I am sitting at my desk reading newspaper accounts of the Negro movement for what they call "civil rights," Jim knocks on my door once again, but this time with greater authority. Has he changed his mind? I turn to him and smile a genuine smile despite a renewed sense of foreboding. As I learn in a second, that sense is justified, but for a different reason.

"You heard?" he asks breathlessly.

"I have been reading all day."

"They got Martin."

"I do not under—"

"They shot Martin Luther King."

I am speechless. I have just been reading of his role in the Negro movement.

"An assassination?"

"Yeah, rifle shots. In Memphis. He was standin' on the balcony. Of his hotel. They got him, Sash, they got him."

"I am so deeply sorry, my dear friend."

"America's gonna burn, Sash. We're gonna see a revolution, we're gonna have a fuckin' revolution."

"Did the security services shoot him?"

"It don't matter who, Sash. The racists got him. Man, oh man, Sash, this country's gonna burn."

"What will you do?"

"Join the revolution!"

"But the Party, what is its position?"

"Don't much care. I quit. Remember? I'm outta here. I'm gonna do what I wanna do."

"Where will you go?"

"To Newark," he says. "Where I'm from. Across the river."

I nod. I vaguely recall having seen the name on some map of New York.

"Can I come with you, Jim?"

"Sure, Sash," he says, "sure. Man, oh man, the place is gonna burn."

Someone has turned on the radio in an adjacent room, and all the comrades are listening attentively. Commentators laud King and speak with foreboding about the future of what they call "race relations" in America. Some reporters interview Negroes in Harlem and other parts of New York. The people are angry. A report from Memphis, a racist city in the American South, features more angry Negro voices. There are reports of riots and insurrections throughout America. Perhaps Jim is right? Perhaps America will burn?

And perhaps I made a mistake in thinking that the true Negro revolutionaries were those young men I met several weeks ago? Perhaps their radicalism is the reason for, as Jim had suggested, their isolation from the working class?

This Baptist minister, this King, appears to have mobilized millions of the Negro race. He is no revolutionary, and he is certainly no Communist, but his bourgeois appeals to equality appear to resonate with Negro workers. I begin to regret having ignored his movement until now. But if I visit this Newark with Jim, perhaps I can better appreciate just what drives the Negro masses.

Jim and I walk a few blocks and board the Hudson Tubes, a train that I had not known existed. In an hour, after traversing a vast expanse of empty marshland and industrial buildings, we arrive at Pennsylvania Station in the city of Newark. The station is full of police, and the streets outside are roiling with mounted officers wearing helmets and carrying truncheons. We hear shouting and gunshots in the distance.

"Let's take the back way," Jim says.

We make our way through crowds of anxious travelers and exit through another doorway.

"This here's the Po'tuguese neighborhood," Jim says. "The cops ain't gonna be here. We'll get to Broad 'long the back streets."

I follow Jim silently, and as we walk along the increasingly dark streets, I sense that his steps are getting longer and his breathing is getting heavier. We walk beneath a train trestle, cross a highway, and enter the Negro neighborhood. A few more blocks and we come upon a sight that I have not seen since the war. A commercial boulevard lined with shops is in flames. Shards of glass cover the sidewalks, and burning cars lie on their sides. Shouts, screams, and chanting intermingle with the neighing of horses and the barking of "pigs." Crowds of Negroes are surging along the street, throwing rocks at the police, smashing windows, looting. The police are amassed in a phalanx, some dash out and swing their clubs, some shoot their guns into the air. Large police trucks are parked at intersections.

"It's burnin', man, it's burnin'. This is it, Sash, this is the revolution."

And Jim runs into the street. He stoops to pick up a rock and I watch him throw it at a mounted policeman. The rock strikes the horse in the head and the policeman turns at a gallop at Jim. My kind and gentle friend, instead of running, picks up another rock and hurls it at the policeman, who raises his right arm and brings down the truncheon on Jim's head. Despite the noise of the crowd, I can hear the sickening crack. I watch Jim crumple to the ground. The horse gallops away, as the policeman swings his club with abandon at the insurrectionaries.

I run to Jim and, seeing that his head is covered with blood, lift him over my shoulder and attempt to bring him to safety.

"Get the fuck outta here, whitey!" a young Negro shouts at me.

"He is injured," I stammer. "He is my friend."

"Leave that brother alone, fuck face!" he cries. "Get your white ass outta here!" He raises his fist threateningly.

"I am a Communist," I plead. "I am a Soviet journalist. Your struggle is my struggle!"

"Fuck you!" he shouts. "Fuck your white Communist ass!" And then he pulls at Jim's body and drops it to the ground. As I stand there, completely uncertain of what to say or do next, he hits me in the mouth—it is one of the strongest blows I have ever experienced—and I stagger backwards and fall to the street.

"Fuck your white ass, whitey!" he shouts and drapes Jim's inert body over his shoulder. I want to protest, to say that Jim needs help, that he may be seriously injured, but I find that I have no strength to speak, and even less to get to my feet.

I return to consciousness as I am lifted onto a stretcher by some medical personnel. I know that I cannot be taken to a hospital—the bourgeois press would be sure to call me an *agent provocateur*—and, as they raise the stretcher to maneuver it into an ambulance, I jump off and run.

"Hey, you!" one of them shouts. "Hey, you!"

But I find new strength and disappear in the side streets before they can follow me. As I come to myself, I realize that the shouting, at least here, has subsided. I hear screams in the distance and conclude that the fighting has moved to another part of the city. The buildings around me are eerily black, and the darkness is interrupted only by the sharp sirens and flashing lights of police cars and ambulances. As I walk, my feet make a crunching sound. Broken glass is strewn everywhere, and the air is thick with the acrid smell of burning rubber.

Like a latter-day John Reed, I have witnessed the beginning of the American Revolution. I only hope that Jim has not been its first victim. But I try to console myself with the thought that, if he is, he will have died for a good cause.

His heroism amazes me. I witnessed the transformation of a mild-mannered Negro *apparatchik*,[32] a disillusioned

---

32   A worker of the Party apparatus.

Communist with no more passion for the cause, into a revolutionary firebrand. How much zeal must have smoldered in his heart! What a tragedy that the American Party was unable to utilize it for the good of the revolution.

Two days later we receive the dreaded news. Jim is dead, killed by the imperialist racists. Gus calls a meeting of the Politburo, to which I am invited. He informs the other comrades of Jim's heroic death on behalf of the oppressed Negro masses. Gus looks distraught, but I know that he is shedding crocodile tears, inwardly glad to be rid of a mole. Morris looks genuinely crestfallen. In the ensuing discussion, the comrades debate how Jim's memory should be best preserved. Someone suggests a peace prize, to be distributed annually to a deserving member of the Negro proletariat. Someone else proposes that a section of *The Daily Worker* be named after Jim. I can see that Gus is uncomfortable with these proposals; he would prefer the name of this traitor to be forgotten. He suggests that a subcommittee discuss the question and report back to the Politburo in several months' time. The matter will die there, I know. Gus has dealt cleverly with this challenge.

We meet afterwards, once the other comrades have dispersed. "Come into my office, Sasha," he says, "and tell me what happened."

"He died heroically," I say. "That is not an exaggeration, Gus. I was there."

Morris and Gus exchange meaningful glances.

"Sasha," Gus says, "the reactionary forces are using Jim's Party affiliation as proof of Communist infiltration of the civil rights movement. Our Negro comrades fear a provocation." Where, I wonder, is this train of thought going?

"We could use the alleged infiltration to our advantage, Gus. We could say that, yes, the Communist Party is a mass party enjoying the support of both white and black toilers."

"The Negro masses won't go for that."

"King," Morris adds, "was a bourgeois diversionary. He preached to the masses about racial oppression and ignored the reality of the class struggle."

"And yet he moved the Negroes," I say.

"But to what end?" Morris asks. "A few days of rioting and what's left? Nothing."

"Unfortunately," Gus continues, "King's propaganda has been effective, and the Negro masses don't trust the Party. I understand our Negro comrades."

"The nationality question is an especially sensitive issue," I say. "Our Party has struggled with it for fifty years."

Gus ignores my diversion and gets to the point. "We must help our Negro comrades."

"Of course." I suspect that by "we," Gus means me.

"We can't claim that Jim wasn't one of us. The police found his Party card in his wallet. But we can let the media know that Jim was—"

"An infiltrator?"

"Yes, an agent of the FBI."

"Sasha?" Morris says.

"Yes?"

"You can help us get the message across."

"Morris, I am unknown here. You know that."

"No, Sasha, not here," says Morris. "In the Soviet Union."

"We want you"—Gus demonstratively points at me—"to write an article exposing Jim for the Soviet press. Our comrades will pick it up and then disseminate the news among the masses, here."

"Sasha," Morris says, "we *must* help the Negroes and we *must* save our Party. This is the only way. You know that."

"Yes, I know," I mumble, "I know. It is an excellent plan."

"We knew you'd agree, dear Comrade Ivanov," Gus says, his face beaming. "Together, we'll win this struggle!"

Morris places his hand on my shoulder.

"Yes," I say weakly, "I am sure we will."

This solution, while brilliant as far as the needs of the Negro comrades and the Party are concerned, is the worst possible one as far as I am concerned. Jim's tragic death at least gave meaning to his life and capped his devotion to the cause with a genuine, even if unnecessary and pointless, act of heroism. But *this*—this supposed expose of a good and honest Communist as a supposed traitor—dishonors his memory and soils my hands. I shall do whatever the cause requires, of course. I am enough of a disciplined Party member to know that. But how deeply repulsive writing this article will be, especially as none of it, absolutely none of it, will be true.

I compose the article in one sitting. It appears several days later, and has the expected effect among the Negro comrades. Gus is also happy, although I notice at the meeting of the Politburo that he is distinctly uncomfortable answering questions about how the Party could have permitted a mole to penetrate its highest ranks for so long. Voices are raised, accusations are made, and at one point Gus even offers to resign. But Morris makes an impassioned speech in his defense and that offer is immediately rejected. The Politburo recommends only that greater vigilance and security be adopted, especially in the headquarters, the "nerve center" of American Communism. I am certain that the real mole is delighted by the outcome of the debate. The wrecker will be able to work undeterred.

I am immersed in reading about the "civil rights" movement of this King. Insurrectionary activity bursts out in New York, Los Angeles, Detroit, Baltimore, Chicago, Boston, Kansas City, St. Louis, and other cities with large Negro populations. Even the capital of imperialist America experiences a Negro rebellion; intense battles take place only blocks from the White House. Everywhere the capitalist authorities expose themselves as beasts. As the peace-loving Negro masses sing, "We shall come over," the police arrest, kill, and maim with abandon. The Negro revolutionaries fight back courageously, but within days of the outbreak of insurrections, the fascist authorities invariably reestablish control. But I suspect that this control is temporary. For what the upheavals have shown is that the potential for revolution among America's Negroes is enormous. Jim was wrong to think that Negroes were afflicted by a trade union mentality. And I was wrong to think that only the self-styled radicals were revolutionaries. In fact, the depth and breadth of revolutionary sentiment among the Negro working class is huge. All it needs is a spark and the leadership of a revolutionary party that will persuade the masses that civil rights are not enough, and that "proletarian rights" are the only solution to the racial question in America. Where is the Negro Lenin?

Seymour, the self-styled student revolutionary, telephones several times, but I am—fortunately—rarely in, and only once do we actually talk. He tells me that the students are getting increasingly radicalized, and that a revolutionary outbreak is imminent. He invites me to attend their meetings again, but I tell him that I am writing about the Negro movement and do not have time for the students or, I want to say, their antics.

"The blacks follow our lead, man. We're where the action is."

"I shall try to visit as soon as I can," I say and know that neither of us believes it.

My liaison with Valeria continues. She usually meets me somewhere on Broadway as I walk to the hotel in the evening. (How ironic, I think, that "broad" is also a colloquial expression for a woman of loose morals.) I suspect she spends most of her days in or near the Factory. How else could she unerringly know exactly when I leave the building?

A disturbing event. One night I go with Andrei, Veeva, and some other Factory colleagues to a night-club called Kansas City. The owner is one Max. Gerald is noticeably absent, and I think that perhaps he left the Factory as he said he might. We sit at a long table in the back. Andrei, as always, is quiet, while the others engage in comradely banter. Veeva, I notice, is unusually possessive of Andrei, applying all her feminine charms to him. Does she not know that Andrei is immune to such blandishments? As the evening progresses, suddenly my Lithuanian mouse appears, wearing baggy trousers and a cap, and shifting nervously from foot to foot as she makes her way among the tables. She is selling some pamphlet, but no one appears interested in buying.

I decide to take pity on her and cry, "Valeria, I will buy one!"

She turns in my direction and shouts, "What the fuck are you doing with that scumbag?"

At that point, Veeva, visibly enraged, rises from the table with a glass in her hand and shouts back, "Hey bitch, come here!"

My Lithuanian mouse, now thoroughly confused by the turn of events, stumbles toward Veeva, who throws the drink in her face.

"You fuck!" cries Valeria.

"Dyke!" Veeva shouts. "You're disgusting!"

I rise, but Valeria pushes past me and runs out. The whole table breaks out in laughter, but I barely hear it. I only wonder whether I should have gone after Valeria and consoled her.

Several days later, while smoking a cigarette in my hotel room, Valeria abruptly turns to me and says, "I mean it. I hate men."

"Then you hate me."

"Not as much as I hate Andy."

"Valeria, do not let bourgeois emotions enslave you. If you looked at Andrei from a proletarian vantage point, you could not hate him."

"He's a fucking man."

"Valeria," I say with great patience, "your obsession with sexual characteristics is indicative of bourgeois thinking. No Soviet woman would speak as you do."

"Fuck Soviet women and fuck you!"

"Valeria, you are smart, you are talented, you are beautiful—"

"So why does Andy treat me like shit?"

"Perhaps you confuse his indifference with disregard?"

"Why won't he do my film?"

"I do not know, Valeria. Have you asked him?"

"Have you seen the chicks in his films? They're his whores."

"Of one thing I am completely certain, Valeria, and that is that they are not his prostitutes."

"I won't let that piece of shit fag ruin my life."

"Then why do you care about his films?"

"Because he's reproducing male chauvinist pig hegemony in them."

"Andrei?" I almost laugh. "How?"

"The women are all sex objects waiting to be fucked."

"But that is Andrei's way of exposing the class and cultural contradictions of capitalist society. And besides, I doubt what you say is true. I saw a film with a woman called Hanoi Hannah. She seemed exceedingly dominant to me."

"Woronow's a fucking bitch."[33]

---

[33]   Mary Woronow, a Warhol superstar who played the role of Hanoi Hannah.

"That I do not know, Valeria. But I do know she seemed supremely sovereign, not at all a sex object waiting to be made love to."

"I said *fucked*, waiting to get *fucked*. You're such a fucking prude, Sasha. Are you in love with Andy?"

"Valeria! That is absurd."

"I bet you two get off each other's cocks, don't you? Or do you like assholes better?"

"Valeria, what has gotten into you?" I try to seize her by her shoulders.

"Fuck off," she shouts, and jabs my chest with the burning end of her cigarette. I withdraw in pain, while she rises from the bed and quickly dons her clothes and runs from the room.

"Asshole!" she shouts as she slams the door.

I am mystified by her behavior, but slightly glad that our liaison has come to an end—even if so unpleasantly. I will be going home one of these days, and it would have been inconvenient for a lovesick woman to have pleaded with me to stay or insisted on coming with me. This end has come more quickly than I would have desired, but it has come, and that is good. Still, her viciousness disturbs me. As I think about this unexpected about-face, it strikes me in the eyes that she has been using me—exploiting me for the information I might give her about Andrei, of course. Andrei is her obsession, and I am merely a means to satisfying that end. How foolish of me to think she might love me. Valeria has her own plans and fixations, and I am only an incidental acquaintance. Good riddance, I think. Still, the jab with the cigarette reveals a capacity for malevolence that I had not suspected. I had always interpreted Valeria's statements about men as attempts at self-affirmation, nothing else. But now I see that she was being straightforward. She hates men, but above all she hates Andrei Warhol who, ironically, is hardly a man.

The imperialist machine is striking back at the European revolutionaries. Rudi Dutschke, a courageous anti-fascist, has been shot by a warmonger in fascist Berlin. It is no accident that this act of violence occurs only days after the workers and peasants of the German Democratic Republic approve overwhelmingly their new constitution. Over ninety percent vote in favor! *That* is democracy. How happy Dean Reed must be. Small wonder that the imperialists are terrified that the peoples of the world will break their chains and follow the socialist example.

Across the avenue from the Kansas City club is a Soviet office, one that I first glimpsed several days ago. The name is a curious amalgam of Russian and English— "Podarogifts".[34] I visit it one day. Soviet souvenirs—electric samovars, gaudily painted spoons and cups and plates, hand-carved wooden toys, and ceramics—lie gathering dust in the window display. There are several desks in the front. One is occupied by a stooped man with a bow tie and mustache, another by a round-faced, gray-haired woman, and a third by a bleach blonde in a black leather miniskirt and tight pink sweater. The man is assiduously punching a calculator: He is obviously the accountant. The little woman is typing with four fingers: She must be the secretary. The blonde is applying bright red polish to her nails. I wager that she is the boss's mistress.

---

34   *Podarok*: Russian for gift.

"*Zdravstvuyte!*"[35] I say.

"Hello," replies the man in Russian, his eyes peering up above his owl-like glasses.

It occurs to me that Pani Julia and Andrei might like these souvenirs.

"I would like to buy some toys."

"Not for sale," the man says. "No retail, only wholesale."

"But surely," I say, "you can sell me one."

"Impossible," he replies and returns to his calculations.

The blonde rises from her desk and, while fanning her nails, approaches me in short brisk steps.

"Leave," she barks, "or I call police!"

"Dina," the man says, "stop."

"Quiet!" she says to him. "And you, dear sir"—she turns to me—"leave. We are not a store for buying."

"Excuse me, comrade," I smile in response, "it was my mistake."

As I open the door, I begin laughing. Outside, I lose all self-control. I have, I realize, just discovered a Soviet island in this sea of capitalism! There is hope, after all.

A day of unpleasant incidents. It begins with a telegram from *Pravda*: it is terse, and I know that this is the editor's way of expressing his displeasure. My article on "Andrei Warhol, An American Socialist Realist" has been rejected. I knew that I would be challenging the received wisdom on America and American art, but I sincerely believed that my reasoning would be persuasive and would merit publication. Is the editor's rejection related to the events in Czechoslovakia? Probably. *That* is a genuine challenge to proletarian internationalism and the leadership of the

---

35   Russian: hello.

Communist Party of the Soviet Union. It is only natural
that the comrades should close ranks and be suspicious
of out-of-the-ordinary analyses. I shall submit the piece
elsewhere—perhaps *Soviet Art*. Or *Soviet Philosophy*?

Bad news from Prague. Comrade Morris is there again.
His talents will be sorely tested. The Czechoslovak Party
is losing control. Deviationist students and brainwashed
intellectuals are growing in strength. The viper Pavel must
be gloating.

Bad news from home. A letter from Katyusha. It is
exceptionally distant and cold in tone. Her style is almost
perfunctory. Work is fine, Leningrad is fine, her parents
are fine. Everything is fine. Within this emotional desert
I sense only one genuinely expressed sentiment—her
enthusiasm for a series of articles by Kelebek about
Czechoslovakia in *Pravda*. Katyusha never reads *Pravda*.
Is this her roundabout way of letting me know that she is
having a liaison with my good friend?

Bad news at Party headquarters. Comrade Gus
informs me that some comrades on the fringes of the Negro
movement have taken offense at my article about Jim as
an agent of the American security services. They insist
that he was an honest revolutionary who could never have
been a turncoat. My article must be a provocation, they say.
Soviet "reactionaries" opposed to Negro civil rights and the
Prague events are, they say, attempting to blacken both
by casting aspersions on Jim. Gus says that he will handle
the controversy, but insists that I be careful about where I
walk. "Avoid dark and empty streets," he says. My distaste
at writing lies about Jim has proven to be fully justified.
Now it is I who am being called a counterrevolutionary—

by none other than the Negro activists I have come to respect!

The only good news is that demonstrations against the imperialist war in Vietnam are intensifying. Various groups—from radicals to moderates—are taking part. Will a popular front emerge? Is this the final assault on the capitalist system?

My troubles deepen. Comrade X telephones me at the hotel. He has never done this before, and the disruption of standard procedures can be explained only by the telegram from *Pravda*. If so, my article must have caused a far greater ideological storm than I imagined. We agree to meet within an hour. He suggests the entrance to the main library at Columbia University. It is a good cover, and I agree.

Longhaired students are distributing leaflets at the University gate, and I sense an excitement in the air that I had not felt before. Groups of students are standing about, arguing, debating, and discussing. Others are running. Some are chanting, "Hell no, we won't go" and "Hey, hey, LBJ, how many children did you kill today?" In the crowd, I think I see the Italian philosopher Dante carrying a sign.

Comrade X is sitting on the stone bench next to the library entrance.

"We appear to be interrupting a demonstration."

"Students," he says dismissively. "Come with me. Inside."

We take the marble stairs to the second floor and turn right. We enter an enormous room containing card catalogues with records of every book. The musty smell reminds me momentarily of Leningrad and my old, now so distant, life. Comrade X leads the way to the letters

U, V, and W, and pauses before the trays marked W. I understand immediately that my forebodings are justified. He runs his fingers along the tops of the cards and stops at Warhol, Andy.

"That article was a mistake, Comrade Ivanov," he says. "There are voices in the Party that insist you should be censured. Some have even talked of expulsion."

I know that I am to say nothing.

"It was not easy to calm the hotheads, Comrade Ivanov. But that has been done. You should be grateful. But the Party insists on a show of remorse."

"An article?"

"Of course."

"Denouncing Warhol?"

"Come," Comrade X says, "let's go outside. I'm glad we understand each other."

As we exit the library, we see a mass of students rushing toward our right. Comrade X unhesitatingly leads the way and, once again, I follow. We are swept up by the crowd, which is chanting, singing, and shouting. The atmosphere is both angry and festive, as the longhaired boys and girls march arm in arm or alone, some drinking—I notice Coca-Cola, beer cans, and wine bottles—some smoking, both cigarettes and what I suspect is marihuana. I share their enthusiasm—how can I not?—but their lack of class discipline disturbs me, reminding me of my last meeting with Seymour and the drunken students in the West End restaurant.

We march through the gate and cross an avenue and keep walking toward the edge of a cliff. And it is there, in the park sprawled out below, that I see that this is no mere student demonstration. Masses of Negroes are assembled with signs and banners and posters. Students are joining them. Everyone is shouting. A lanky student is standing amid the crowd with a megaphone. I can make out only bits and pieces of what he says, something about the University and capitalism and a gymnasium and racism. At some point, Comrade X, who has been carefully surveying the crowd, pokes me in the side and whispers, "Come, let's go, the police are coming." And indeed, as I look toward the campus, and north and south of the crowd, I can see armed police, mostly on foot, some on horseback, approaching.

We dash down the hill and through the park. I have been here before, I realize, but last time I went up the hill. The park is filthy, strewn with bottles, glass, cans, and needles. At the bottom of the hill, I glance upward. The buildings of the University resemble a fortress.

"Quickly," says Comrade X, "we must hurry."

We turn right and walk south along the park. The crowd above roars like the ocean. The streets are empty, except for a few drug addicts and drunks sitting on the benches. But then, at One Hundred Eleventh Street, three large Negro men, all dressed in coats and ties and hats, block our path. We withdraw into the park.

One of them points at me and says, "It's payback time for Jim, you white scumbag."

They surround us and then remove blackjacks and brass knuckles from their pockets. These are, I realize, professionals who will not shirk from leaving us physically maimed. They circle us carefully, occasionally lunging at us, laughing, calling us "motherfuckers." I look to Comrade

X for guidance. He is observing them with a steely calm, his right hand lodged in the pocket of his coat. And then he acts. He removes a gun from his pocket and fires off three bullets in rapid succession. His gun has a silencer and, as the three men hit the ground and lie there motionlessly, it is almost as if they fainted. I am shocked and incapable of movement, but Comrade X takes me by the arm and pulls me toward the exit.

"Fucking niggers," he mutters. "Go!" he whispers in my ear. "Do not run. I have diplomatic immunity. *You* do not. And you have work to do."

I walk away, surprised to see that no one appears to have paid any attention to us. At One Hundred Tenth Street, I turn to look at Comrade X and see that he has moved the bodies behind some bushes.

I manage to arrive at the hotel on my own strength. I rush upstairs and bolt my room shut. I make short shrift of the nearly full vodka bottle and immediately fall asleep.

I have a dream, but not the one about the dead man near the lift. This one is quite new, and I remember all the details.

Kolibri is at the wheel. I am afraid, because he likes to drive fast, especially on winding country roads that can barely accommodate one car. I am sitting next to him. At every turn, my right foot presses an imaginary brake.

We have been traveling, virtually without pause, for ten hours. When Kolibri drives, he does so obsessively. His concentration affects us, and we have spent all that time in almost complete silence. The usual banter and joke-telling ceases and each of us seems lost in his thoughts. I watch the road approach, curl up, and then extend itself—over and over again. I try to stop the trees by following them rush by with my eyes. They slow down, but never for more than a second. And the rush backward resumes. The radio is turned off. We hear only the sounds of traffic, the occasional screeching of tires or the blowing of a horn, a cough or sniff or clearing of a throat.

We are traveling east, not west. The signs are in German, and the roads are potted. The countryside looks odd to me. Where are we? The fields seem sparser, larger. The villages look more secluded, the houses more run-down.

As if reading my thoughts, Kolibri breaks the silence. "We are in the East," he says.

"Look." Kelebek points at some man. "Look, there goes a Communist."

"Or a fascist," says Kolibri.

"No, he's definitely a Communist."

"How can you tell?"

"He's slouched. See? And he's wearing old clothes."

"Is he up to no good?" asks Kolibri.

"He might be plotting something," I say. "Perhaps an act of sabotage?"

"Or maybe he's going to a meeting of his cell?"

"Look at his face," says Kelebek. "There's no expression on his face. It's blank."

"He is hiding something," says Kolibri. "His plans, he is hiding his plans."

The man crosses the road and disappears in the mist on our left. Kolibri presses the accelerator and suddenly turns left.

"Let's follow him," he says. We say nothing.

The man is walking on the right side of the road and we are following him, discreetly, some twenty meters behind. He turns to look at us, but does not appear to have become suspicious. We are in a village and all the vehicles are driving slowly.

"What's he holding in his hand?" asks Kolibri. "See? He's holding something in his left hand. It looks like a wrench."

"It's a hammer," says Kelebek. "I think it's a hammer."

"Why would he be walking with a hammer?" I ask. "Did you notice that no one greeted him? They all walk by. They don't know him."

"He's not from around here," says Kolibri.

"But he looks like he knows where he's going," I say.

"Of course," says Kolibri. "He's a Communist. He has plans. He knows the layout of the village."

"And he's up to no good," I add.

The man stops, removes a packet of cigarettes from his right pocket, places the hammer beneath his knees, and lights the cigarette.

"He's not using a lighter," says Kolibri. "Did you see that? He used matches."

We all see him strike his right hand against a matchbox several times.

"He's a Communist," says Kolibri. "He's definitely a Communist."

"Slow down," says Kelebek. "Or he'll see that we're following him."

"No, don't slow down," I say. "If we do, he'll know that we're following him."

Kolibri stops the car. We wait for the man to finish

lighting his cigarette. He takes a deep drag and exhales. He resumes walking, the hammer in his right hand. We resume following him. This time he turns around and stares at us for several seconds.

"Our cover is blown!" cries Kelebek. "I told you not to slow down. Now he knows we're following him."

The man continues to stand, looking at us. As we approach, he raises his right hand and hurls the hammer at us. Kolibri sees it and swerves to the right, but it strikes the side of the car. The man runs.

"Follow him," shouts Kelebek, "follow him!" But Kolibri needs no encouragement. He slams on the accelerator, our tires screech, and we lurch forward.

But the man is gone.

"Stop the car," says Kelebek. "Let's follow him on foot."

"No," I say, "he's gone. We'll never find him."

"We have to be more vigilant next time," says Kolibri.

"Next time we have to be prepared," says Kelebek.

"Yes," I say, "next time we *will* be prepared."

After I awake, it strikes me in the eyes, with exceptional force, that Comrade X has killed three Negroes in cold blood. They may have been out to kill us, but he fired before they did anything. His efficiency impresses me: three bullets, all presumably through the heart. And a rapid escape, with no trace of the police on our tails. Still, he has committed murder. To save me, a Soviet journalist. I would like to believe that he acted so ruthlessly in order to advance the cause of the revolution. In reality, his final comment, about my having work to do, says it all. He saved me because I must denounce Andrei.

I turn on the television for some distraction from these thoughts. A somber-faced news announcer is speaking of mass riots and seizures of buildings at Columbia University. Apparently, a demonstration against the University's plans to build a fitness center—so that was what the chanters meant by a gymnasium!—turned into a spontaneous effort to seize the campus on behalf of the people. I am reminded of Seymour's words and of the discussion in the bar. The television shows students waving banners from the windows of the University's main administrative building. The doors are shut, and jostling about below are hundreds of supporters and police. How this will end, and to what end it was initiated, is unclear to me. Although I still expect the worst, I am impressed by the students' drive and determination. If nothing else, their efforts will contribute to a weakening of the capitalist structure. I also feel chastened. I have misunderstood the student radicals no less than I misunderstood the Negro leader King. Is there anything about this country that I understand? I turn off the television.

But these are all minor questions. I must figure out what to do about the killings. Who pulled the trigger? Comrade X, not me. I committed no crime. Comrade X did. I must also remember that the three men Comrade X shot could have killed me. In a manner of speaking, Comrade X was acting in self-defense. True, he need not have killed them— shots in their legs would have sufficed to protect me—but Comrade X's crime, his real crime, is to have overreacted, not to have reacted. Had he not reacted, I might have been lying in a pool of blood—as dead as the bald man in my dreams. So, two conclusions leap up at me. First, I am guilty of nothing. Second, Comrade X is guilty at most of having gone too far. That he shot three Negroes is objectively a tragedy, especially as they appear to have been allied with the comrades who support Jim. On the other hand, they could hardly have been normal comrades. They may have been hooligans, or they may have been members of some internal security service. Either way, they were ready for violence.

There is also the question of just how to respond to these killings, *if* I felt that some response were mandatory. Were this a Communist society, I would go to the militia and expect class justice. The process would be fair, and the outcome would not be preordained. But here, in New York, I can only go to the police—that is, to the repressive arm of the bourgeoisie. They engage in daily repression of the Negroes and other workers, and they would decide whether a crime had been committed. The absurdity of such a move is obvious.

Even more absurd is the question of whether I would receive justice. Bourgeois justice, yes. Proletarian justice, no. Indeed, if the repressive apparatus were to lay its hands on two representatives of the Soviet working class, it would use us to promote class oppression, racial hatred, and the repression of the Communist movement. Objectively, I would be abetting the bourgeoisie in the international class struggle. I would be joining the side of inveterate anti-Sovietism and anti-Communism. I would be betraying the cause of the world proletariat and international Communism. So what should I do about the killings? The answer is obvious: nothing, exactly as Comrade X recommended.

There is a related problem. What if the American police pursue an investigation and point the finger of suspicion at Comrade X—or me? How likely is that? Not very. First, the shootings took place in a few seconds. Second, no one saw us, and no one responded to the shots. I remember looking in the direction of the bodies from some fifty meters away and noticing that no crowd had gathered. Third, the killings are likely to be attributed to Negro criminal elements. In this sense, the racism of the police will work to our advantage. Fourth, the police were focused on the demonstration at the top of the park. Last, I pulled no trigger. Comrade X did.

These reasons give me some comfort, but I remain acutely aware of the possibility that a police investigation could lead to us. What to do? I shall have to speak to Comrade X as soon as possible. Has he reported the killings to the consul, or to the station chief? I doubt it. After all, the killings were unnecessary and professionals like Comrade X are not supposed to engage in unnecessary actions. And they could embarrass the Soviet Union, and that too is an undesirable outcome. Comrade X will stay quiet, using his many contacts in the American underground to shift suspicion onto someone else. Comrade X moved the bodies for some reason. If I know his methods, he probably planted drugs on the dead men's bodies or left other telltale clues. And I am certain that he wiped the gun clean and dumped it somewhere in Harlem. I should be safe—at least for the time being. In any case, I shall have to take the risk. I cannot leave just as revolution is breaking out in America. I must be as brave as John Reed and Dean Reed.

But the question of Andrei Warhol remains. I know that

I have no choice but to write that article. It is as simple as that. After all, that is the essence of Communist morality— always and everywhere placing the cause of the revolution above all personal concerns. Were I not a Communist, I could waver. But I am, and I dare not. So it is settled. I shall denounce Andrei.

I turn on the television. After a few minutes of advertisements—these pathetic Americans must buy commodities even as their streets are burning—a newsman reads a report of a "gangland-style" killing of three Negro "drug dealers" in Harlem. Comrade X has done his job well. The report shifts to the student uprising at Columbia University. The siege continues. A reporter interviews a young man, Shapiro, evidently of Jewish nationality, sitting with a cigar in his mouth and his legs stretched out on the desk of the president of the University. The student's cockiness is admirable, and I wish only that it were directed into more organized channels of revolutionary activity. As I watch the footage of the student radicals, I become more and more persuaded that they will fail—if only because their occupation cannot last forever. At some point, probably in a few days, they will have to surrender, and the forces of reaction will claim triumph. Another reporter is attending a meeting of the Students for a Democratic Society. The hall is packed, and the excitement is palpable even on the television screen. But so too is the chaos. Some students shout slogans, others whistle; still others clap their hands and sing songs. The camera shifts to the stage and there I see, of all people, Seymour. He is an effective public speaker, pacing up and down, gesticulating, pausing, hastening his delivery, asking rhetorical questions. The audience responds, though chaos predominates. My last encounter with Seymour in the West End comes to mind.

Shall I denounce Andrei? What if I delay writing the article? Moscow will be angry. What if I produce an extensive series on the coming American Revolution—in order to win time? Who knows what the mood will be like in a few weeks, or in a few months? After all, what purpose would a denunciation serve? I know that Andrei is not a counterrevolutionary. I know that he is a revolutionary. So denouncing him would, objectively, be a counterrevolutionary act. But the Party wills that I denounce him, and how can I act against the Party's wishes? But the Party *really* wills that I demonstrate my loyalty. The article is just a vehicle prompted by my piece praising him. Is there any way for me to remain loyal to the Party *and* to Andrei? Can I reconcile the dialectic? Come what may, I can refrain from writing the article for a few days. And perhaps then my thinking, or the circumstances, will be clearer.

I reach for the bottle of vodka and empty it in a few minutes. Again I fall asleep. Upon awakening—it is already dark outside—I open a third bottle. Again—sleep.

The lift dream again. This time, I recognize the man who is lying in the pool of blood. But, as before, Kelebek, Kolibri, and I return to our table, where Katyusha is still waiting.

How long have I been drinking and sleeping? Sixteen empty bottles are arranged neatly on my night table. How many days have gone by? I have no idea. I reach for another bottle.

The students of Paris have taken to the streets! Has another French Revolution erupted? There are riots and demonstrations in Germany and Italy as well. All of Europe is in turmoil. Opposition to imperialism is growing. So is opposition to capitalism. Even the working class seems to be forming alliances with the students. Still, despite the good news, I have a foreboding of doom. Is it just my own mood, or is my analysis of student radicals correct? As I feared, the seizure of Columbia University ended after a week. The police entered the buildings through subterranean tunnels, and the students capitulated. And where are they now? Probably drinking beer in the West End café again. Probably dreaming of action and spontaneity and revolt— without the Party and without the working class. I hope that Seymour has learned his lesson. For all his stubbornness, he could become an excellent comrade one day.

I have a conversation with Comrade Morris about his recent trip to the fraternal socialist states. He says that reactionaries are leading Czechoslovakia away from socialism, and that there is growing talk of stopping the counterrevolution with whatever means necessary. I am furious and angry and utterly powerless to change anything, to do anything. Communism—*my* Communism—may be collapsing in a fraternal state, and I have no strength, no energy, no passion. What is happening to me? Where is Andrei? His love of life would revive me. And then the dream. I have never before experienced a recurrent dream. Always the elevator, always the same pool of blood.

A day of terrible things. I decide to visit the New York

Public Library in order to read some books about Negroes in America. I am sitting at a large wooden table in the main reading room, as two men sidle up to me, one on my left, the other on my right. One is tall and husky and has large jowls. The other is of average height and build, and has a determined look on his face. The average one, to my left, says, "Hello there, Mister Ivanov." He pronounces my name AY-va-noff, and from the official way in which he speaks I know that I am dealing with American government agents.

"Hello," I say dully.

"Mister Ivanov," he continues, "there's a little problem we'd like to talk to you about."

"Yes?" I say.

"Not here. Outside."

"But I have to return these books first."

"No you don't, Mister Ivanov."

We exit the library, with each American at my side. I may not be under arrest, but I see that I have been apprehended. I have no doubt that Comrade X's killing of the three Negro men is the reason these agents are here. We descend the stairs in front of the library and turn right. At the street, we turn right again and after we reach the back of the library, we enter a dirty little park. I have not been here before, but I am struck by its resemblance to the park on the slope between Columbia University and Harlem. Drug dealers and drug addicts appear to be the only occupants. From my captors' point of view, the park is ideal for a clandestine conversation.

"Mister Ivanov," the stocky agent says, "my friend Carter here thinks you have a problem, but I don't think you do."

"Excuse me," I say, "what problem?"

"My friend Carter thinks you're in deep shit"—the man called Carter laughs at the obscenity—"but I think you're just fine."

"I am afraid I do not understand."

"Of course you do, Mister Ivanov."

"But how can I if you do not tell me what this problem is?"

"Three dead niggers ain't no problem?" Carter asks.

"Now you see, Mister Ivanov, I don't agree that three dead niggers are a problem. I think of them as an op-por-tu-ni-ty." Carter's friend pronounces the last word very carefully.

"What three dead Negroes?" I ask.

"Don't fuck with us, Ivanov," Carter says. "We know your pal shot them and we know you were there. An accessory to a crime is what we call that."

"You see, Mister Ivanov, my friend Carter thinks that's a problem. Do you?"

"I, I do not know." I am stuttering, I know it, and my heart is pounding.

"You see, Mister Ivanov, those three dead niggers are just three dead niggers. Or"—he grabs me by my elbow—"they're your ticket out of jail."

"Killing niggers is a crime in this country," Carter smiles. "Didn't you know that?"

"But we could overlook it," says his friend, "if—"

"If what?" I ask.

"If you did us a favor."

I say nothing. What am I to say, as I wait for the other shoe to drop?

"Now let's just say," he continues, "you did something for us. We might just be inclined to forget those niggers."

"Hey, Ivanov," says Carter, "even I might forget them!"

"What would I have to do?" I ask.

"That's the spirit, Mister Ivanov! What would you have to do? Carter, tell Mister Ivanov what he would have to do."

"Piece of cake, Ivanov. You know that creep, Warhol. We don't like him, but we could get to liking you if you—"

"—reported on him?" It is all too easy to finish the sentence.

"Now that's really quick thinking, Mister Ivanov, ain't it, Carter? What do you think, Carter, do you think we could use Mister Ivanov's kind offer to keep us up to date on Mister Warhol?"

"Sure could, boss."

"See, Mister Ivanov? Carter thinks we sure could. I'm inclined to agree."

"What do you want?" I know that I am caught, and I know exactly what they want.

"*You're* asking *us*, Mister Ivanov? Just pretend you're in Russia."

"Yeah," says Carter, "we trust you, don't we, boss?"

"Written or verbal?" I ask.

"Verbal, of course."

"Where? And when?"

"Every Friday at three in the afternoon. We can meet—"

"Hey," Carter interrupts, "I know where. The Nathan's on Forty-Third and Broadway. You ever had some real American food, Ivanov?"

And so it has come to this. I am now in the impossible position of being both Andrei's friend *and* enemy, of working against him for two ideological enemies—the Soviet Union and the United States. The contradiction strikes me in the eyes and I cannot rid myself of the sensation that I have, like little Alicia, fallen into some extraordinary wonderland. Is this a metonym for the absurdity of capitalist existence? Is my fate reflective of the alienation and loss of identity that inevitably befall all laborers under conditions of capitalist exploitation? (I am reminded of how Andrei's masterful *Below Job* affected me.) Or have I just been careless, stupid even, and blindly walked into a series of traps? I humor myself by wanting to believe that both capitalism and I are equally at fault.

But the contradictions are no less anguishing in light of this rationalization. Because, whatever the reasons for my predicament, the fact is that I must now betray Andrei. And yet I love him, not in the way he loves, or thinks he loves, other men, but as my brother and countryman, as my comrade-in-arms and co-revolutionary. I love him like I love all good Communists and like I love all good Ukrainians. And now I must spy on him, inform on him, and betray him. I must denounce him in the Soviet press while delivering information to the American imperialists. Do two evils cancel each other? Andrei will know nothing of my meetings with the Americans. And I know that I can persuade him not to take my article in the Soviet press seriously. He may not care. He may even find it amusing. Still, I will be doing the devil's work. I will be Judas. That Andrei will not be crucified is my only solace.

Is there any way out for me? The Party demands my

loyalty, so I must write that article. And the Americans can associate me with Comrade X's killings of the three Negroes. So I must cooperate. I have no choice. Or do I? What if I were to declare to both sides that I refuse, absolutely refuse, to betray Andrei? The Americans would arrest me and my comrades would denounce me. An unsavory prospect for me, but an equally unsavory prospect for the cause of Communism. The revolution would lose one of its most ardent defenders; the workers of the world would lose a propagandist. The imperialists would win a major propaganda triumph. I can see the headlines in the American press, exposing the evil deeds of the "Commies" against the oppressed American Negroes. And Andrei? The Americans would still be on his trail. After all, he embodies proletarian freedom and creativity, and they hate freedom and creativity. My comrades would find someone else, in all likelihood a hack, to denounce him. Everyone would be worse off, and I would never see the light of day again—unless, of course, my comrades would exchange me for some American spies. A humiliating prospect. I have no choice. I must give Andrei the kiss—no, two kisses—of Judas.

A ray of light in this gloom. Is capitalist France about to topple? Students have liberated the Left Bank of Paris, and millions of workers are supporting them. This is the way revolutions are made! Workers and students, manual laborers and intellectual laborers, united, with a steely resolve, committed to overthrowing capitalism and ushering in a new life—and under the dedicated leadership of the Communist Party of France. The fascist De Gaulle must be trembling. There are pitched battles between the revolutionaries and the forces of repression. France is reclaiming its revolutionary legacy. But a timid voice within me asks: Is this 1917 or 1848?[36]

Nine million workers are on strike in France! My mind boggles at the number. De Gaulle has called for a referendum. The Bourse has gone up in flames. This is 1917, I am certain. Once France joins the socialist camp, the capitalist regimes of Germany and Italy will topple with ease. Even if America does not follow suit, Europe will be socialist from the Atlantic to Vladivostok! Good-bye, NATO militarism! Good-bye, American imperialism! My head spins at the prospect.

In a remarkable breach of security, Comrade X calls me at Party headquarters. He knows the telephones are bugged. He wants to know how my article about Andrei is proceeding. I tell him that I am making excellent progress, but that I still need to collect more information. Comrade X seems blissfully unaware of the fact that the Americans know he shot three Negroes. When I ask, indirectly, about the consequences of the shooting, he simply says that I should not worry. But how can I not worry? The Americans are already using me, and I have no doubt that they will also try to use him. Were our roles reversed, our secret services would pressure him into cooperating and perhaps even working as a double agent. Should I tell Comrade X of the danger he is in, or should I try, first and foremost, to save myself?

---

36   1917: the glorious year of Russia's successful Bolshevik revolution;
        1848: a tragic year of unsuccessful revolutions in Europe.

We meet later in the day on the seventh floor of a large department store called Macy's. Comrade X said to go to the area where sofas are on display. And indeed, I find him sitting on a large, black-leather couch. We exchange a few formalities—"Waiting for your wife?" I say, "Yes, I hate shopping for furniture," he replies—and I sit down next to him.

"Should you be approached by the Americans," he intones, "say nothing, admit nothing."

"About the events?"

"Say absolutely nothing." He strokes his chin. "At first."

"At first? I am not sure I understand, comrade."

"As far as you know, nothing happened, absolutely nothing." Comrade X makes as if he is looking impatiently at his watch. "Let them court you. Let them come to you."

"To what end?"

He says nothing.

"Ah," I say, "I see."

"Don't worry," he says, "everything is under control. But be on guard. This is imperialist America, after all."

"And where will this courtship end?"

"Moscow hasn't told me," he replies, "but one can guess. Where all courtships end, I suppose." He looks at his watch again. "I trust life in America appeals to you."

"It is not home."

"Nothing is, Comrade Ivanov, but we do what we have to do."

"Yes," I say, "we are Communists." This time I look at my watch and feign a look of annoyance. "They may have been following me that day."

"Possibly. But remember, you saw nothing."

"Are *you* not worried, comrade?"

"Why should I be?"

"I was there," I say. "I saw what happened."

"Muggers, drug addicts," he says dismissively. "A clear case of self-defense."

"But will the imperialists see it that way?"

"Do not worry about me, Comrade Ivanov. Whatever happens, you just do what you have to do."

A tired-looking woman carrying shopping bags approaches us and Comrade X rises to kiss her. "Good-bye," he says to me, and they depart arm in arm. I remain sitting for several minutes, dumbstruck by the nauseating prospect of becoming a defector to, of all places, the United States of America.

At night, thoughts of endings, thoughts of betrayals, thoughts of despair. I am in an impossible situation—in a Zugzwang unlike any I have encountered playing chess. I have no move. How can I betray Andrei? How can I not betray Andrei? How can I cooperate with the Americans? How can I not cooperate with the Americans? Should I warn Comrade X? Should I not warn Comrade X? Should I accept the American advances? Should I reject the American advances? The world is upside down.

Knocking on my door awakens me. It is gentle at first and then, after a few minutes, it turns insistent. My first thought is of the American security services. If it has come to this, then so be it. I don a fresh shirt, run my fingers through my hair, and notice from the stubble on my face that several days have gone by since my last shave. I place the empty bottles into the carton and kick it under the bed. I also open the window. Then I go to the door and jerk it open. If I create an impression of self-confidence, perhaps the Americans will be taken aback.

Instead of burly government agents, I see Pani Julia and Andrei.

"Andrei!" I cry, with joy and relief in my voice. "Where have you been, my dear, dear friend?"

"Uh, California," he says, a broad smile covering his face. "Mama was, uh, worried."

"Sashenka," she says as she takes my face in her hands, "where have you been all this time? I have been so worried. And a beard?"

"Mama wanted to, uh, invite you for pierogis—"

"—and I called and called your office, but no one knew where you were."

Andrei is smiling his gentle smile.

"So she, uh, figured—"

"—that we'd come here!"

As she says this, she bolts inside, my hand in hers, and Andrei follows, carrying two shopping bags.

"This room is a mess," she says, "like Andik's. Sit down, Sashenka, and you too, Andiku. And open the other window. It stinks in here."

As we obey, she sets the two bags on the table and begins removing the contents.

"Borsch," she says as she places two large red jars on the table. "And sour cream. And"—she turns to us and chuckles—"varenyky. I made them of potatoes and cheese, and meat, and Andik's favorite, blueberries. Those were very hard to find," she says as an afterthought, "but I found them. They are still warm." She removes the plastic wrap. "Sit and eat," she commands.

"You know Mama," Andrei says.

She ladles the borsch into soup bowls, dumps a spoonful of sour cream into each, and pushes them in our direction. As Andrei and I attack the borsch, I realize that I am ravenously hungry. She refills our bowls and, her face glowing, removes a small bottle of vodka from her purse.

"You have had too much, Sashenka, but a little nip won't hurt."

She places the varenyky into our soup bowls. "No need to stand on ceremony," she says, "right, Sashenka? We're all *nashi*[37] here." Then she covers them with mounds of sour cream. We start with the potato and cheese varenyky, work our way through those filled with meat—she sprinkles them with generous amounts of black pepper, which she keeps in a small plastic bag—and then are treated to a few blueberry ones. "Dessert," she smiles as she dusts them with a powdery sugar.

By the end of the meal, I am in excellent spirits.

"You go sit on the bed, boys," she says. "I want to sing some songs. Will your neighbors mind, Sashenka?"

Her voice is frail and high-pitched, but she sings Ukrainian folk songs—mostly of disappointed love and none of which I have ever heard before—with a tenderness and depth of feeling that wrench my heart. Eventually, she moves on to well-known songs, and I join in. I have not sung them since I was a boy in Kyiv, but I find that I have not forgotten the words. Even Andrei sings along, usually only a few mumbled words at a time, but I can see

---

37   Ukrainian: our own kind.

that he is enjoying himself. His singing is off-key, but that does not matter. Finally, at least one hour after we began, Pani Julia says, "That was my entire repertoire," and we all break out laughing.

"Oh, my boys," she says and takes us in her arms. "I feel home."

"She means the, uh, old country," Andrei says.

"Yes," I nod, "I know."

"I feel young again," she says. "My God, what I wouldn't give to be back home!"

Andrei rolls his eyes, but I know exactly what she means.

"We had nothing, Sashenka, we were poor. But we were so much happier."

"You were young, Mama."

"Yes," she says wistfully, "I was young then. But that's not all. You understand me, Sashenka, don't you?"

I nod.

"I knew everyone in our village, Sashenka. You couldn't walk down the street without being greeted by everyone. And we sang all the time. You know what I mean, Sashenka. Here, the young people"—and she gestures with her eyebrows at Andrei—"only listen to loud music. But we sang, we always sang. Did you know, Sashenka, that I had a beautiful voice? I sang in the choir, and everyone said I had the best voice. And we used to dance, Sashenka, all the time. A little village in the Carpathians, but we used to dance the waltz and the fox trot and the tango. Can you imagine that, Sashenka? Poor peasant boys and girls dancing the waltz barefoot on rough wooden floors! And the accordionist and the fiddler provided the only music!"

"They still do," I say, "in that part of Ukraine."

"Ah, what I wouldn't give to be there again."

"You'd be on the, uh, first bus out," Andrei giggles. "If they, uh, have buses."

"I still have family there," she says. "They write, I write. But this one"—she looks sternly at Andrei—"this one hasn't written a postcard, even a postcard, in ages. You know, Sashenka, we used to send them the shoes Andik designed."

"Back in the, uh, fifties," Andrei says.

"Very fancy shoes," she continues, "the kind fancy women wear on Fifth Avenue."

"Or, uh, on muddy streets."

"And we used to send them Andik's drawings and watercolors. They must have enough for a museum."

"Have you been there?" I ask Andrei.

He shakes his head.

"You should visit," I say. "It is breathtakingly beautiful country. Mountains, streams, and the air is the best in the world."

"Uh, better than Pittsburgh's?"

I laugh. "And," I continue, "your Mama is right. The people are friendly. If does not matter that you are a stranger. They invite you into their homes, the tables are immediately covered with food, and by the time you leave, you are all the greatest of friends, laughing, singing."

"Andik traveled around the world," Pani Julia says proudly. "But"—she casts a scolding glance at him—"he didn't have time to make a stop at home."

"Mama," Andrei says, "*this* is home."

After Pani Julia returns from the bathroom, she joins us on the bed. Andrei has kicked off his shoes and stretched himself out, his hands beneath his head. Pani Julia places his feet on her lap and rubs his toes.

"You know, Sashenka, my cousin in Czechoslovakia writes that life has gotten better now. That they can breathe freely. Even go to church again."

I tense up. "But a restoration of capitalism will only make everything worse, Pani Julia."

"Capitalism? Oh, Sashenka, my cousin doesn't know what that is. And neither do I. She just wants to be able to pray."

"Why is that so important to you, Pani Julia?" I ask with a slight tone of impatience. "I am an atheist," I say hesitantly, "and I have never been able to understand the appeal of cults."

"I go to Mass." Andrei lifts his head—"Every week"—and drops it back onto the pillow.

"Andik even has an altar in his bedroom. With candles and icons."

My surprise must be painfully evident, because Pani Julia says, "Sashenka, you look as if you've seen the Holy Ghost!" Then she laughs. As does Andrei. After a few seconds, so do I, though nervously.

"Why, Andrei?"

"Uh, I guess I believe. In, uh, God."

"But *why?*" I sense that I sound desperate.

"Uh, I dunno."

"I go to Mass *every* day," Pani Julia says proudly. "On Fifteenth Street and Second Avenue. It's our church. Have you ever been to Mass, Sashenka?"

"No, of course not."

"Then come with me one day."

"I am a Communist, Pani Julia."

"The priest won't eat you," she fires back.

"Maybe I could, uh, film you?" Andrei lifts his head from the pillow.

"A film? Of me in a church? That will never—"

"Sashenka," Pani Julia says, "why are you Communists so afraid of church?"

"Pani Julia, religion is the opiate of the people."

"What is," she says tentatively, "opiate?"

"A drug, Mama."

"A drug?" she asks, her eyes round. "But all we do is pray and sleep through a sermon and gossip with our friends. We don't drink or take narcotics. The alcoholics and addicts—I've never seen them in church," she says triumphantly.

Andrei looks at me. "Mama's, uh, got a point."

"But that's not what Marx—"

"Groucho?" Andrei asks.

"Excuse me?" I say.

"Groucho Marx?"

"I meant *Karl*, Karl Marx."

"Oh," Pani Julia interjects, "that Groucho Marx is so funny. But I don't always understand what he's saying. He talks so fast. Does anyone understand him? Thank God, Sashenka"—and she strokes my face with such maternal gentleness that I almost imagine she is my own mother—"that you speak *po nashemu*. Oh," she says, almost as if she has just remembered something important, "do you know the song, *Ridna maty moya*?"[38]

---

38   Ukrainian: *Oh, My Dear Mother.*

"It is one of my favorites."

And she breaks out into a solo rendition, her emotionally charged, almost cracking thin voice lingering over each word, each syllable. I start crying. I always do when I hear this song of a Ukrainian mother who awaits her son's return. I recall that my mother used to sing it, too, as she soothed me after a nightmare. Katyusha hates the song, calling it sentimental and syrupy. And she is right. But sentimentality and syrup speak to the Ukrainian soul, which she lacks and will never understand.

Andrei, I notice, has stopped smiling. The playful look on his face is gone, and I think I see tears in his eyes.

Pani Julia finishes and heaves a deep sigh.

"*That* is why I want to go home," she says. "Sashenka?"

"Yes, Pani Julia."

"I just had a wonderful idea, and you must say yes."

"Uh-oh," Andrei says. "When Mama has, uh, wonderful ideas...."

"Why don't you come live with us? We have space, several spare rooms. You could even have your own bathroom. And we could sing and talk and laugh whenever we wanted to."

"Well," I begin to say, "I do not know what—"

"We wouldn't disturb you, Sashenka. Andik is always working. He's always away. And I'm just an old woman."

Why not? I think. I am tired of the hotel, I would save money, and no one could object to my infiltrating the bourgeois "enemy." I do enjoy Pani Julia and Andrei. And I would have the opportunity to learn everything about his life, regardless of the purposes to which I would then put my knowledge.

I smile broadly. "How can I say no to you, Pani Julia?" And then I embrace her and Andrei.

As I pack my things, I realize with some sadness that I am leaving the place and the neighborhood that have been home to me since my arrival in New York so long ago. I recall the discomfort and alienation I felt as Comrade Sam drove me to the hotel, my initial impressions of the room, the streets, and the poor people who inhabit them. Somehow, without being aware of any point that marked a shift in my views, I have progressively, unnoticeably, come to feel at home here. Marx was right. Man is the product of material conditions. They form his consciousness of himself and his surroundings, and after a while he comes to accept his surroundings as natural. I feel wistful, almost nostalgic, as I arrange my clothes in the suitcases. It strikes me in the eyes that this is the origin of trade union consciousness. The routines of material existence impress themselves on man, and he comes to see himself and his interests only in their light. Only the Party, armed with an ideology that sees above these mundane circumstances, can infuse the worker with revolutionary consciousness. The great Lenin knew that subjectively. The great Warhol knows that objectively. Will I ever be able to move his consciousness in a subjectively revolutionary direction?

Several postcards from Andrei await me at Party headquarters. What a surprise! The first card depicts a beach in La Jolla, California. (I wonder if Andrei knows that he was in former Russian territory?) The second is of muscular young men, their tanned bodies glistening against the bright blue waves of the Pacific. The third shows some local landmark, a villa inhabited by a Hollywood actress. The fourth contains colorful illustrations of kittens ("Mama's favorites," he writes). And the fifth, really a photograph converted into a postcard, shows a skinny Andrei in a bathing suit, his arms raised in the style of a muscleman. How innocent and idyllic these scenes appear, how peaceful and trouble-free. I am reminded of vacations in the Crimea, the promenade in Yalta, the endless bottles of dry champagne, and the merry-making of three great friends and comrades. Oh, how I miss Kelebek and Kolibri!

I decide not to tell the comrades just yet that I will be living at Andrei's. Since Jim's death, I no longer feel quite at ease at Party headquarters. I miss Jim. I miss his kind Negro smile, his Negro sincerity and warmth, his deep commitment to the Party and to humanity. Working at the Party office meant seeing him on a daily basis. With him gone, I feel as if I have lost a piece of myself. He was, I realize, a true friend. Did I fully appreciate that when he was alive? And to think that I denounced him. I am ashamed. But what choice did I have—objectively? None. If I must choose between the Party and my sentiments, I will always choose the Party. But how tragic that such choices exist and must be made.

My first evening at Andrei's. Pani Julia shows me to my room, which has a private bathroom and is much larger than my accommodations at the hotel. After I unpack, she gently knocks on my door and asks if I would like to join her and Andrei for supper. Of course, I say, and smile at her excessive care not to overstep the bounds of hospitality.

As I sit down, Andrei grins and says, "I have, uh, a surprise," and points at a film projector. "Footage of you. When you were, uh, here."[39]

---

39   This film is not in the Andy Warhol Film Archive and appears

He turns it on, and as we dine on Pani Julia's cabbage rolls, we watch the flickering images on the bed sheet hung above the bookcase. The film is grainy. It is shot from one angle only. Most of us are visible, although the back of Pavel's head is on screen most of the time. I watch Gerald's confessions mesmerized, a piece of cabbage suspended on my fork. There is no plot, and there is no acting, and yet Andrei's film is more riveting than anything I have ever seen. Gerald's striptease before the camera is almost painful to watch. What truth! No less painful are the almost thuggish methods of interrogation that Pavel and I applied to the poor, flustered boy.

"Ah," Pani Julia sighs, as Andrei turns on the light, "the end of love is always so sad." She looks at me with loving eyes. "But at least you and your wife are happy."

"Pani Julia," I say, "I am not quite sure about that. Katyusha's letters have changed. I feel cold after reading them."

"My poor, poor Sashenka," she says. "Is there"—she hesitates—"someone else?"

"I think it is my good friend Kelebek."

"And that doesn't trouble you, Sashenka? Or anger you?"

"No."

"Then you no longer love your Katyusha," Pani Julia says flatly.

"I know. I have not, I think, for some time now. Since last year. Maybe the year before."

"Life goes on, Sashenka."

"Katyusha does not worry me, Pani Julia. Kelebek does."

---

to be lost.

"Of course," she says, "he betrayed you."

"Only outwardly."

"Still, you were close friends."

"But that is just it," I reply. "I feel no anger toward Kelebek. None at all. He remains my close friend and I love him. *That* has not changed."

"So what troubles you, Sashenka?"

"I feel empty inside, Pani Julia. And I have never in my life felt that way."

"Oh, Sashenka, my poor, dear Sashenka."

Suddenly Andrei grins. "Welcome, uh, to my world." Then he laughs. "Veeva, uh, saw you with that Solanas girl."

How grateful I am for this timely diversion from my subjective difficulties!

"A small lapse, Andrei. It is over. She is a very disturbed young woman."

"You mean a whack job."

"Who is Solanas?" Pani Julia asks.

"Uh, a lousy actress."

"But she can be sweet," I say. "There is something oddly vulnerable about her."

"You, uh, *would* say that."

"She hates you, Andrei. Do you know that?"

"Uh-huh."

"I think she could be violent."

"Uh-huh."

"Well, at least you are not letting her worry you."

"Andiku?" Pani Julia says. "Stay away from this Solanas. I don't like her."

Another dream, my second at Andrei's. I am sitting on some beach. Predictably and unsurprisingly, the waves creep up onto the sand. Sandpipers taunt them. The sand bubbles as the water recedes. The other side of the bay, enveloped in a blue mist, is barely visible. There too, I think, are waves. Is there a point, perhaps in the geometric center of the bay, where the water is perfectly still, where the waves are generated or, possibly, where they cancel each other out? I rise to my feet, brush the sand off the bottom of my trousers, and approach the rowboat slouched on the shore. I shove the boat into the water—the waves resist—and step inside. I attach the right oar to the right side and the left oar to the left side—or is it the other way around?—dip the oars into the foam, and pull as hard as I can. The boat seems to stand still, despite my greatest exertions. This is going nowhere, I think. But then, after raising my head, I am surprised to see that the shoreline is already quite distant. But if I am not moving, I wonder, how can I be going forward? I row harder, but, unsurprisingly, seem just as stationary as before. And yet, several minutes later when I look again, I notice that I *have* moved. And then another strange thing happens. The waters grow suddenly still, the bay is as placid as a mountain lake. I am in dead center, I think. If I stop rowing, I would stop moving, and if I stop moving, I would stay here indefinitely. But then another strange thing happens. Before I can say stop or go, the boat moves and the stillness disappears, replaced by predictable and unsurprising waves and wavelets.

I row the boat back to the beach. The bow plows into the wet sand. I carefully place the right oar at the bottom of the right side of the boat and the left oar at the bottom of the left side. For a moment, I consider, mischievously, placing the right oar on the left side and the left oar on the right, but decide against it. As the waves beat against the boat, the oars rattle. I slowly rise to my feet, extend my right leg and drape it over the side of the boat, soon feeling the wet sand against the sole of my foot. Then, one leg inside the boat and one leg outside, I hold the boat with both hands and, my lips puckered and a slight whistle emanating from my mouth, I lift my left leg and, almost as gracefully as a ballerina, turn on my right heel and place both legs onto the sand.

I sleep badly and awake in the morning with a terrible headache. If I were still in the hotel, I could stay in bed all day. Did I make a mistake coming here? Where is my revolutionary fervor?

The meeting in Nathan's, a garish, cavernous, typically American restaurant. Large neon signs, walls painted a mustard yellow, boys and girls in uniforms and white caps serving endless amounts of sausages and other unpalatable foods. I enter this capitalist utopia and glance around me. The large man called Carter is standing at a small counter with plastic pumps that dispense mustard and ketchup.

"Upstairs, Ivanov," he says. He carries two gray paper boxes containing hot dogs and containers of what I assume is soda. His colleague is waiting for us at a corner table.

"Hello, Mister Ivanov," he smiles. "Glad you could make it. What's that you got there, Carter?"

"Bunch of dogs. Two apiece. You like hot dogs, Ivanov?"

"Naturally," I say.

"And that stuff ain't rum, Ivanov. It's Coke. You like Coke, Ivanov?"

"Of course."

"So tell us, Mister Ivanov, what's Warhol up to?"

"What would you like to know?"

"He's a faggot, ain't he?" Carter asks.

"Yes, I believe he is."

"Hey," Carter eyes me suspiciously, "you're not—"

"No, of course not," I say.

"Who does he consort with?"

"Excuse me?"

"Who are his pals?"

"Mostly artists. Like him."

"No Communists?"

"Except for me," I say.

"None at all?"

"As I said, except for me."

"Ever seen this fellow?" The American shows me a grainy black-and-white photograph of Pavel, shot from an angle that betrays a hidden camera.

"He came to dinner once."

"And he ain't a Communist?"

"He is Slovak!" I try to say with disdain. "They have betrayed Communism."

"Have they? And this here fellow, he betrayed Communism?"

"As far as I could tell from our brief conversation. We did not get along."

"Funny," Carter's colleague says. "Funny that you two old comrades didn't get along."

"Why is that funny? There are many genuine Communists I do not get along with."

"Hey, Carter, I think he really doesn't know!"

"Yeah," Carter laughs.

"What?" I ask.

"Your pal is KGB."

Everything is suddenly clear to me. Of course! I have been such a fool.

"I did not know," I say—very, very quietly.

"You know, Mister Ivanov, I believe you didn't. Something must be wrong, right? Your pals wouldn't normally cut you off, would they? You know what, Carter, I believe our friend here is in some serious shit with his employers."

Carter laughs. "Here," he says, "have some ketchup."

The Americans' laughter rings in my ears after they leave. I stay in the Nathan's restaurant and nibble on the sausage. Carter is right. It does taste better with mustard and ketchup.

An American saying comes to mind: I am in a pickle. Indeed, that is exactly where I appear to be—in a pickle. The translation into Ukrainian strikes me as absurd, but no less accurate. My predicament, which seemed bad enough, has gotten appreciably worse. It is possible that they were lying about Pavel, in the expectation that I would be unnerved, as indeed I have been. But I do not think they were lying. I know we have many assets in the fraternal socialist countries, so there is no reason that Pavel could not be a chekist. His presence at the dinner—ostensibly as a family friend of the Warhols—struck me even then as suspicious. Why would Pani Julia's childhood friend need to visit her just as counterrevolution is breaking out in Czechoslovakia? It makes far more sense to think that he was there, first, to spy on Andrei and, second, to spy on me. His confrontational attitude comes to mind. Was he trying to provoke me—to see how I would respond to his defense of counterrevolution? Now the answer seems obvious. I only wonder why I did not see through his game. And his anger at Andrei's filming—that, too, was only a subterfuge, an excuse to feign outrage and leave before we could question him.

In any case, the fact is that he is who he is and that I knew nothing about him. Normally, I would be informed of a meeting, even a chance meeting, with a comrade from the security services. I would be told beforehand, or the comrade would let me know during our encounter. This time, nothing. I was purposefully kept in the dark. Carter's thuggish friend was right. I am not trusted in Moscow.

That means my situation is much worse than I had imagined. The Party no longer just insists that I make amends for my article on Andrei. It is no longer certain that I would make amends *sincerely*. Am I on the verge of expulsion? Is this why Katyusha has cooled toward me?

So my Zugzwang is complete. Is this why Comrade X encouraged me to go along with the Americans? But I *cannot* stay here, and I do not *want* to stay here. *I am a Communist.* Even if some in the Party disagree, I am a Communist and I have only one Motherland.

And then it strikes me in the eyes. This is 1918. The German imperialists and Russian counterrevolutionaries are all around me, and I have declared no peace and no war. I shall have to sign my Brest-Litovsk[40] and beat a strategic retreat. So what shall I do? Nothing. I shall simply do what

---

40   The Treaty of Brest-Litovsk, signed by the farsighted Bolsheviks
      under the leadership of the great Lenin and Germany in March 1918.

everyone expects me to and nothing more. I shall talk to
the odious hot-dog eaters, and I shall talk to Comrade X
and work on some article about Andrei. I shall also write
other articles—and simply go on as if everything were
normal. It is not, I know that. But I am to stay here for six
more months. During this time, much can happen. Leaders
may come and go. Crises may take place. Who knows how
the revolution will unfold in America? Who knows how the
Soviet Union will respond? Who knows how the national-
liberation struggle of the Vietnamese people will proceed?
Who knows what will happen in Europe? Who knows
how the Americans will react? I have time. I can wait. I
can wait for these competing forces to alter political and
social reality. And as that reality changes, I shall remain
vigilant. Opportunities will present themselves. I will be
ready. Things will get better.

"Sasha?"

It is Morris, his head protruding into my office. "May I
have a word?"

He enters and sits down without waiting for my reply.

"Sasha." He looks straight into my eyes. "I know."

"Know what?"

"We have a comrade in the FBI," he says, almost in a
whisper. "I know they're trying to recruit you."

I am embarrassed and can think of nothing to say.

"Let them," he says.

"But—"

"Let them, Sasha. Do that, and the Party will take you
back."

"But I—"

"Just let them, Sasha."

Morris leaves as quickly and as quietly as he came in, and I know that all my hopes of a Brest-Litovsk are an illusion. This is Tannenberg.[41] I am trapped and have no way out. I am lost.

A welcome distraction in the evening. Andrei suggests I go with him to hear a musical ensemble known as the Velvets Under Ground.

"You met, uh, Lou," he says. "Remember? In the hotel."

I gladly agree, just to forget my worries. We leave the house and Andrei hails a taxi. We turn left on Eighty-Sixth Street and then right on Second Avenue. We catch a wave of changing green lights and reach Ninth Street in a few minutes. As we leave the taxi, I notice that we are in the heart of the New York area most favored by the hippies. Here, everyone has long hair. I look around and see that the large squat gray building across the avenue is called the "Ukrainian National Home." How curious, I think, that the nationalists and the hippies should be living side by side.

"Look," I point at the building. "Did you know that, Andrei?"

"Know, uh, what?"

"The Ukrainian National Home."

"Uh-uh."

"It is probably a hotbed of anti-Communism."

"Uh, Sasha—"

"And look, Andrei, there is a bar inside. Do we have time for a hundred grams?"

---

41   Battle with Germany in August 1914, in which Russia suffered
      enormous losses.

"Uh, what?"

"Vodka."

"Uh, sure, I guess."

The inside resembles a typical New York bar in every way except that the patrons speak some combination of English and Ukrainian. They are loud and laugh heartily, and the round faces and mustaches remind me of Soviet faces.

I order a vodka, Andrei a Coca-Cola. A group of young men and women walk in and place themselves at the bar next to us. They order drinks and the oldest of the group, a fat man with a walrus mustache, turns to me and introduces himself in Ukrainian.

"My name is Roman." He resembles a collective farm chairman. I can see that he is no pederast.

"Sasha," I respond.

"Ah," he says, "you're from the Soviet Union."

"Of course. How did you know?"

"No Ukrainian émigré would be named Sasha."

"Well," I say as I lift my drink, "then let us drink to friendship."

The others join us in the toast. Only Andrei stands quietly to my right.

"Are you a tourist?" Roman says.

"A journalist."

"From Kyiv?"

"Leningrad. And you, Mister Roman?"

"Also a journalist."

"For a nationalist newspaper?"

"For a notoriously anti-Communist one," he smiles in assent. "Here's my card."

"West End Avenue?" I ask. "Where is that?"

"Near Columbia. We could have dinner some day. Do you have a card?"

"No, but you can always reach me at the Party office—"

"On Sixty-Seventh Street?"

"No," I say, "not the Mission. I have an office at the American Party headquarters."

"On Union Square."

"Yes," I say with some surprise, "you know."

"Of course, I know."

"Of course?"

"Of course."

"I see," I say.

Our conversation reminds me of a game of chess. I see that Andrei is leaning against the wall and fidgeting with his glass. It is time to go.

"Very well, Mister Roman. I hope we meet again."

Andrei says nothing but I can see from his unusually quick steps that he is in a hurry.

"Are we late?" I ask.

"Uh, no, I don't, uh, think so. It's just that Nico gets, uh, nervous."

I decide not to ask who Nico is. Once we get to where we are supposed to be, I know that I will find out. We cross the avenue and wend our way through throngs of longhaired boys and girls swinging their hips. I am certain I smell marihuana. We walk past discordantly decorated stores and restaurants and then Andrei stops, a puzzled look on his face.

"Uh," he says, "I can't find it."

"What are we looking for?"

"Some place on Second Avenue. Uh, one-forty, I think."

"We are below one hundred, Andrei. Let us go back."

As we walk through the crowds again, this time I stop.

"Andrei, we are such fools. Did you say one hundred and forty?"

"Uh-huh."

"We were just there!" I cry. "There! See? The Ukrainian National Home!"

We climb a carpeted maroon staircase and enter a dark hall packed with gyrating bodies. There is barely enough space for us to make our way to the stairs that lead to a small balcony. Andrei's Factory comrades are sitting and standing, with drinks and cigarettes in their hands. The hot air is almost unbreathable. Andrei seats himself in a corner and motions to me to join him.

"A few more, uh, minutes," he says.

A young woman in a miniskirt and tight sweater kisses Andrei on the cheek.

"Baby Jane!" he cries. "You look fab."

"Who's your gorgeous friend?"

"Sasha Ivanov." I say. "I am very honored to meet you."

"Andy, this guy's too much!" she laughs. "Where'd you find him?"

"Sasha's a blast. He's staying with, uh, me."

"So that's where you've been hiding him." She winks at me.

"I am a house guest, Miss Baby Jane," I say. "Andrei and I are friends."

"Andrei?! Since when are you Andrei, Andy? Man, that is too cool. Andrei," she coos, "may I call you that too, Andrei?"

Andrei smiles. "Look," he points.

The ensemble is assembled on the stage and I recognize the man I met once before in the hotel lobby. (How many encounters have I had in that fateful place?) A tall Nordic blonde—she is evidently the singer—stands among the men, who are tuning their guitars or adjusting the amplifiers. To my surprise, I see Gerald on stage as well, and he is snapping an enormous bullwhip.

"Does Gerald sing, Andrei?"

"Uh, no," he says. "Just watch what—"

At that moment, the hall explodes with sound and I cannot hear a word of what Andrei says. Colored lights flash and illuminate the walls, ceiling, floor, and crowd. Insistent rhythms, wailing, screams, and the barely audible voices of the blonde—who must be this Nico—and Dean Reed's namesake merge into an overpowering blast of noise. And that blast never stops. It is one long explosion. I think that this is what ceaseless bombardment must be like. Nico is almost motionless as she sings, while the other members of the ensemble confine their twitches to the spaces on the stage they occupy. How curiously inert they all look, and what a contrast their inertness forms to the cacophonous attacks and counterattacks around me. And then I notice Gerald, who is dancing madly, almost uncontrollably, and swinging and snapping the whip.

I am terrified. I look at Andrei, but his eyes are closed—he has actually removed his sunglasses—and he has a blissful smile on his face. Baby Jane is swinging her head rapturously from side to side. The others on the terrace are dancing, or moving their bodies rhythmically. But there is no rhythm here! I want to shout. There is no melody! This is just noise!

"Uh, have a drink, Sasha. You're uptight," Andrei says. "Can someone get us a bottle of, uh, vodka?"

A minute later, I am pouring myself two hundred grams. After three glasses, the music no longer terrifies me. Andrei is smiling visibly now. Baby Jane is dancing; her thigh brushes against my shoulder. I drink again.

When it is all over, and the second bottle is empty, Andrei and Baby Jane help me down the stairs. I stumble outside and realize that I can barely hear the cars and people. They take me by my arms and lead me away. In a few minutes, we are sitting in a small restaurant; its walls are lined with signed photographs of smiling people. Gerald and Nico and Dean Reed's namesake have joined us. Except for Andrei, they are all talking and laughing, but I can hardly hear what they are saying. The blonde woman called Nico keeps whispering at me, but I just point to my ears, shake my head, and shrug my shoulders. A waiter brings a large metal plate and, after moving the beer bottles to the side, deposits it onto the table.

"Garbage pizza!" cries Gerald, and I cannot help but think of the mountains of refuse that greeted me on my arrival in this city.

Everyone takes a piece—the singer Nico gives me one— but only Andrei does not. As we eat, I watch him watch us. He still has a dreamy expression on his face, exactly the same as at the musical performance. The pizza lying on the plate before me brings to mind my first days in New York, my bumbling attempts to understand capitalist culture, the isolation and alienation I felt. And now, several months later, how things have changed. I am surrounded by people with whom I feel comfortable (even if they are Andrei's friends, not mine). I am eating this "garbage pizza" (Gerald calls it that because every manner of food, from bacon to mushrooms to olives and much, much more, can be found on its surface). And I finally understand America.

After the meal, we turn quiet. Nico is nodding her head, as if to some internal rhythm; Andrei is smiling. I realize that I can hear again.

"Mister Reed," I say.

"Lou."

"Lou," I continue, "what do you call that music?"

"I don't call it anything, man."

"Then what is it?"

"It's my music, man. That's what it is."

"It is very, uh, interesting."

The table breaks into laughter.

"Very *interesting*? Hey, man, you're supposed to say it's—"

"Amazing!" Nico whispers.

"Plastic!" Gerald cries out.

"Uh," Andrei concludes, "inevitable."

I rise to go to the bathroom, which is somewhere in the corner farthest from our table. As I am negotiating my way past the flirtatiously occupied boys and girls, I hear a vaguely familiar voice say in Ukrainian, "Hello, comrade." I turn. It is the stout man with a large mustache named Roman. Has he been following me?

"Hello, Mister Roman. What are you doing here?"

"I should be asking you that," he says. "Don't you know that the Orchidia is a Ukrainian restaurant?"

"I came with my friends."

"You're welcome to join *my* friends."

"Perhaps for a minute," I say. A slim brunette with a cigarette moves to the right to make room on her chair. I squeeze in.

"Beer?" Roman asks and, without waiting for my response, pours me a glass from a large pitcher. "So," he continues with a grin, "how is life in the imperialist West?"

"Interesting," I say.

"Have you encountered the class struggle?"

I can see from his use of Marxist terminology that he is familiar with Soviet ideology. This is no crude nationalist, but a refined opponent.

"I find the revolution exhilarating."

"Which one?" he asks slyly, while stroking his mustache. "Here or in Czechoslovakia?"

"Here, of course." I resolve not to take his bait.

"There is also some trouble in your homeland, isn't there?"

"Yes," I nod, "the harvest is always a problem."

"And the nationality question."

I wave my hand dismissively. "*That* was solved by Lenin many years ago."

"Ivan Dzyuba[42] disagrees."

"Your émigré politicians are of no interest to me."

Roman smiles again. "He's from Kyiv. A Communist."

"Even Communists can be wrong, Mister Roman."

"Like Nikita Sergeevich?"[43]

"Yes."

---

42   Ukrainian so-called dissident who incorrectly criticized Soviet nationality policy.
43   Nikita Sergeevich Khrushchev, of course, a world-famous Communist leader.

"Like Iosif Vissarionovich?"[44]

"The cult of personality was a tragic mistake."

"Like Vladimir Illich?"

"Lenin made no mistakes," I say firmly.

"He chose Stalin as his successor."

"He was ill."

"He adopted War Communism."

"But then he rescinded it."

"He crushed Kronstadt."[45]

"They were counterrevolutionaries."

"So, will Soviet tanks also crush the Prague Spring?"

"Only if the working class of Czechoslovakia invites them."

Roman pours me more beer. He is an agent provocateur, but I am glad to have resisted all his provocations.

"Thank you," I say, "I must go."

I make to rise but Roman seizes me by the hand and purrs, "Stay, comrade, stay for a few more minutes." I pull my hand back and accidentally knock my elbow against some man.

"Excuse me," I say. It is Dean Reed's namesake.

"Hey, man," he says, "this guy giving you shit?"

"A friendly misunderstanding," Roman says.

"Fuck you," Lou says. "Fuck you and stay fucked, you fat fuck." He takes me by the arm and leads me back to our table.

"We missed you, *Liebling*," Nico coos.

"That means darling in Deutsch," Gerald says. He winks at me.

---

44   Stalin.
45   The site of a counterrevolutionary rebellion crushed by the heroic
      Bolshevik forces in 1921.

"Sit down." Lou almost pushes me into the seat. "Some fucking asshole was giving our pal here a hard time."

"Did you, uh, whack him?" Andrei asks.

"The fucking asshole? Nah."

"Thank you, Lou," I say.

"Forget it. Here, have some vodka. Fuck it all."

"Thank you, yes. I will. I think I will fuck it all."

A restless night. I am exhausted and drunk, but the effects of the music and my conversation with the fat man named Roman keep me awake. The relentless beat of the bass guitar and drums also gives me no sleep. I can hear it distinctly. And I can hear the sadness of Nico's wails and the taunting quality of Dean Reed's voice. And I see Gerald, whirling and jumping like a mad Hungarian czardas dancer. And among these images and noises, there is the insistent questioning of the Ukrainian bourgeois nationalist agent provocateur. In retrospect, I am less pleased with my performance. Why did I meekly answer every one of his questions? Why did I let him question me? Why did I not turn the table on him? Although I did not let myself be provoked, I did let his provocations go unmet.

Something else worries me. His provocations were grounded in some kind of logic. Even I, his ideological enemy, have to admit that. The way he guided our conversation from some errant Marxist in Kyiv to Khrushchev and Stalin and Lenin was masterful. And he has a point, although it is one that only Kolibri has ever raised. If we know *now* that our past leaders made mistakes, how can we know that our current leaders are not making mistakes? Perhaps, in ten or twenty years, we, or our children, will speak of *their* cults, of *their* hare-brained schemes? And then there is Vladimir Illich. Surely our propaganda cannot be right to insist that he *never* made any mistakes. After all, even Lenin was human.

Take my views of Andrei. I am absolutely certain that I know him better than anyone in the West, and certainly better than anyone in the East. I have no doubt whatsoever that he is a genius—as a working class artist and as a proletarian revolutionary. The Party appears to disagree with my views of Andrei. As a Communist, I will publicly denounce Andrei. I have no choice.

As a human being, he is deeply flawed. He is sexually perverted. He does not confide in friends. He is too dependent on his mother. But we are all flawed, as human beings, and so with Andrei, as with Kelebek and Kolibri, I look the other way and forgive them their peccadilloes. (Can I forgive Kelebek his liaison with Katyusha? I may be indifferent to her, but can I forgive my very close friend such a betrayal? Yes, I can.) I have often watched Andrei. He moves his hands slowly, perhaps raising one hand to his chin and scratching it, perhaps dropping the other to his side. Andrei turns his head just a bit, he blinks, he purses his lips, he turns his head again, he tugs at his earlobe. He inhales and exhales, he is silent, he grins, he is quiet. Andrei walks across the room, holding a paintbrush in his hand. He takes slow, measured steps, moving first the right foot, then the left foot, then again the right, and then again the left. This movement is not, for most people, unusual, but for Andrei it is. I am amazed by the fact that he can walk and move his arms and legs and hands. That he can speak and say things is nothing short of miraculous. And yet, he is a great *vozhd*.[46]

I am torn by the contradictory demands being placed upon me by American imperialists, Soviet comrades, and American Communists. And now this Roman reminds me of my own doubts—no, *questions*—about Communist ideology and practice. I can imagine that our Politburo is facing a no less painful dilemma. Should it acquiesce in the revisionist ideological developments taking place in Czechoslovakia? Or should it impose its own, correct, view on our errant Czech and Slovak comrades? Neither alternative is satisfactory; both lead to trouble. Perhaps the Party, like me, is hoping that the difficulties will blow over, that, one day, it will wake up to see a cloudless horizon and infinite vistas? Sooner or later, it will, I am certain, have to choose. Alas, sooner or later so will I.

Once again I sleep badly. Once again I dream of the dead man in the hotel.

It is light outside when I awake. Andrei and Pani Julia are either away or still asleep, so I have a coffee and a slice of bread with cheese and then head for the subway. My head is bursting with pain, and I feel nauseous from the hangover. At Union Square, I exit at the northwest corner of the park and buy a Coca-Cola at the stand. As I am paying, I notice Valeria standing nervously near a tree, drinking from a paper cup. It is almost two months since I last saw her. I recall the circumstances of our parting only vaguely. She is, I see now, still obsessed with Andrei.

"Valeria!" I cry out to her.

---

46   Russian and Ukrainian: leader.

She does not react.

"Valeria!"

She turns in my direction, grimaces, and discards the cup. Uncharacteristically she is wearing lipstick and mascara. Her hair is neatly coiffed, and she is not wearing a cap. She finally looks like a real woman, one who is about to meet the man she loves.

"Valeria!" I approach her with outstretched hand. I have decided that kissing her would be inappropriate.

"Fuck you, Sasha," she barks. "Get lost!" Her right hand is in her pocket.

"Valeria," I say gently, "it is good to see you."

"Fuck off, scumbag!"

"Valeria," I say and reach for her right shoulder. She turns to avoid being touched and, as she does so, her hand comes halfway out of the pocket. She is holding a gun.

"What is that for?"

"Fuck off," she says and brushes past me. I grab her by the shoulder and she spins around.

"For the last time, Sasha, fuck off!"

"I will not, Valeria," I say. "What is that for? What are you planning to do?"

And then it strikes me in the eyes: Andrei! Valeria will use the gun against Andrei.

She pushes me to the side and I almost fall to the ground. Then she runs across the street. I follow and catch hold of her sleeve just as she is opening the door to the building.

"Valeria!" I cry. "Give me that gun!"

The door closes behind us, and she shoves me. But this time I am prepared and I hold my ground. I shove back and reach for the gun. She steps back and turns to climb the stairs. I run after her and trip, but not before I manage to grab the heel of her right boot.

"I will not let you do anything stupid!"

And then she does something unexpected. She takes the gun from her pocket, cocks it, and points it at my groin.

"Your choice, asshole."

This is, I think, the time for heroism. This is the time I have trained for all my life, when all my Communist discipline and self-sacrifice can be put to good use. All I have to do, I realize, is pull her heel. In all likelihood, she will attempt to shoot. In all likelihood, she will miss. In all likelihood, I will emerge unscathed. But oh, the pain in my head!

I release her heel. She kicks my head with her boot and I tumble down the stairs. I hear her rise and run up the stairs. As the sound of her footsteps recedes, it strikes me in the eyes: I am saved.